HEX MARKS THE SPOT

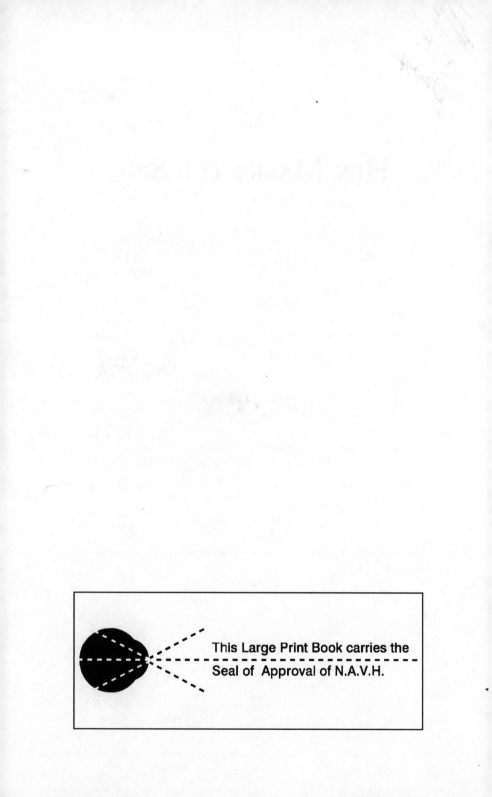

This Large Print Book carries the
Seal of Approval of N.A.V.H.

HEX MARKS THE SPOT

MADELYN ALT

WHEELER PUBLISHING
A part of Gale, Cengage Learning

GALE
CENGAGE Learning

Detroit • New York • San Francisco • New Haven, Conn • Waterville, Maine • London

GALE
CENGAGE Learning

Wheeler Publishing Large Print Cozy Mystery.
The text of this Large Print edition is unabridged.
Other aspects of the book may vary from the original edition.
Set in 16 pt. Plantin.
Printed on permanent paper.

LIBRARY OF CONGRESS CATALOGING-IN-PUBLICATION DATA

Alt, Madelyn.
    Hex marks the spot / by Madelyn Alt.
        p. cm. — (A bewitching mystery) (Wheeler Publishing large print cozy mystery)
        ISBN-13: 978-1-59722-726-1 (hardcover : alk. paper)
        ISBN-10: 1-59722-726-9 (hardcover : alk. paper)
        1. Witches — Fiction. 2. Cabinetmakers — Crimes against — Fiction. 3. Amish — Fiction. 4. Large type books. I. Title.
PS3601.L45H49 2008
813'.6—dc22   2007051868

Published in 2008 by arrangement with The Berkley Publishing Group, a member of Penguin Group (USA) Inc.

Printed in the United States of America
1 2 3 4 5 6 7 12 11 10 09 08

For Mom and Dad, for always believing in me,
no matter what . . .

And for my boys of assorted shapes and sizes . . .
Love you always . . .

ACKNOWLEDGMENTS

So many people go into the successful creation of a novel. Friends, family, business associates, treasured partners, *readers* — the Bewitching Mysteries would be nothing without you.

That being said, there are a few who have gone above and beyond the call of duty with me:

Jessica Wade, my beloved editor, whose editorial pencil is sharp but never cutting . . . and who seems to know instinctively how to draw out the best from me.

My agent, Peter Miller. Peter, quite simply, you rock. Many thanks to you and your team for everything.

Every single person at Berkley who has had a hand in the finished product. You all are amazing, and I enjoy working together so much.

Steve, Matthew, Josh, Caleb, and Alex . . . you are what this is all about.

Mom, Dad, Jerry, Rhonda, Cindy, Brian, Chuck, Bart, Tammy, and the nieces and nephews. Love you all.

LorHen, CinLon, DavStu, AshKuc, Mik-She, FreShi, ScoDen, DavLee, RoxWer, JefKin, KimTho, JefCam, RonSla, JayFri, RonThi, JefMai, WilMin, JefSea, DusOus, MonHer, AdrPla, JerBos, SherBos, AnnFar, JenLea, BriLux, MikKam, TerMue, PauCar, and oh, heck, all of my Pyro peeps for never doubting that I could and would do this.

My Witchy Chicks: Yasmine Galenorn, Terey Ramin, Lisa Croll Di Dio, Linda Wisdom, Annette Blair, Kate Austin, and Candace Havens . . . sisters of my heart, all.

Dorothy Morrison, Ellen Dugan, Edain McCoy, for so much inspiration.

My GB crew, including The Man himself, but with a special shout-out to Trudy Lancaster, Deborah Ann Barnum, Ann Luongo, Jennifer Hupke, Jen York, and all the rest of the Indy Girls, and to the HSBCers. Oh, and of course, to Mum Margaret for the very special gift you presented to the world.

And last, but definitely not least, I honor YOU, the readers. For every single one of you who has purchased a copy, talked about the series with others, blogged about it, reviewed it, and/or perhaps even sent me a note of support . . . I am continually humbled and amazed by your encouragement and appreciation for Maggie's ongoing adventures. Because of you all, word is spreading, and I am so very grateful.

They say, "Everything's all right."
They say, "Better days are near."
They tell us, "These are the good
times."
But they don't live around here.

— WARREN ZEVON,
"THE INDIFFERENCE OF HEAVEN"

CHAPTER 1

My name is Margaret Mary-Catherine O'Neill — Maggie to those who know and love me best — and I have a secret. A big secret. The kind of secret few here in my hometown of Stony Mill, Indiana, would understand, let alone accept or even tolerate.

Big breath here. You see, I am an empath. An intuitive who can feel another person's emotions, and sometimes even know the reasons behind them.

For those of you whose only exposure to the world of an empath was through *Star Trek,* allow me to explain. I can't read your mind (well, not *often*), and I can't see what you had for dinner last night (unless you're still wearing it on your tie). A psychic I'm not. It's just that sometimes I feel things, in the same way that you feel them. As though your emotions and motivations are my own, residing within my own body. And, well, sometimes I sense things — *disturbances* — in the world around me.

I won't go into the dreams. Everyone has dreams . . . right? Mine can't be *that* different.

Can they?

I know what you're thinking. I've been where you are. In fact, until six months ago I would have called myself an outright skeptic. Heaven knows I wasn't raised to think any of this was even possible, let alone normal. Being an empath, as you can see, is not something I'm especially comfortable with, but as my Grandma Cora always said, we all have our crosses to bear. There have been many days when I've wanted nothing more than to sink back into the comfort of ignorance. To go back to the time in my life when skepticism reigned supreme.

Truth be told, I've seen and felt too much lately to have the luxury of skepticism ever again.

My name is Maggie O'Neill, and this is my story.

The winter had been a hard one — two brutal deaths and several months solid of howling winds and bitter temperatures were enough to break the backbone of even the most stalwart personality. But the snows had at long last receded and, if the robins twittering in the thickly budded bushes along the streets of Stony Mill could be considered definitive proof, spring had sprung. *For better or for worse,* I thought as I maneuvered my 1972 Volkswagen Bug (long ago christened Christine due to her testy mechanical idiosyncrasies) through town toward River Street and the line of Rockwell-esque storefronts that included Enchantments Antiques and Fine Gifts. In other words, my place of employ and home away from home.

If my mood that morning seemed overly fatalistic, I had my reasons. I'd worked at the unique gift shop/antique store/witchy emporium since the autumn just past, and I'd come to love the peaceful environment, not to mention having the most perfect boss a girl could ever wish for in Felicity Dow. No matter that she called herself a modern-day witch and follower of the Old Ways, and by every indication appeared to be telling the truth. All the same, ever since Christmas when a much respected Stony Mill resident had broken our trust in the worst way imaginable, I hadn't been able to feel comfortable in my own skin. I felt . . . on my guard. On edge. Always watchful, always anxious, always waiting for the proverbial axe to fall.

Except that it hadn't. January had passed without anything more gruesome than a few fender benders caused by icy roads and blowing snow. When February eventually drifted into March without incident, by all rights I should have been able to breathe a sigh of relief and resume the carefree and somewhat frivolous life of an almost thirty-year-old single girl on the lookout for the ideal life . . . but I couldn't. Something was wrong in Stony Mill. *Something.* And I knew that eventually it would raise its head again.

The question was, when?

And that was the problem. I didn't have an answer to that question or any of the other questions that had been plaguing me for months. I'd been completely knocked out of my comfort zone, and I wasn't sure how to handle anything anymore.

To be fair to myself, I didn't know many who would have felt comfortable with all that had happened. But I'd come to accept that people without the gift of sensitivity had no idea what was happening right beneath their noses. Not one. Loosely translated, that amounted to about 99.8 percent of the town proper. While your average Stony Millers went on about their daily lives — working, shopping, going to basketball games, and hitting the Elks Lodge on a Saturday night — the level of spirit activity in town was getting worse. Outside of Felicity and the N.I.G.H.T.S., the Northeast Indiana Ghost Hunting and Tracking Society, and perhaps a few nameless and faceless others, the town was clueless.

The N.I.G.H.T.S. could best be described as Stony Mill's version of the Ghostbusters. All of them friends of Felicity's and now of mine, all talented in some area of the paranormal, and all sensitive to the same types of strangeness I had been picking up on. With Felicity as my mentor and the N.I.G.H.T.S. as a kind of metaphysical posse, I had been on a mission to understand the whispers, feelings, and thoughts my newly realized empathic abilities had brought into my life. But as the winter passed, a new reticence had overtaken me, and I had found myself conjuring up excuses whenever Liss had raised the subject of tutoring me. I'd even begged off the last few N.I.G.H.T.S. meetings, inventing family obligations so I wouldn't have to chase down pesky spirit orbs.

Call it a change of heart. Call it self-preservation. Call it spinelessness, if you must. You probably wouldn't be too far off the mark. All I knew was, I was being led down a garden path toward an uncertain future, and I wasn't at all sure the shoes I was wearing were sturdy enough to stand up to the muck.

And yet, I have always been a sucker for a good mystery.

It was a sunny April Saturday morning, and for once my mind was as far from floating orbs and spirit messages as it could be. Enchantments was my first destination, but not for my usual pre-opening rituals of filling the coffee and tea makers with fresh water and checking for new Web orders. Instead, this was to be the first Saturday in six months that I would not be manning the cash register. That honor would go to my two young protégées, Evie Carpenter and Tara Murphy, while I accompanied Liss to the opening day of the county farmers market/craft bazaar in search of new local goodies for the store.

I felt like a newbie mother leaving her baby with a sitter for the first time. Despite knowing I needed to give myself a little time to refresh and renew, like any new mom I was exhibiting the first signs of separation anxiety well before the deciding moment. But I forced myself to be strong and persevere. Going to the bazaar had been Liss's idea, and I would drink a gallon of root beer before I would let her down. Besides, on some level I was hoping to absorb some of the spiritual peace that seemed to surround my lovely employer like a mantle of light. Regardless of whether or not I embraced her religious beliefs (and the jury was still out on that), there was a lot I could learn from her about life, the universe, and everything.

Who needed Douglas Adams when you had a new witch in town?

"Morning, girls!" I sang out as I sailed through the back entrance into the store office. As usual, it was piled high with boxes to be opened, receipts to be filed, bills to be paid. I dropped my purse onto the desk, transported as always as I breathed in the store's cinnamon bun scent. God, I loved this place. I loved everything about it. Perhaps that was the reason for the reticence I felt at the thought of abandoning it this morning.

Slouched in the desk chair with a ginormous cup of coffee sheltered in her hands, Tara scarcely turned a heavily mascaraed eye my way. "G'morning," she muttered. Or at least, I thought that's what she said. The words did kind of melt together. For all I knew, she might have said gallbladder . . . or goose mallow . . . though I suppose those would have made slightly less sense.

"Are you and Evie all set for today?" I asked in the same breezy voice I would have used to persuade my pretty little nieces to put smiles on their faces. "I don't know if we'll be away the entire day or not, but you can reach us on our cells at any time."

"Yeah, yeah. We got it. No worries." She yawned wide, her jaw cracking with the effort.

"Great. Thanks." I paused and looked around the office, half expecting to see Evie slumped on a chair in a different corner. "Where's Evie, by the way?"

Right on cue, I heard light footsteps tap-dancing down the floorboards in the front of the store. "Here you are," Evie sang as she swept past the purple velvet curtain that separated the front of the store from the back office. Catching sight of me, she waved but did not falter in her mission. "One great big cup of double fudge mocha, complete with whipped cream and a thick caramel swirl, just for you, Tar. This'll open those sleepy eyes right up."

Tara gave her the evil eye. "You've been taking lessons from Maggie, haven't you, Swiss Miss?"

I laughed. I was beginning to think our Tara was not a morning person.

"All right, all right. Enough with the maligning of our characters," I scolded good-naturedly. "Besides, it's after nine. The store opens in a little under half an hour. Is everything good to go? Do you need my help with anything before I take off?"

Evie snapped to with a mock salute. "Everything is ready, Cap'n. Water's on for coffee and tea, the morning delivery of scones and cookies has been lodged in the glass cabinets, the dusting has been done, and the floors vacuumed. The only thing we need from you is the key to the cash register, and then that will be humming right along, too."

I raised my brows. "My, you have been busy. What time did you girls get here?"

"*Evil* here picked me up at seven o'clock," Tara grumbled. "On a Saturday!"

I mock whispered to Evie, "Soooo, Evil, do you think a scone might help? Or should I go to Annie's to pick up a fritter to sweeten her disposition?"

"I heard that," Tara said, scowling. "For your information, my disposition doesn't need sweetening. It just needs more sleep. S-L-E-E-P. Haven't you people ever heard that a teenage girl needs her beauty rest? Sheesh!" Then she sighed. "I'll have a cookie. Chocolate and macadamia nut."

From the depths of my purse, my cell phone began blaring the "1812 Overture," my ring tone of the mo'.

Evie headed for the front. "I'll get the cookie, you get your phone."

There was something insistent about phone calls in general, and cell phone calls in particular, that made me feel just a little bit anxious, as though I was being tested on how quickly I could answer. I grabbed for my bag and made my usual desperate scrounge through the contents at the bottom. At last my fingers closed around the sleek case, and I flipped it open.

"Hello?"

"Maggie? Liss here. Listen, ducks, I know I'm supposed to be on my way there, but . . . is there any way you could find it in your heart to pop out to pick me up?"

"Of course I can. Is anything wrong?"

An exasperated sigh whispered over the phone connection. "It's the Lexus again. One would think the expense of the bloody thing would prevent such trials. The dealer promised me they'd fixed it last time, but I should have known better — Mercury is retrograde, you know."

Mercury, the planet whose cosmic path rules communication and technology in the astrological scheme of things, is reputed to trail chaos and carnage in its wake several times a year when it makes an about-face toward the sun. It is this troublesome reverse path that affects anything of a mechanical or communicative nature, causing cars to break down, computers to crash, telephones and printers to malfunction, and relationships to stumble. Cosmically speaking, Mercury in retrograde is a planet having PMS, and the only help for it is to let it run its course.

I made a mental note to delay buying that new vacuum cleaner — the last thing I needed was a Suck-O-Luxe run amok. "Hang tight. I'll be there with bells on." By that time Evie had returned with the cookies, and she and Tara were munching away. "Sorry, girls, I have to get going. Have one of those for me, would you? And call me if you need me."

So yes, I probably did sound like an overprotective mom, but I wasn't about to apologize for it. I loved the store, loved my job there, and I had learned lessons from my own mother all too well. I would be hard-pressed to keep myself from checking in every hour on the hour.

That cell phone had to be good for something.

Right on cue, my phone blared again

23

almost as soon as I had exited the store. I shuffled through my handbag, trying to find it. At last my fingers closed around it — *success!*

" 'Lo?"

"Hey there." My stomach made a warm and squidgie little bobble when I heard the voice of my quasi-boyfriend, Deputy Tom Fielding of the Stony Mill Police Department, on the other end of the airwaves. "You on your way to the farmers market?"

"Yeah. My first free Saturday in months. I'm both looking forward to it and missing the store already."

"Sounds like fun."

"You could come out." But I knew better.

"Unfortunately, I have a boatload of paperwork to catch up on. Damned schoolkids sure have been acting up like crazy."

"Nothing particularly strange about that." Every year as the school year wound down, the student population wound up. Pranks and practical jokes flew around the county like spells gone awry. Mailboxes, fences, garden statuary, and garage doors were bashed, dashed, kidnapped, and spray painted. Typical Friday night highjinks.

"No, but I've been spending most of my time chasing high schoolers out of Alden

24

Woods and the city parks after hours rather than upholding the laws of the community. You'd think I'd have better things to do with my time."

"Aw, poor baby," I sympathized. And I did, really — I knew how tedious it was for him to have to deal with the petty stuff, day in and day out. But surely it was better than the alternative. Methinks I was going to have to have a talk with Tom soon about being more careful with random wishes.

"Sooo," he said, "see you later?"

"Tonight? Well, I'll have to check my schedule."

"Aw, come on, Maggie . . ."

"Hmm. Looks like I'm free. My place? Whenever you get done?"

"I'll be there."

Oh, goody. The night ahead was definitely looking up.

I called him my quasi-boyfriend. What I really meant is that he's my sometimes-maybe-kinda-sorta boyfriend. Why the equivocation? It wasn't that I didn't think we could be compatible. It wasn't that he didn't light my fire. It wasn't even that I wasn't ready for a serious relationship. I mean, for heaven's sake, my thirtieth birthday was a little more than two months away, and all I had to show for it was . . . not much at all. Seeing my nieces playing at the feet of my younger sister, Melanie, sometimes gave me a physical ache. Not so deep down, I wanted the life that my sister had — perfect girls, perfect home, perfect husband — and I wasn't ashamed to admit it. And yet . . . truth be told, this time around *I* was the one holding back. For the last four months, since my near fatal accident at Christmas, Tom had gone out of his way to make it very clear, at least verbally, that he wanted to give things between us a try. And yet, between my hesitation and his never-ending busy schedule, our relationship never seemed to quite get off the ground. Maybe he wasn't as ready as he thought he was. Maybe the weirdness factor of my friendship with Liss and the N.I.G.H.T.S. was too much for him to take after all.

We'd first gotten together when Tom was investigating the murder of Felicity's sister, Isabella — and he'd fingered Liss as the prime suspect. Of course, she'd been cleared of all charges, but Tom still didn't trust her, and he didn't trust any of the paranormal activities she was involved with, either. That had never set well with me. And of course, there was the fact that he was only separated from his wife and about to start divorce proceedings.

Maybe we both had issues with trust that needed to be worked through.

"Enough," I said aloud, shaking my head to break free of the serious thoughts and lifting my face to the midmorning sunshine streaming through the car windows. Now was not the time to crawl through the cobwebs of my subconscious.

Before I knew it, I had crossed town and ventured onto Victoria Park Road. Once lined with working farms, this meandering stretch of byway was now the gold coast of Stony Mill's surrounding countryside, as evidenced by the occasional happily situated residence punctuating the picturesque isolation. But it wasn't until I approached Liss's manor-style home that I realized how long it had been since I'd last driven the road's narrow curves. Had it really been six months since Liss's sister had been killed? At one time I might have labeled Isabella Harding's death the spark that set fire to my intuitive sensitivities and abilities, but looking back now, I couldn't be so sure. I had the slow, sneaking suspicion that things had been happening in town all along. Was it just that I'd been too busy to notice? To really see?

I drove slowly past the architectural monstrosity that was the Harding estate, barely visible behind the elaborate six-foot iron fence that protected the house and grounds from the outside world. From the outside world, yes, but the bigger threat had come from within. I couldn't help wondering how Jeremy Harding was filling his time these days, now that both his wife and his daughter had abandoned him for . . . other eventualities. Something told me the grieving widower was too busy following his bliss through the ministrations of his able-bodied assistant, Jetta James, to be missing the dear departed Isabella . . . but maybe I was being too hard on the man.

Eh, probably not.

I slowed down as Harding's grandiose fencing transitioned to Liss's classic fieldstone. The entrance to Liss's property was already open as I approached — a sign, perhaps, that whatever ghosts Liss had been suffering had finally been laid to rest. I hoped so. Turning onto the smoothly paved driveway, a welcome change from the crushed limestone most often found in these parts, I tooled up the wooded stretch that began just inside the gates, turning the wheel this way and that until I rounded the last bend and burst through to the stretch of green lawn and burgeoning spring gardens that surrounded the English-style manor house.

Liss hurried out to greet me as Christine sputtered to a halt beneath the carriage port.

"Record time," she enthused as she folded herself into the bucket seat next to me.

Known for her retro-antique fashion sense, today Liss had chosen an outfit that was actually on the mod side: a pair of khaki linen slacks and a bouclé jacket. She paired it with a gorgeous embroidered silk frame purse with a snake chain handle that was something my grandmother might have used as a young woman. As for me, I'd worn my usual safe uniform of turtleneck, jeans, and wool jacket — worn open, as a concession to the season. Spring may have sprung, but summer heat was not exactly forthcoming, and in my mind, comfort was king. Or at least queen.

"Onward?" I suggested.

"Absolutely. Oh, Maggie, I'm so looking forward to this — great Goddess, it's been a long winter! This is going to be just what the doctor ordered."

"I feel a little guilty, leaving the store to the girls," I fretted as we bumped along county roads still pitted from the winter frost heave.

"Spring is all about renewal," Liss said,

patting my hand on the stick shift. "Women tend to put the needs of everyone and everything before their own. We all need to refill the well from time to time."

The annual kickoff to the upcoming summer season was opening day of the county craft bazaar and farmers market. It was a big deal, highly attended by Stony Millers, well-to-do and poor alike. Not so many years ago the bazaar was little more than an informal assembly of pickup trucks and tents gathered around the courthouse square on Thursday mornings, until the traffic had gotten bad enough to necessitate a more spacious venue. The 4-H Fairgrounds at Heritage Park fit the bill nicely, so long as one didn't mind the smelly animal barns and deeply trenched demolition derby field also on the premises.

We left Christine in one of the parking areas, then made our way toward the tents where the bulk of the festivities were to take place. Ropes of brightly colored flags pointed us in the right direction along straw-covered paths. Not that we needed them with the unmistakable smoky aroma of Port-a-Pit chicken wafting our way. Lunch, I hoped . . . or maybe a brat . . . or a tenderloin . . . or . . .

I was still thinking about my stomach

when I realized just how many Stony Millers had turned out for the opening day. People, great throngs of them, milled about between the myriad tents and tables. I faltered a moment when I saw them. Crowds aren't exactly my favorite things in the world, mostly because people en masse give off an amazing amount of energy, and I still hadn't quite mastered the ability to completely shield myself from the cumulative effects. But at least I'd prepared for this possibility today — as much as a fledgling empath could. Some of the personal wards I had put into effect earlier. Just a few last-minute preparations were needed now.

As Liss had taught me, I took a moment to center myself, to call for the white, protective light to fill me, surround me, keep me safe from harm. That and a deep, steadying breath . . .

Not as effective as a personal Taser, perhaps, but on a spiritual and emotional level, it was the next best thing.

"Better?"

I opened my eyes to find Liss watching me, her blue eyes smiling kindly. I flushed a little. "I . . . well, yes. Thanks."

She leaned in a little as she took my arm and we began walking again toward the crowds, two sensitives united against the outside world. "Don't resist so much. Let the energy flow through you. Recognize it for what it is, acknowledge it, and let it go. You'll feel better."

Letting it go sounded like good advice, but it was going to take a little practice.

The first tent we came to was filled to bursting with chatter and the predictable "kuntry" crafts so many found charming these days. Cows, chickens, gingham, too many items decorated with that watered-down and ubiquitous blue that had been popular for at least a decade . . . Even miniature two-seater privies for the country girls who had everything. And then there was the proliferation of bunnies of all shapes and sizes, phony eggs, and baskets with pastel grass, proudly displayed side by side with the crosses adorned with plastic Jesus figures, just in time for the upcoming holiday. I smiled to myself, wondering what they would say if I told them the bunnies and colored eggs stemmed from the pagan festival of Ostara, a name that had been shamelessly usurped and revamped by the early Church leaders. Not that it would make a difference — they wouldn't believe me anyway.

I drifted from table to table, nodding politely at the vendors (mostly middle-aged ladies trying to make a buck or two to justify their favorite hobbies) as they proudly demonstrated the tchotchkes they had made at their kitchen tables, but I knew we were unlikely to find anything suitable for Enchantments in this particular tent. Still, Liss took her time, speaking personably with each vendor, exclaiming over their wares and even buying a particularly florid rooster that she insisted was the mirror image of one her own wee mum had owned when she was growing up at their home in the Trossachs area of Scotland. Personally, I suspected she was just making nice with the natives, but then again, that was Liss. God love her for it.

Eventually we moved on to other tents with more crafts, as well as a few antiques and collectibles. But the booth Liss had really come for was yet to be seen — a display of handmade Amish furniture made by your friend and mine, fellow N.I.G.H.T.S. member Eli Yoder.

Speak of the devil . . .

"Eli!"

I had caught sight of our friend where he had set up his tools and projects in an open horse barn across the way. I waved cheerily and immediately headed in his direction, knowing Liss was only seconds behind me.

Most days when I saw Eli, he wore a pair of black pants held up by a pair of suspenders, a black coat with black buttons, and a white shirt, topped off by a round, flat-brimmed hat. Today he wore — wait for it — a pair of black pants held up by suspenders, a black coat, and a white shirt topped off by a round, flat-brimmed hat. I've heard tell that when he really wants to mix things up, he wears a shirt that's robin's egg blue or pale green, but I've never seen him look anything but, well, plain.

In the dusty shade of the barn Eli bent over a piece of wood stretched between two well-used sawhorses, his thick hands delicately sanding the wood to a state of perfection.

"And how are you this bright and beautiful morning?" I said as I drew near.

Lifting his big head, he smiled at me, his hands continuing their task. *"Gut. Wunderbar! Und Sie?"*

I held up my hands in protest, laughing. "And now I wish I'd paid more attention to Frau Nielson in first-year German class. Why is it that life is always clearer in retrospect?"

"It is just the way of the world, *ja?*"

"So it would seem. What are you doing?"

"I am preparing the wood. See? You try."

He ran his hand over the wood, motioning for me to do the same. "What do you feel?"

I smoothed my hand over the piece of wood. It was warm, and slick as glass. "Nothing."

"Then it is ready almost."

Liss sidled up beside me. "There you are, Eli. We've been looking all over for you and your wares."

I could have sworn I saw Eli blush beneath the brim of his hat. "I have been here. Just so."

"I see that." She ran her gaze over the gleaming tables, bookshelves, and rocking chairs that surrounded us in the dusty shade. "My, you have been busy this winter. These are lovely, Eli. Just lovely."

"I am glad they please you."

"Oh, they do. They do. You are a real master of the woodcrafting arts. And — oh!" She caught her breath. Holding her hand to her breast in awe, she nodded in the direction of an armoire at least seven feet high that was being hefted onto a furniture dolly by two knot-shouldered men in Amish garb. "Is that yours?"

Eli grunted as he straightened his spine. "The cabinet? *Ja.* It is mine. For now."

Unlike Eli's other pieces, the cabinet was ablaze with color and chased delicately with carvings that looked almost Celtic in origin. "That is amazing work," Felicity sighed.

"Ah." Eli dusted his hands off on a thick bundle of cheesecloth. "That would be Luc's handiwork. Lucas Metzger," he said by way of explanation, nodding toward the departing armoire. "That is Luc, just there on the left."

I glanced at the retreating backs of the two men. The man on the left was just another man in Amish garb, made nondescript by the homogeneous uniform.

"A friend of yours?" Liss asked politely as she ran practiced hands over the joints of a chair. "Or a business partner?"

"Not partners. Luc, he used to work with his brother roofing houses, but he left off doing that for a job at the RV factory in town. But this winter was hard — his hours were cut at the plant, and he is a proud man and would not go back to his brother. I have been giving him extra work whenever I can spare it."

Honorable Eli. "That was a very nice thing for you to do," I told him, and meant it.

Eli gave a modest shrug. "He had the need, I had the means. A good arrangement for the both of us. But the cabinet . . ."

"The color and carvings," Liss commented as she studied the retreating piece with the attention of a scholar. "Like something straight out of Celtic Europe. I've never seen you do that before."

"No. It is not plain," Eli said, quieting his voice as though reluctant to allow the admission to go beyond their earshot. "Luc, he was raised in a Pennsylvania order of Amish. Some things they do not do the same way that we do here." He looked down at the ground, deep in thought, then shrugged. "It is not plain, the cabinet, and so it is not something I could in good faith sell as my own . . . and yet it would be wasteful to dismantle it. That is why I donated it for the auction today. Someone will put it to good use."

"Auction?" Liss's ears perked up at the use of one of her favorite words.

I had almost forgotten. The highlight of opening day was an auction that raised money for a different charity selected by a governing committee every year. The committee identified the best from those items offered by the local crafting community. To be one of the chosen few was a big honor, and free publicity for the artisan in question.

Liss was eyeing the armoire's retreat with a gleam in her eye. "I know just where I could use something like that."

I giggled. I knew well what the look meant. "Should I call my father and ask whether his pickup will be free?"

Liss laughed, too. "Maybe so. I suppose it all depends on how successful I am at the bidding." She turned back to Eli. "What time is the auction?"

"The big reveal is at eleven o'clock," I said, reading from the schedule I'd picked up on the way in. "Don't worry, you have plenty of time."

Liss leisurely selected several items from Eli's stock, including a solidly crafted plant stand that she said would be perfect for an altar. While Eli slapped Sold signs on them and grumbled good-naturedly about letting things go under cost, Liss and I hightailed it over to the main pavilion where the auction was to be held.

The pavilion was shrouded with white sheets to give the proceedings an air of anticipation and mystery. A crowd had formed around it, whispering together, wondering what offerings the committee had selected this year. The comprehensive list of donations that some organized soul had thought to post was a thing to behold and made one thing abundantly clear: Our little town boasted its share of craftsmen, artisans, and closet artistes.

Kind of made a hometown girl proud.

Liss looked at me and smiled.

The white curtains at the front shivered, then parted briefly as the committee chair stepped through to the podium. At the helm was none other than . . .

Jetta James?

Jetta James, not-so-secret paramour of Liss's not-so-grieving ex-brother-in-law, Jeremy Harding.

Six months had not allowed for much change, I noticed as I surveyed her from the anonymity of the crowd. Same brassy hair, same penchant for tight clothing and teeter-totter heels, same hard eyes.

"Ladies. And. Gentlemen." Her voice rang out over the crowd. "Welcome, one and all, to the opening day of the Stony Mill Farmers Market and Craft Extravaganza! We, the members of the Stony Mill Planning Committee, want to thank you for your support of this vital part of our town's continued economic growth and vigor. We are extraordinarily proud of the improvements we have been able to make in the last few years, and with your ongoing support we will continue to do just that. And now . . . without further ado" — an important shuffle of the papers — "let's move on to the moment we've all been waiting for. Committee members, come forward, please."

Several Stony Mill notables emerged from the crowd to join her. The hush of anticipation became a ribbon of energy that snaked from person to person, circling the pavilion. I felt it first as a flicker in my solar plexus that made me expand my lungs to take in more air, the very fiber of which felt distinctly alive. It was always like this when people joined together. Good vibes, bad vibes, neutral vibes, but always something.

Beside me, Liss smiled blandly, seemingly untouched by the exchange of personal energies. I did my best to emulate her calm.

"Come on down, committee members, don't be shy," Jetta teased, beckoning with her free hand. To the crowd at large she said, "These people have put in untold hours, and I think they deserve a round of applause from us all, don't you?" The crowd obliged her politely. "Bill Childers, Catherine Neely, Bob Dixon, Olivia Manning, and our selfless leader, Jeremy Harding. We thank you all for your dedication to the success of this year's festivities."

Jeremy Harding? Liss's self-serving brother-in-law a selfless volunteer?

Behind Jetta, the curtains trembled once, twice, then fell in a puddle to the weathered

40

floorboards. Delighted titters of excitement rose from the crowd. Auction junkies eager to strike.

While everyone else leaned forward as one to get a better look at the goods, I scanned the committee faces I'd thus far ignored. Sure enough, there Jeremy was on the end, all well-tailored suit and pretty-boy hair, the only man in town who went in regularly for a manicure. But as for the selfless part, I didn't believe it for a minute. He wasn't the altruistic type. And for that matter, neither was Jetta. Which raised the question of why they were both serving on the SMPC.

Hmm.

But there was no time for speculation. Jetta was busy introducing the crafters and artisans who had created the show's auction prizes. With all the glib savoir faire of a game show model, she made a flourish at each prize, describing it in enthusiastic detail and giving a short introduction of the artist. I couldn't help beaming like a proud mom when Jetta presented Eli's work to the crowd.

"And isn't this armoire just gorgeous?" she enthused. Amazingly, most of the audience seemed to be hanging on her every word. "The quality in this piece is unparalleled, I'm telling you. You simply don't get solid wood like this nowadays at just any old furniture store. You're lucky if you get a thin veneer of real wood pasted over a piece of particle board, even though you're paying the same for the pleasure. This, ladies and gentlemen, is one hundred percent solid oak, from stem to stern. And this hand carving and painting is truly unique, all by the artist, Eli Yoder —"

"Excuse me, ma'am."

Jetta paused in mid-rave. "Did somebody — ?" She held up her hand as a staying measure. "I'm sorry, there will be a question-and-answer session at the end of the reveal."

"Ma'am, it is not a question." Like everyone around me, I searched until I located the source of the voice as Eli came into view. When had Eli joined the crowd? Flushing from the sudden attention, he removed his hat and stood turning the brim round and round in his hands. "What you said just now is not the case. The carving, the painting . . . it is not mine."

Momentarily flustered, Jetta frowned. "I'm sorry, what did you say?"

"I am Eli Yoder, ma'am, but I did not do the carving. I built the cabinet, but the carving, the painting, it was not done by my hands. It was Lucas Metzger that did the artistry. Luc, you out there?" Eli held a hand up to shade his eyes and squinted into the crowd.

The curious crowd moved as one to follow his lead. I found myself turning with them to look for the Amish man I'd seen earlier only from behind.

"*Ja,* there he is. Knew I'd find you here. Luc, raise up your hand."

There he was. Leaning up against a post like an . . . Amish James Dean.

Good golly, Miss Molly. Handsomer than a man sporting a jawline-only beard had any right to be, he was broad in the shoulder, narrow at the hip, and fully hubba-hubba. Funny, I'd never seen an Amish man who made me take a second look — I'd never been able to get past the trappings. Shame on me. Was this what I'd been missing? I blinked, certain I was just imagining things, but the angelic vision remained, all golden hair, twinkling eyes, and ruddy, sensual lips.

A man of few words, Luc Metzger gave the crowd a stoic nod, then lowered his hat over his brow and crossed his arms again. Knotted muscles bulged beneath the rolled-up sleeves of his collar-free shirt.

"Lord Jesus," came a hushed female voice from somewhere behind us.

43

The rest of the predominantly female crowd simply hummed with approval.

This man made suspenders and utilitarian garb look good. And I wasn't the only female to notice. If one more woman in the crowd sucked in her stomach, I was afraid the entire area might implode.

Even Jetta straightened her shoulders as, with a practiced eye, she measured the length and breadth of him.

"Well, then," she said at last. "Stony Mill, I give you the exquisitely talented team of Yoder and Metzger, whose beautifully crafted cabinet has been selected to receive our Opening Day Award of Excellence." She paused a moment to allow for applause. Liss and I clapped loudest of all, which brought a flush of embarrassment to Eli's weathered cheeks. "I encourage all interested parties to dig deep into their wallets. This year all profits will go to the newly formed Isabella Harding Foundation. As you might recall, Mrs. Harding's life was sadly cut short last autumn, and her family has donated generously to be sure that the causes near and dear to the late Mrs. Harding's heart do not suffer from her loss."

I glanced surreptitiously over at Liss, wondering what was going through her mind. Did it bother her to hear Jetta pseudoeulogize her sister, even in such a perfunctory manner? If it did, she wasn't showing it. Typical British stiff-upper-lip reserve.

"Finally, the committee would like to thank all participants in this year's competition," Jetta droned on. "Without you, none of this would be possible. And now, I'll let you all browse this year's selections until we're ready to start the bidding."

Liss immediately headed toward the podium to get a better look at the goodies being offered. Being rather short of cash, I remained behind, choosing instead to take part in one of my favorite pastimes: people watching.

Liss would have me believe that it was all part and parcel of being an intuitive/sensitive in general, and an empath in particular. Whatever the reason, it was an indulgence I catered to regularly. For instance, the pair of older ladies sporting head-to-toe pastel outfits and practical shoes. The one in pink was an Enchantments regular and a member of my mother's favorite church group, St. Catherine's Ladies Auxiliary — perhaps I'd say hello. I wandered closer under the guise of buying a raspberry lemonade from the nearest stand. As I did so, a scrap of their conversation floated over to me.

"Never quite seen anything like that cabinet," the woman in periwinkle was saying.

"Never mind the cabinet," Pink Lady, a.k.a. Mrs. Mansfield, murmured. "Did you get a load of that Luc character?"

"I did. That's a good-looking young man. Too bad he's Amish."

"I know. No fraternizing with the regulars. A shame, I say. It's been an awful long time since I've done a little fraternizing myself, if you get my meaning."

"Grace!" Periwinkle hissed. "You could be his mother! And almost his grandmother."

"Doesn't mean I'm too old to appreciate the form of a fine man. Besides, I don't consider myself old. I'm just experienced. Big difference. And some men like a little experience on their women, you know. That's what I need to find me. A man of discerning tastes."

"A man too vain to wear his glasses might work."

"Hmmph. I think *you* could use a little fraternizing, Frannie. You're getting a little pinched in the kisser."

On second thought, I mused, hiding a grin behind a giant lemonade, maybe I'd say hello later.

Liss was running her fingertips over the

46

cabinet's joints and hinges, so I moseyed over to see what other things had been offered up for auction. There was a nice watercolor of the County Courthouse by Miranda Goldson; a wrought iron arbor from Owen Thorsley, blacksmith to the Amish community and iron artisan in disguise; a garden bench made by one of the Gordon sisters, Janet or Ruth, with their trademark trompe l'oeil treatment; a huge grapevine wreath with autumn leaves; blown glass and charm jewelry in all sorts of lovely colors by someone who operated under a business name of Phantom Dreamer (I made a mental note to show these to Liss — at last, something with Enchantments potential!); a gargantuan birdhouse built to look like an old-time prairie church complete with steeple and stained glass window; and so much more.

My browsing for the moment complete, I was about to beat a retreat to less crowded confines when I felt a hand on my shoulder.

"Got spooks?"

CHAPTER 2

I spun around with a smile on my face. "Marcus! What are you doing here?"

Marcus Quinn and I had become close friends over the last eight months. A member of the N.I.G.H.T.S. and Liss's magical partner (*and possibly more?*), Marcus was a bit of an anomaly in my eyes. With his penchant for black leather and his dark, shoulder-length hair, sometimes pulled back, sometimes not, he looked every inch a threat to a good girl's equilibrium. But the moment he removed his shades to reveal sparkling blue eyes above a saucy grin, the world started to spin for a whole 'nother reason, drat him. He was fun, he was smart, and he liked to give as good as he got when it came to male-female banter. I liked that in a man.

"I wanted to scope out the scene. See what I was turned down for," he answered, slinging his arm companionably around my shoulders and giving me a friendly squeeze.

I peered up at him. At six foot two, he was a good eight inches taller than me. "Turned down? You mean, for the craft bazaar?"

"Mmhmm. Turned down flat."

It was hard to believe — from the long list of contributors, the committee didn't seem to be too discriminating — and yet I knew Marcus well enough to trust that he was telling me the truth. "Soooo . . . what kind of, er, *craft* were you planning to present?"

His eyes twinkled — he knew what I was getting at. "Knives, darlin'."

"Knives. You mean, like kitchen knives or —"

"No, I mean like knives I made. It's what I do, Maggie. What I like to do, I mean, hobby-wise. I'm a knife artisan. Didn't you know?"

Honestly? No, I didn't. I racked my brain, trying to remember some lost bit of information that I'd misfiled in a dark corner somewhere, but I couldn't seem to dredge it up. "You know, I don't think I ever did know what you did. Outside of your fiddling with the band, of course."

That little piece of info I'd discovered just by chance around Christmas. Marcus, it seemed to me, enjoyed maintaining a web of the mysterious around himself at all times. Whether it was intentional or not, I wasn't quite sure. Maybe it was his military intelligence background — never be too forthcoming.

"Yeah, well, it's not my music they had a problem with. They denied my app because someone on the committee thought that by selling knives, they were opening themselves up to all sorts of legal liabilities. The L word is none too popular these days, if you know what I mean."

Well, geez, if Owen Thorsley could sell iron fireplace pokers and other sharp instruments of potential torture, I didn't see why knives should present a problem. "What kind of knives are they?" I asked with an eye toward politeness.

"All kinds. Mostly high-end outdoor and tactical knives that I market worldwide on my website and through Internet usegroups and forums. I haven't quite mastered pocket knives with any great success. They're a little tricky. Fixed-blade knives are more my area of expertise. I have some right here, if you'd like to see —"

Uh-oh. I recognized the double-bladed (*heh*) edge of passion in a man's voice as well as the next woman. Usually in reference to sports, sporting equipment, tools, technology, or anything that went *vroom vroom* . . . and yet always there was room for just one more obsession.

I started to panic as he began rooting around in a messenger-style bag he had strapped across his chest.

"This one — Damascus steel with a convex edge. The handle is rosewood, nice and simple — and what a beauty of a wood. Tooled pins holding the lot of it together, brass and leather spacers. See?"

"Gee, those are nice, Marcus. You made them yourself, did you?"

"From the carving of the handle to the forging of the blade itself. You see, there's more to knifemaking than you might expect. It's an art form that goes way back. I've always liked the idea of doing things the way they've been done for millennia, before automation and machines. The Army is what got me interested in them in the first place. Every soldier has to have his idea of the perfect knife; it's a question of survival. What makes the perfect knife, now, that's where the discussion comes in. Anyway, I took classes with some of the acknowledged masters of our time, found I had a knack for it, and a few years and an honorable discharge later, here we are."

So. This must be the way a man feels when

a woman starts discussing the problems she's having with her hair.

"Ah," I said. Retreat. Retreat was the only answer. I started to back away, s-l-o-w-l-y.

Knives. It must be a learned obsession. Who'da thunk they could hold such a fascination?

He was still blathering on about various sharpening methods as he followed me. We met up with Liss outside the pavilion office.

Her face lit up the moment she saw him. "Marcus! What a surprise, darling. I didn't know you were going to be here this morning."

"Neither did I."

"How nice — synchronicity."

Marcus laughed. "Hardly. I just wanted to see what I was being turned away from."

"You mean . . . ?"

"Yeah. I was going to donate Big Ben for the auction, but they turned me down."

Liss gave me a secret look. "Has Marcus introduced you to his knives yet?"

"Just today."

"Ah. I should have warned you."

"Funny. Very funny." Marcus made a wry face. "I'm being serious, you know."

"Oh? Did they say why they turned you down, ducks?"

"The usual nonsense about liability and

community ethics. You know the drill: *We can't have you selling these to the local youth, we'll all be murdered in our beds.*" All of a sudden he looked stricken. "I'm sorry, Liss. That was a thoughtless thing to say. I wasn't thinking about Isabella."

If Liss had taken offense at the slip, she wasn't showing it. "Never mind that. Besides, she wasn't killed in her bed, was she? I really think you should appeal that decision, Marcus. It's too late for the opening day celebration, obviously, but there's no reason you should be discriminated against in the future."

He shrugged. "I'm thinking it's not worth it. It doesn't look like I'd have many clients lurking about. Most of my sales come through the Internet anyway. Direct to consumer marketing. No big deal."

Prejudice was always a big deal, but maybe preserving one's dignity was equally important. No one wanted to admit to being downtrodden. Especially when the one in question happened to be male and macho to the max.

"I don't care one iota that you didn't realize teaming up made a difference." The anger in the female voice that rose sharply from inside the building we were standing next to was unmistakable. It was also unmistakably Jetta's.

Without a moment's qualm, Marcus, Liss, and I shushed each other and strained to hear through the screen door.

"You made me look like a fool, and I have to tell you, Mr. Yoder, I find that unforgivable. You're lucky I didn't decide to snatch the award out of your hands on the spot. As it is, I'm not sure the misrepresentation of your status is not actionable."

"Jetta —" Jeremy Harding's voice, a softer warning.

"Fine, maybe not actionable, but at the very least it's seriously unethical," she fumed. I could hear her high heels clattering none too gently against the wooden floorboards as she paced. "Just what were you thinking when you decided not to come clean about your project being a team effort?"

"I did not mean to mislead anybody." That was Eli, calmly trying to explain. "The paper, it did not give much space for names —"

"Excuses. You could have said something *before* I started singing your praises."

"Jet, let it go," Jeremy urged. "None of this is important right now. We need to get the show on the road."

"The show will be a circus if we allow

54

things like this to happen, and I have no desire to be the clown who falls off the bike."

"You won't be. Let's just get back out there."

"All right. Fine. But this is not over. Not by a long shot."

The three of us managed to break apart and leap away from the doorway just as Jetta shoved her way through and burst back into the sunshine. She froze as she flew past us, turned to glance back, then stiffened in recognition. Her fury at being overheard showed as two splotches of high color that burned beneath her angular cheekbones . . . then she recovered herself, turned sharply on her heel, and stalked toward the microphone. I'm not sure what she was muttering under her breath along the way, but without a doubt it wasn't pretty.

Jeremy followed quickly on her heels, passing Marcus and me with scarcely a glance. He did take note of Liss, though. His face went still for a moment, and then he changed direction and scurried away like a scared little bug being chased by a cat's paw.

Left to his own designs was Eli. He stopped when he saw us and gave a shrug. "That went *gut, ja?*" Shaking his head, he moved off in the opposite direction, away from the pavilion and the pending auction.

Liss cleared her throat and smoothed her hand down her shirtfront. "Well, I suppose I've dallied long enough. I'll be off to the auction, then. I have an armoire to win."

I wasn't sure I could watch more of Jetta and Jeremy behaving like lord and lady of the proceedings. "If you don't mind, I think I'll go pick up something from the bake tables I saw being set up," I told her. "My grandpa has a real sweet tooth, and I saw some oatmeal raisin cookies that have his name written all over them."

"Have fun, then." She patted me on the shoulder. "While you're at it, perhaps you wouldn't mind picking up a loaf of that Amish sourdough bread for me. Oh, and maybe a loaf of cranberry cinnamon swirl as well?"

"Done!" I said, relieved to be off the hook for the Jeremy and Jetta show. "What about you, Marcus?"

"Hmm. Do you think they have sugar cookies alongside those oatmeal raisin cookies? I'm a sucker for a good sugar cookie."

"There's only one way to find out."

He gave Liss a quick kiss on the cheek. "Knock 'em dead, Liss. We'll check back shortly."

Away from the crowded pavilion, the day

seemed lighter, brighter, and a lot less frenzied. Marcus and I wandered in silence a moment, soaking in the burble of light-hearted people energy. A number of tables had been set up along the main path while we were scoping out the pavilion's goodies. Church groups, mostly, along with tables full of Girl Scout cookies and a sign encouraging all to "Support Troop 84!" I picked up a box of Thin Mint cookies for myself (*so* good frozen!) and two boxes of Short-bread cookies for my dad because I knew they were his favorites, and made a promise to stop by the old homestead to drop them off for him later that day, along with Grandpa's.

Down the way, Marcus had stopped by a long table covered, unlike all the others, by full-sized quilts in cheerful colors and patterns, and loaded with basket upon basket of loaves of bread in all different shapes and sizes, trays of cookies, bags of homemade egg noodles, and more. Behind them was a booth from which the most wonderful smells emerged, manned by three no-nonsense Amish women garbed in utilitarian cotton dresses that reached to just above their sturdy shoes. I edged closer, trying to identify the food smells. Chicken, for one. Possibly stewed with egg noodles and sage.

Bundles of the savory herbs hung from the rafters of the booth, easily identified by the silvery green of its dried leaves. Yes, there was the sign: Stewed Chicken and Noodles, $2.50 Per Cup. Those not counting their carbs too closely could add a scoop of garlic mashed potatoes for an extra fifty cents.

I glanced at my watch. Eleven fifteen. Was that too early for lunch? My stomach didn't think so.

"Can I help you?"

I looked up. The youngest of the three women had noticed me eyeing their sign. Round of cheek and breast and hip, she was the picture of robust good health that hard work and clean living can give you. Perhaps a bit broader than Hollyweird's skewed definition of perfect female beauty, but I doubted most men would mind. I smiled at her. "I was just trying to decide whether my diet could stand a cup of the noodles. They smell wonderful."

"Ah. What is a cup of noodles on a day like today?" she asked in a soft voice reminiscent of the wisest oracles of long ago. She lifted the lid on the closest pot and stirred the contents. The languorous movements raised a snake of steam that beckoned as it tantalized. "It is but a few quick steps down the lane to burn it off. A row in the garden to be weeded. A loaf of dough to be kneaded. Not so much." Her bright gaze glittered as it lifted, and she cocked her head to one side like a bird. "You are a slim girl. Not yet a mother, I do not think. A little meat and egg noodles would do you some good. Put some color in your cheeks and make your skin glow." She paused and glanced over my shoulder, her eyes twinkling. "Would you not agree, Luc? She could use a little fattening up, *ja?*"

I turned to find Luc Metzger watching us both from one of the nearby picnic tables. In the sunlight, his hair and chin-only beard glowed like a mixture of burnished gold and copper, and I was struck again by his resemblance to some pre-Raphaelite angel. For a moment his face was without expression as his eyes met mine. Then, as the woman turned away to ask another to reach the stack of cups, his gaze lowered as I watched. Slowly. By the time he had brought his gaze back up to mine, my cheeks were hotter than the noodles in the pot. His ruddy lips quirked up at the corners, as though he was aware of my schoolgirl discomfort and was amused by it.

Holy sheep.

"I take it you found the bread."

Marcus appeared at my elbow, a large

waxed paper sack dangling from his fingers. I nodded toward it. "I take it *you* found the cookies."

"Three dozen of the best damned sugar cookies you could ever hope for."

"Oh, good," I said faintly, glancing back to where Luc Metzger had been giving me the eye. But he was gone now, no doubt scared off by Marcus's sudden appearance. I gave a sigh of relief. Whatever the reason for his little game of cat and mouse, I wanted no part of it. "I was about to yield to the call of the Carbmonster and indulge in a cup of this lady's chicken and noodles for lunch. Want some?"

"Sure, why not? We can take a cup back for Liss."

I stepped back to the booth, waiting my turn. It didn't take long.

The rosy-cheeked Amish woman smiled at me. "You have decided, *ja?*"

"*Ja.* I mean, yes," I said, blushing at my slip. I had a knack for picking up the speaking habits and dialects of others without even trying. Sometimes it made for an uncomfortable moment — after all, you never knew when someone would think you were poking fun at them. "I'll take three cups of the noodles. With mashed potatoes," I added as an afterthought. If a girl was going to go all the way, the least she could do was enjoy it.

"Three? Well. You *are* a girl who makes up her mind." She laughed as she scooped up three servings of mashed potatoes and ladled the thick noodle, gravy, and chicken concoction over them. "A woman after my own husband's heart. He is the same way. My Luc. Once he makes a decision, that is the way things are going to be . . . for better or for worse."

"Oh," I said with some surprise as I dug in my purse for my wallet. "So you are Luc Metzger's wife?"

"Ja." She smoothed back a lock of shining red hair that had slipped from beneath her white cap as she gazed at my face more closely. "You know him?"

I shook my head. "Only from the auction. I was at the pavilion when they announced that Eli Yoder's cabinet had been chosen for the top award in the charity auction. He does really nice work, your husband. Have you been together long?"

"We have been married for over nine years now."

Perhaps that was the reason for her pink cheeks. If his smile had meant what I thought it did, Luc Metzger had a healthy interest in the female form, perfect or not.

61

"Children?"

She nodded, now gazing distractedly over my shoulder. "Two daughters, eight and four, and two sons, six and two."

Every two years, just like clockwork. "What a blessing. Oh, you know, I'll also need two loaves of bread — one sourdough, and one cinnamon cranberry — and a dozen oatmeal raisin cookies."

She gathered the items together for me, but it seemed to me that her peaceful façade of moments ago had fled. I wondered why, but it was not my place to ask.

"Thank you," I told her, handing her a twenty-dollar bill. "Keep the change."

She held the money in her hand, staring at it blankly. I was about to walk away when she reached over the counter and stopped me with a hand on my shoulder. Her dark eyes bore into mine, hot and insistent, almost wild. "There's trouble here ahead for us all. A sickness, settling in. We who see must be very wary and vigilant."

She released me suddenly, muttering to herself. The other two ladies in the booth, I couldn't help noticing, had backed away and were now watching her, senses on edge, fear in their eyes.

"Thank you," I said again, even though I knew she would not hear me.

Odd woman, I thought to myself. Nice, but odd.

I tried to brush off her warning as I rejoined Marcus and handed him his cup of noodles. It didn't mean anything, no matter that it was an echo of some of the things I had been thinking and feeling for weeks now. Things were better in town. They were. The dark months were gone. The time for concern was long past. There was no reason to fear.

But despite what I was trying to convince myself of, the Metzger woman was just one more notch on Ye Olde Worry Belt.

"You okay?" Marcus asked me as I walked in silence beside him, a frown tightening my brow. "You seem kind of distant."

"I'm okay. I . . . Marcus, what has been going on with the N.I.G.H.T.S. lately? What have I been missing?"

He gazed at me, quietly assessing. "Well, now, why the sudden interest?"

I shrugged, blushing. "Well, it's not like I haven't been involved. I've only missed a few of the meetings."

"Eight, Sunshine."

Eight. Had it really been that many? Liss had never said a word, never once questioned me about my absence from the informal get-togethers. What would I have told her, if she had? That I was afraid? So unnerved by my experience on the lake in December that my only way of dealing with it was to withdraw? I had tapped into something that night, something stronger and more powerful than anything in my wildest imaginings. Something . . . primal.

And the worst thing was, I had not a single clue how I had done it. And that scared me more than anything. I was afraid of myself, and the only way I could think of to deal with it was total and utter avoidance.

To give up the ghost, as it were.

I cleared my throat and shrugged away my feelings of guilt. "Fine. Eight, then."

"Want to talk about it?"

"I — There's something wrong, Marcus, and I don't understand it. I don't understand any of it, and it scares the crap out of me. I mean, you and Liss and the others, you've been a part of this for a while now. You've had time to adjust, right? But I . . ." I took a deep breath as the panicky feeling welled up in my chest. I closed myself down, purposely, to combat it. "I don't want to talk about it right now. I can't."

"Hey, hey." He stopped me when I would have walked away. "I didn't mean to make you feel like I was giving you a hard time. If you're not comfortable, it's okay to take things slow. Whenever you're ready, we'll be there. We're not going anywhere."

Because the spooky stuff wasn't going anywhere. Maybe that was a part of what I was most afraid of. That what we had been experiencing was more than a blip on the radar screen. Maybe, just maybe, it was a bona fide trend.

I thought it, but I didn't say it. Instead I attempted a smile. "Thanks, Marcus. I appreciate it."

We started walking again, and he began to fill me in. "We had baseline readings on most of the sites in the area where people have reported strange experiences. That's nothing you haven't heard before. But what you may not realize is that all of the places we have investigated have shown marked signs of growing worse. And we're receiving more reports all the time."

It was as I had feared. Sensed. "But why?"

"I don't know."

"That doesn't really make me feel better, Marcus."

"At least we can try to understand what's happening. That's a start."

But was it enough?

As we reached the pavilion and stopped to search for Liss, we were enveloped by a wave of applause that had the air of completion about it. The auction was just ending.

Liss saw us at the same time that we caught sight of her. We met somewhere in the middle, people milling about all around us. In the pavilion, the armoire and other large items were being manhandled into position on furniture dollies.

"Done already?" I asked Liss, handing her a cup of noodles.

"Mmm. Thanks. They smell lovely."

"Taste lovely, too. So," I said, nodding toward the armoire, "how much did it go for?"

"Five thousand, two hundred and seventy-five."

Marcus broke in with a long, low whistle. "Wow. Kudos to the team of Yoder and Metzger. Maybe I should rethink this foray into the knifemaking business."

Somehow I couldn't quite picture Marcus as a sedate and sedentary woodworker. The idea had me smiling. "Stick with the knives and the band," I recommended. "Much more your style." To Liss, I asked, "So, should I call my dad and enlist him and his pickup for furniture-moving duty?"

"No need. I didn't win it."

"What? Oh. I'm sorry. I know how much you wanted it."

"C'est la vie, ducks. Someone will love it,

and that's all that's important. There will be other armoires for me. The woman who won it looked thrilled to have it."

I cast my eye around. "Who was it? Do we know her?"

"I don't see her just now. An older woman — not quite my age — who was here with some friends. It was adorable, really — she squealed like a young girl when the auctioneer announced her the winner. Obviously the right woman won."

I was still stuck on her description of herself. I looked askance, trying to see it. "You're not old, Liss. You're as young and hip as any of my friends."

"Tell that to my knees and back," she quipped, chucking me affectionately beneath my chin. "They put up quite the fuss every time I try to weed my garden. One of these days they might just win the battle, too. But until then, I quite enjoy thumbing my nose at them, just for the spite of it."

That's one of the things I like best about Liss. She's as much a rebel at heart as I had always longed to be.

"Maybe we could get Eli to build you an armoire to spec," Marcus suggested. "I'm sure he'd be thrilled."

"It's a nice thought, but you heard Eli. His armoires are meant to be plain. What attracted me so much to this one in particular was the carvings."

"They're very unusual for a piece of Amish furniture," I conceded.

"That they are. In fact, I don't know how closely you looked at them, Marcus, but they appeared almost Celtic in design. Knotted vines, circular patterns, interlacing features, and I even saw crescent moons. Definite symbolism in use there. It might be interesting to talk to this friend of Eli's."

Nature symbolism? Well, the Amish are known for their ties to the land, so in a way that made sense. Or perhaps Luc Metzger was a creative personality locked within an austere belief system. Just because a person was born Amish didn't mean that he could completely go against his inner being.

How well I was beginning to understand that myself.

"I met his wife just a little while ago," I commented as an aside.

"Oh?" Liss's whip-sharp gaze turned my way. "And Luc?"

"Mmhmm, I kinda-sorta met him, too." And I wasn't about to elaborate on that one. I was still a bit shell-shocked over the unexpected tractor-beam eye lock.

"Well, lead on, dear girl. If I can't have the armoire, at least I can tell the man how enamored I am of his work."

"Sure."

The three of us left the pavilion together, wending our way amicably among the shoppers and festival junkies, the teenagers who were there for the food and the party atmosphere, the retirees who steadfastly avoided them, and strolled back down the walkway toward where the Amish women had set up shop with their baked goods and aromatic egg noodles. High above us the noonday sun shone brilliantly in a sky clear and devoid of the April showers that had been plaguing the area of late, as per the dictates of the season. I lifted my face to the sky, trying to feel the heat of the sun, but there was none to be had. In its stead a chill slithered across my cheek, taunting and cruel. I shivered at the reminder that while spring had arrived, summer was not yet within our grasp.

Marcus noticed, and threw his arm around my shoulders, then slung his arm around Felicity's waist for good measure. "Can't let my two best girls get cold, now, can I?"

I felt more than a little bit guilty at the flush of warmth that radiated from that simple touch. Marcus was one of those guys who can throw any woman for a loop, and I was definitely not immune. I was human, and he was a charmer, through and through. It was his nature. But it was all innocent fun. Marcus was taken, and so was I, for all intents and purposes, and to dwell on the sensations would be wrong. So I did what any self-respecting good girl would do: I pushed them from my thoughts and tried to focus on the quilt-covered table just ahead. F-O-C-U-S.

Unfortunately, Mrs. Metzger wasn't behind the table anymore. I stepped up to it, waiting for one of the other bonneted ladies to attend to me. The first to finish with her customer was the little dark-haired one with the pale, drawn face. She looked at me and gave a little smile that did nothing to warm the wariness reflected in her features. "Can I help you?"

I cleared my throat. "Hi, there. I was here a little while ago and was helped by a Mrs. Metzger. Luc Metzger's wife. I was wondering if you knew where they've gone. My friend here" — I indicated Liss behind me — "wanted to meet them."

The dark little Amish woman leaned to one side to catch a glimpse of Liss, then exchanged a private glance with the raw-boned matron who was working the table with her. Before I could wonder what the glance meant, she began straightening and restacking the loaves of bread on the table. "She went off looking for her man. There." With nothing more than a flick of her gaze, she indicated the path the Metzger woman had taken.

The three of us headed in that direction, not certain of where we were going, but Heritage Park wasn't overly large or grand, and I felt sure we could spot her eventually.

As it turned out, we hit pay dirt. We found them both.

The beautiful Amishman was just where I might have expected him to be — standing in the door of one of the big barns, beside an open buggy. His wife stood facing him, her hand on the horse's neck. It was an iconic scene that might have appeared in any number of romantic advertisements for Amish Country, USA . . . except they were embroiled in conversation, and from the tension that wavered like a heat mirage in the air around them, it was not pretty.

All three of us seemed to notice at the same time, and we hesitated as one as words floated back to us, audible even through the festival babble.

"You promised me, Luc. No more. Are you forgetting why we came here? Why you went to work at the factory?"

"Are you saying we do not need the

money, Hester? That our children do not need new shoes? That we do not have repairs to make to the farm?"

"Are you saying that money is the most important thing?" she countered, her chin quivering but set in determination.

"Of course not. But I will not stand by while they want, either."

"We are fine. We do what we can do. No one can do more. You *are* working, Luc. You are supporting our family. The children need a father more than they need material things." She paused a moment, then said, her voice vibrating with emotion, "I need their father, too."

His jaw tightened. "Hest —" A warning, no comfort to be found.

Watching, listening, was perhaps wrong, but the three of us were held fast in the grip of the couple's private torment, unable to turn away. Tears sprang to my eyes as I felt the depths of the young woman's need, a need that went unmet. Didn't he know what she was feeling? Couldn't he understand? I bit my lip as raw emotion coiled into a knot just below my ribs.

"Luc, please. Please."

Suddenly his demeanor changed. Anger melted away from his features, replaced by a softer, chiding tenderness. "Hest, it is a simple job, just for the afternoon. Do you think I will fly away from you so quickly?" Abandoning the customary public reserve our Amish are known for, he reached out for a moment and stroked his thumb along the creamy line of her jaw before withdrawing to a more respectable distance. "I will be home by supper, and next weekend we can buy some of the things we have been needing. We'll make a day of it. Lunch by the lake in the park. Won't that be fine?"

She didn't want to say yes. She didn't want to give in. And yet, watching her, I was just as certain that she could not help herself. "All right. Just this one last time, Luc?"

His face broke into a smile meant to be reassuring. Then, in one heartstoppingly masculine motion, he turned and, with a flex of mighty shoulders, lifted down a heavy, old-fashioned bicycle that was held fast to the back of the buggy. A toolbox soon followed suit and was strapped to the bike's back fender. "Keep supper warm for me."

As he pedaled off, he gave a shrill whistle over his shoulder. At the sound, the fuzzy head of a medium-sized pooch popped briefly into sight above the rim of the buggy. The dog leapt down and was after him like a shot, a blur of muted browns in motion.

Still caught up in the drama we had accidentally witnessed, none of us had thought to move before Hester Metzger turned away from him. It didn't seem to matter; if she recognized me, she gave no indication. Lost in thought, she smoothed her hand over her cheek once — to hold dear the memory of his hand or to wipe away all hint of tears, I could not tell — before straightening her shoulders and disappearing within the darker depths of the barn.

"Poor lamb," Liss said under her breath.

"Men," I grumbled by way of agreement.

We both turned to give the lone male in our vicinity the evil eye.

"Hey, hey," Marcus said with a laugh, holding up his hands in surrender. "I didn't do it."

There was something about watching a good woman get taken advantage of that made most other good women snarl. Wine, women, or song, the reason didn't matter. It was the end result that was so painful to watch, compounded by the residual fear that it could one day be us. I didn't know what Luc Metzger was about that afternoon, or why Hester was afraid. I didn't need to. The situation, whatever it was, was one that resonated in the heart of every woman, everywhere. We'd all been there at some point in time. Some of us might even be there again in our lives, and therein lay the rub. "Guilt," I sniffed, "by association."

Marcus looked at me mournfully. "You are a hard, hard woman."

Liss laughed. "That's the thing about women. Any one of us can be hard and unyielding, when provoked. Best to remember that, ducks. It will keep you out of trouble."

CHAPTER 3

We turned back toward the heart of the festivities, but my heart was no longer in them. The sunlight, once bright and warming, now felt harsh and unyielding. The chill in the air now possessed teeth. The laughter, no longer cheery, seemed instead to have a predatory edge, one that wound and circled through the proceedings, watching for a chance to strike. And it had struck, hadn't it? Hester Metzger had felt it. Who would be next?

I shivered and closed my jacket more tightly around me.

The afternoon's joy tainted, I was glad when Marcus raised his hand and shouted, "Hey, Aunt Marion!"

I glanced up just in time to see Marion Tabor, librarian extraordinaire, coming toward us. Marion was Marcus's favorite aunt and a long-standing friend of my mother. By all outward appearances she was a maiden-lady scholar — just so long as one overlooked (a) her tendency to ogle every male who came into view, and (b) her unfortunate penchant for mixing animal prints into her wardrobe in every way possible. This afternoon, her choice in animal prints included a pair of faux-zebra cowboy boots that would give any old-school rocker heart palpitations, a shearling-lined jacket, and a leopard print purse. All in all, pretty reserved for Marion.

Marion held up a hand from which dangled several plastic bags loaded with goodies. "Howdy, neighbors!" she shouted, smiling with pleasure at the lot of us. "Fancy meeting you here."

"Always good to see my favorite auntie." Marcus wrapped his aunt in a big bear hug, then kissed her with a resounding smack on the cheek. "And just what are you up to today?"

Marion held up the bags. "Shopping, shopping, and more shopping," she confessed. "I think I broke the bank. I found the cutest little rooster and hen salt-and-pepper shakers in one of the antiques and collectibles tents, and a Victorian-style mirror that will be perfect at the bottom of my stairs. And the food! Lordy, lordy, lordy. I'll have to diet for a month when all is said and done . . . but it'll be worth it," she said with a wicked little wink. "Did you all find what you were looking for?"

That and a little more, I thought, picturing Hester's sad face. "I bought a few cookies for Grandpa G," I told her. "Not much else, though. And Felicity —"

"I totally missed my mark," Liss inserted with a sigh. "Completely outdone at the auction, I'm afraid. I had so wanted that armoire. Although I did pick up quite a few lovely wood pieces from Eli Yoder for the store —"

"So the day wasn't a total loss," I finished for her.

Marion chuckled at the exchange. "Do you two always think in tandem? No wonder you have such a good working relationship. Louisa Murray won the armoire, I hear — I just ran into her down the way. She's one of my library regulars, and of course your mother and I know her from church. She's over the moon about it! Nice lady." She paused for a moment. "You know, Marcus, I'm glad I ran into you today. I have a little situation at the library you might be interested in."

"Oh? What kind of situation?" Marcus asked.

"Well . . . I don't want to go into it here.

Little pitchers, and all that. I wouldn't want anyone to get the wrong idea. You know how people can be . . ."

"You mean like those little pitchers with the big ears, way over there by the ice cream booth? Spill it, Aunt Marion."

She gave a self-conscious laugh. "I'm not usually this tongue-tied, don't know what's wrong with me. The truth is . . . our ghost has been acting up again."

"Boiler Room Bertie?"

"Right. I've lived with the man for a long time now — the last twenty years at least — and he has always been a gentleman. Very respectful, low-key, never frightening. But lately — lately things have been different."

"Different, how?"

"I don't know how to explain it. Maybe it would be better if you saw it for yourself. You and your, uh, friends."

She meant the N.I.G.H.T.S., of course. Which left me wondering. I wasn't sure that I had known Marion was aware of the work of the N.I.G.H.T.S. Was she also in the know about Marcus's religious leanings? Had she learned of his relationship with Liss? Despite the lack of sophistication that her choice of clothing and favorite pastime (Manwatching, with a capital M) perhaps suggested, Marion was highly educated and

intelligent. She could also be highly percep-
tive.

And *that* was scary.

Marcus lifted his brows questioningly at
me and Liss. I don't know what Liss's face
told him, but the message I sent was decid-
edly neutral.

"Why don't I stop in this week, sometime?" he suggested. "See what kinds of
things are going down."

Marion patted his cheek. "Perfect," she
said, relief and gratitude evident on her
face. "You're a good boy." She shifted her
bags on her wrist in order to see her watch.
"Oh, my goodness, is that the time? I'm going to have to run. I've promised to put in
some time at the soup kitchen this evening,
and I need to get these things home beforehand. See you all later. Enjoy your day!"

We walked about a bit more, but the
exuberance of the earlier part of the day
was gone. I was relieved when Liss asked
whether Marcus and I would like to join
her for afternoon tea. But even leaving the
park behind us, Liss and I happily ensconced inside my aging VW and Marcus
following on his rumbling motorcycle, did
not help to alleviate the unease that slithered
at the pit of my stomach.

Something was up; I knew it. But I could

not imagine what.

Liss and I made a quick detour by my parents' house to drop off the cookies. My grandpa accepted his with a gleam in his eye that made it seem like I'd handed over the keys to a treasure chest. Then again, considering the bland, mushed-up foods my mom insisted on feeding him to keep him regular, maybe I was. He made me promise to keep the cookies on the down low from my mom, who at that moment was visiting with Mel and the girls. I did, but I told him he had to share with my dad as a price for my silence.

The deal struck, I gave him a kiss and a hug good-bye, and dragged Liss out of there before Grandpa's gleam turned in her direction.

Tea ended up extending into a wonderful dinner of grilled vegetables and cheese omelets, perfect with a cup of spicy chai and animated conversation. The sun was making a hasty descent toward the horizon when I finally rose from my seat at the kitchen table with a lazy stretch and announced that I had to be heading for home.

"Would you like to stay?" Liss offered. "It would take me only a moment to turn down a bed for you."

"Oh . . . thanks . . . but I have a couple of

stops to make on the way. Thanks for the offer, though," I said, feeling not a little guilty. I was putting her off, and I knew it, but I couldn't seem to help myself. The last and only time I'd stayed over had been nearly six months before, the night that Liss's sister, Isabella, had been found dead on her property just up the road. The memories of that time were not exactly conducive to a good night's sleep . . . especially when I remembered Cecil, the big black hound who had disappeared — literally — into the night. A guardian of the spirit kind, Liss had said. But was that a positive thing? The jury was still out, in my mind.

"Well, you're welcome any time, you know. Marcus?"

Marcus was in mid-gulp, polishing off the last of his chai. He set the cup back on its saucer with a clatter and pushed to his feet. " 'Fraid I've got an early morning, luv. Uncle Lou is needing some strong-armed help setting up at the church before people start arriving for morning services. They're having an ice cream social tomorrow afternoon to raise money for the local firehouse. I promised I'd lend a hand."

Liss smiled indulgently. "Always the noble

one. Do tell your Uncle Lou hello from me, then."

"Will do."

Marcus followed me out. I shivered the moment I left the warmth and security of the big house, and did not dawdle. The night air had gone crisp again — a frost tonight seemed a done deal. And after the sunny beauty of the day, too! It didn't seem right, but that was the Midwest for you. All seasons at once. Standing in the open doorway in a golden halo of light, Liss saw us off, her slender hand raised in soft farewell as I started Christine's engine. Was it a trick of the light that I saw a shadow hovering like a sentinel at her feet? I almost hoped so — Cecil might not be very reassuring to me, but I'm sure he made Liss feel as safe and secure as a witch can be.

Giving one last wave, I pulled forward down the paved drive, across the green, and through the thick expanse of trees that were twisting and swaying violently all around me as I moved through the night.

Too violently — the spring breezes of the day had all but abated while we made merry around Liss's table, so what was going on? Nervously I darted a quick glance to the left and to the right, but the glow from my headlights did nothing to cut through the thick blackness the trees were now sheltering.

Mother Mary, what a strange night. If I didn't know any better, I might have thought there was energy moving. Big energy. A great, wallowing river of it.

As I drove, I took comfort from the single wavering beam from Marcus's motorcycle following close behind. The old county roads were narrow, with no shoulder, and were rutted from the winter frost heave, so I was proceeding at a veritable snail's pace, not wanting to risk damage to one of Christine's ancient axles. Unfortunately, my slower progress meant I had ample time to survey the landscape around me, and it was dark as pitch out there. Acres and acres of fields stretched on either side of me, some already harrowed and disked and planted, others still rough with their winter stubble, probably destined for a fallow season. In the summer, Indiana is a green place, thick and lush with vegetation. Tonight, arid and cold beneath the endless night of the new moon, it might have been moonscape.

Two junctions later, and I was on County Road 500, another road that was all too familiar to me. Joe Aames, a big teddy bear of a man I knew from the N.I.G.H.T.S., lived on this road, next to a graveyard that was long out of commission to all but the spirit world. As I'd found out in December, spirit activity ran high among the weather-worn gravestones. In December we'd recorded magnetic field disturbances, EVPs (electronic voice phenomena — in other words, ghostly voices recorded where no voices should be heard), and plenty of spirit orbs, those invisible floating balls of energy that seemed ever present where spirits liked to tread.

And yes, it had scared the bejeebers out of timid little me.

Tonight the old cemetery appeared at rest as I passed it — thank goodness — the tombstones silent sentinels in the night. I shivered and motored on, grateful not to feel the cold nudge of the dead attempting to make contact.

Another turn. Somehow the road ahead was even darker than the one I'd just turned off. Geez-oh-pete, didn't anyone out this way believe in security lights? The view of the road was limited to the sickly glow of my headlights wobbling around in their old chrome frames. I leaned forward to peer more intently through the windshield and into the syrupy dark. I knew I was passing houses here and there, as evidenced by the limestone driveways and plain aluminum mailboxes my high beams picked out. I didn't even need to see the names on the mailboxes — Schultz, Schwartz, Metzger, Ritter, Lutz — to know I was passing through an Amish farming community. The lack of security lights and electric power lines gave proof enough. All of the inhabitants, I decided, must have hearts of stone. Mine would have succumbed to a fear of the dark long ago.

A flicker of red in the road ahead caught my eye. And then another, and another. I eased off the gas pedal. What was it? Animal eyes reflecting in my headlights? Oh, but they reflected green, didn't they? Not red. And the flashes seemed kind of big for eyes . . .

Slowly the scene ahead came into view. The red flashes weren't eyes. They were the rear reflectors on a congregation of buggies blocking the road in front of me.

I slowed down to a crawl, barely creeping forward by inches as I tried to decide what was going on. Marcus pulled his motorcycle up beside me on my left and motioned for me to roll down my window.

"Stay here," he told me. "I'm going to go up and find out what's going down." He started to push his bike forward, then paused. "Why don't you turn on your flashers? We wouldn't want anyone rear-ending the lot of us."

"Gotcha."

He parked his bike in front of me and thrust down the kickstand while I fiddled in the dark for the flashers. There — *got 'em.* I had left my window down, and now wisps of conversation were floating back to me as Marcus hailed someone I couldn't see.

"Evening," he called out, his tone friendly but neutral. "Is there a problem here? I'd be glad to help if I can."

I didn't hear the answer, but I saw Marcus's stance go from loose-jointed and casual to a kind of stillness I'd never seen from him. It certainly didn't make me feel any better. I peered through the windshield, willing my headlights to reach farther into the darkness. What was in front of the buggies? Marcus made his way carefully between them, then disappeared from sight.

Stay here, Marcus had said.

Hey, wait a minute! I thought, exasperated with myself. I was a grown woman, and it was obvious that a group of law-abiding Amish men was not something a girl needed to fear on a dark spring night. The only thing keeping me in the car was my own overdeveloped sense of propriety and duty. Marcus was fulfilling the role of overly protective male, as usual, and that was nice, but I was not at risk here. And that being the case, there was no reason I couldn't just find out for myself what was going on.

Right? Right.

Sometimes a girl just has to take charge of her own destiny.

Before I realized I'd come to a decision, my hand was on the chrome door lever and the door was swinging wide on creaking hinges.

Outside, my headlights were making a valiant attempt at dispelling the creepiness of the dark surroundings. Unfortunately, the repeating red flashes of my taillights were counteracting the soothing effect, casting a gaudy carnival glow over all. Clearing my throat, I edged toward the buggies, my desire to assert my independence somehow less resolute now that I had left the security of my car. The closer I came to the buggies, the more I found myself rising on tiptoe.

Not to see over them. To quiet my steps.

Marcus had taken a zigzag path between the old-school vehicles, but I didn't follow. I couldn't. The horses were shifting their weight nervously, their movements constantly realigning the buggies and backing them closer together. As I had no wish to become a Maggie sandwich, I closed in on the nearest one, a low-slung model that looked short enough for me to see over. But not short enough, so I climbed onto the running board, gripping the sides for balance.

There were still more carriages off the road. Their positions were heedless and haphazard, which somehow unnerved me even more, but that was nowhere near as unsettling as the circle of men I saw standing on the edge of the field, huddled together as though for protection.

This was not some kind of Amish rendition of a Chinese fire drill.

I watched one of the men hunker down, stretching his hand toward a shadow on the churned earth. After only a moment or two he rose again, shaking his head. As he walked back toward where I stood behind the grouping of buggies, even before he encountered the glow from the headlights, I could tell by the shape of the man's body and by the way he moved that it was Marcus.

"What is it?" I called out softly.

He glanced up and stopped in his tracks, and I felt him staring at me. Then he ducked and arched his way around the buggies until he reached me. "Maggie, I think you ought to go home."

I frowned, turning to look at the huddled men. Why weren't they coming back to their buggies? Why weren't they going home? "What's out there, Marcus?"

Marcus shook his head. "You don't want to know, love."

It didn't matter. In that moment the truth came to me, unbidden. It wasn't a what. It was a who lying at the edge of the field just ahead. "Marcus?"

He took my hand in his. "Don't ask, Maggie. It will all come out soon enough."

But I couldn't help myself. The need to know, to understand, had always run strong in me. To the bitter end. "Tell me."

He blew his breath out, the male urge to protect running a strong counter to my very female need for truth. His jaw clenched — once, twice — but his eyes on mine never wavered, ice blue flames in the night. "It's Luc Metzger."

CHAPTER 4

Mother Mary.

Luc Metzger, the talented Amish furniture carver I had met only that afternoon? Whose angelic face and earthly form could launch many an admiring female? Husband to the pretty Hester and father to their four children? Eli's friend Luc?

I shook my head, trying to wrap my mind around it. "We just saw him. Hours ago."

"I know, love. I know." Marcus squeezed my fingers gently and pulled until I followed him back toward Christine. His hand felt warm and reassuring against mine, but I was shivering and I couldn't stop. Questions were forming in my head like machine-gun fire. I couldn't stop them, either. "Was it an accident, Marcus? He was riding his bike earlier, and it *is* dark out here. It wouldn't be too hard to sideswipe a bike on this narrow road. And . . ."

My voice trailed off when my seeking eyes

connected with his. The breath squeezed out of my lungs. The air around me felt used up. As dead as the air in a room that's been closed off for years. As dead as the man lying out there on the cold, wet ground. *"God."*

Marcus was digging his cell phone out of his jacket pocket. "God or Goddess, neither had a part in this."

Marcus punched numbers onto the dial pad of his cell phone and turned away from me. Thank goodness we had lucked into cell coverage. It was usually pretty spotty out here, away from town — service could drop without notice, and often did. I wrapped my arms around myself, trying not to think of Luc Metzger lying just beyond the jumble of buggies.

Marcus spoke quietly into the phone before pressing another button and signing off. "They'll send someone out right away, along with an ambulance."

I turned my head and gazed out toward where I knew Luc must be. "It doesn't seem right, leaving him out there while we wait for the police to arrive."

"There's nothing else we can do."

I knew he was right, but still, it felt coldhearted to let him lie. "What about the others?"

"They won't disturb anything. They're

praying over his body."

At least he had friends with him now, watching over him. People he must have known. I would say a prayer for him tonight, too. It couldn't hurt. Sudden tears of sympathy welled in my eyes as I thought back to earlier today. His pretty auburn-headed wife, and the pride in her eyes when she had spoken of him as her husband. What would she and her children do now?

A headache, sudden and intense, struck me from behind, expanding outward like a violently red rose with viciously barbed thorns. I bit my lower lip against the rush of pain and the waves of nausea it brought along with it. "I-I think I'd better sit down."

Blindly I turned back in the direction of Christine, closing my eyes when the brilliance of the headlights hit my face. I foundered there a moment, uncertain which way to turn, the pain in the back of my head so intense that I feared I wouldn't make it. My knees buckled beneath me.

"Whoa there, girl. Hold on to me."

Strong arms closed around me, supporting me all the way back to Christine's worn bucket seat. As soon as I was sheltered within the old Bug's confines, I began to feel a little bit better.

"You okay, Mags?"

"I will be."

I was still sitting there, catching my breath, when a squad car squealed to a halt, sirens screaming. The sirens cut off suddenly, making the silence that followed feel harsh and abrupt. I lifted my head just in time to watch Tom Fielding in full cop mode step slowly from the vehicle, awash in the red-blue wigwags of police lights. His leonine coloring and stoic gray eyes suited him in a way I couldn't help but admire, in more ways than just the physical. Something about his stance — poised, controlled — spoke to me. Always. Ever the professional, he was practicing the first rule of smart police work: *Assess Your Situation Carefully Before Acting.*

His gaze passed slowly over the buggies, motorcycle, Christine. It snagged there a moment on me, slouched and shivering with the driver's side door open, but I got the distinct impression the pause had more to do with Marcus crouching at my feet than anything else. His expression unreadable, Tom turned away to speak briefly into the radio clipped to his shoulder harness before moving our way.

"You call this in?" he asked Marcus, avoiding my eyes.

Marcus nodded. "Over there," he said

with a jerk of his head. "The others are watching over him. Don't worry, they know not to touch anything."

Tom's gaze barely flickered in my direction. "Keep her here."

He needn't have worried. I wasn't going anywhere. The last thing I wanted was to see the destruction someone had wreaked upon one of Stony Mill's inhabitants. But that didn't mean I wasn't going to keep my eyes and ears open, and it didn't mean I was too far gone to feel miffed by his high-handed attitude. As though I was somehow both fragile flower and unnecessary annoyance in the night's doings.

As Tom picked his way carefully around the horses and buggies, I cast an accusing stare at Marcus.

Marcus held up his hands. "Hey, I'm just doing what I was told."

"Like you do that often," I grumbled under my breath. Especially where Tom was concerned. It hadn't exactly escaped my notice that the two of them didn't like each other much. He wasn't fooling anyone.

Within moments Tom was back, ushering the Amish prayer force away from the crime scene and heading to his car to talk to Dispatch. While he was occupied, an ambulance and a sheriff's cruiser pulled up behind his squad car, ripping through the stillness with the relentless onslaught of their dual lights and sirens. The sheriff's deputy quickly set out safety flashers and barricades before heading for Tom. In the meantime, the emergency medical technicians bustled about, poetry in motion as they got down to the business of gathering the tools of their trade. Tom pointed the way for the deputy, then headed over to intercept the EMTs. After only a few words the urgency drained from their movements — their healing skills would not be needed tonight. Resignedly they pulled the minimum of gear — a bag, a portable gurney that jackknifed open from a flat position, a couple of small stainless steel cases — from the back of the ambulance and followed Tom through the maze of buggies, leaving Marcus and me and all the Amish behind to scuff our feet against the chip-and-seal surface of the road, wondering what we should be doing to help.

"Stay?" I whispered to Marcus.

"You'll have to now," he whispered back. "He'll want to talk to you, too, I'm pretty sure. Do you need to call someone? Let them know you'll be late?"

I ran through the short list of people I *might* call. Tom and Marcus were both here, and I saw no reason to involve Liss or any of the N.I.G.H.T.S. My best friend Steff, a nurse, was working the night shift at the local hospital. My little sister was no doubt waiting up for her workaholic husband to get home, but calling her would only serve to spread the word far and wide — there wasn't a single soul in Stony Mill outside of my family's reach when it came to gossip. My brother lived too far away to help. Grandpa Gordon? Well, I wouldn't put it past him to try to hotfoot it all the way out here in his electric wheelchair, orange visibility flags flapping in the breeze. And there was no way I was going to wake my parents with something like this.

I shook my head.

Our Amish counterparts had been doing some quiet talking among themselves. Like one mind, one body, they began to straighten the haphazard positioning of the buggies and pull them off the road. Marcus went over to help. When they were finished, one of them offered his hand, enveloping Marcus's none-too-tiny extremity in a massive, pawlike grip.

"Jacob Ritter."

"Marcus. Marcus Quinn. Good to know you . . . but a pity that we had to meet on a night like this."

"A pity, *ja*."

"All of you knew Luc Metzger, I take it?"

The big man nodded. "*Ja*. He is Amish. A part of our congregation. He is . . . was . . . a cousin to my wife, Johanna. We are family."

He spoke in the short, perfunctory sentences typical of the men of his community, but his demeanor of strength, sturdiness, and hard work hinted at so much more than a picture postcard image can provide.

"We all knew Brother Luc," another of the men said, stepping forward. "What happened here tonight . . ." His voice trailed away in quiet sorrow.

By that time I had found my sea legs again, so I made my way over to where the men stood stamping the cold and uneasiness from their big, booted feet. I put my hand on Marcus's shoulder to let him know I was there.

"Pretty shocking," Marcus said as sympathetically and nonintrusively as possible. "No one ever thinks it will be someone they know, do they?"

I knew what he was doing. In his own laid-back way, he was working the crowd, making them receptive and putting them at ease.

"I've seen death before," Marcus went on, "but I don't know that I've ever been as surprised by it as I am tonight. I can't seem to wrap my mind around it. Why Luc Metzger?"

"It is God's will," intoned a stocky man with rawboned features and dour brown eyes. "Who are we to judge?"

God's will, the stocky man had said. Something told me God would have been appalled to have his name associated with this. It was the Amish way to treat with mercy and compassion even the most reviled of men, but it didn't sit well with me, not with Luc lying cold on the ground a scant ten yards away. Maybe I was missing something.

I cleared my throat. "Excuse me. What, exactly, did happen to Luc?"

Men . . . they're funny creatures. There they were, discussing away without concern. Insert one lone inquisitive female into the mix, and they seal up tighter than a humidity-swollen door. And Amish men appeared to be even more closemouthed than most. It wasn't so much that they were eyeing me with wariness or suspicion — actually, they weren't looking in my direction at all.

"It's not that we think you can't handle it." This from a beardless boy of seventeen or eighteen who, although he spoke with the tiniest bit of German inflection in his English, was dressed in jeans, trainers, and an Indianapolis Colts T-shirt. *Rumspringe*, the Amish called the custom that allowed their young people to experience life in the secular world before dedicating themselves to the traditional way. Seeing him on the street, I would never have guessed him to be Amish. "It is that the way that Luc died is unseemly."

Okay, most boys his age didn't use the word "unseemly." Definitely Amish.

"Unseemly." I turned my attention to Marcus, who had been watching my efforts with amusement. "And to the rest of us, that translates into . . ."

All traces of humor faded from Marcus's eyes. "Definitely not accidental. Blunt force trauma. Apparently someone mistook his head for a birthday piñata."

"Bad?"

"Yeah."

Nice.

My stomach gave a nasty little lurch, and my head began to throb again. I had known it was no accident — from the moment I'd stepped from the car, I'd felt the frenetic, unsettled sensation of dark energy on the move — but still, the glaring truth left me grasping for a handhold against the flow to keep from being swept away.

To the rest of us, the Amish were the Gentle People, love thy neighbor, honor peace not war, turn the other cheek. They were the last people who came to mind as victims when random acts of violence came a-knockin' at the door of life . . . because you'd have to be some kind of cretin to pick on an Amish man or woman who wouldn't lift a hand to defend themselves. Most of the good ol' boys around here had too much pride to lower themselves to that level. I gazed over my shoulder to where Tom and the EMTs were working in the bright light of floodlamps. "Who would have done such a thing?" I wondered aloud. "And why, for heaven's sake?"

"I do not know," came a grim voice from behind me. "But I will pray for him, of that I am certain."

I turned to the voice. It was the stocky man from before. "For Luc, you mean?"

"For his attacker."

"Well, *I* will not pray for him. Whoever he is." The teenager in the Colts tee stepped forward, his smooth features twisted against the fury he was only just repressing.

"Jonah!" Jacob Ritter hissed. "Be still."

"I will not. Whoever it was does not deserve our prayer, and he does not deserve

101

God's blessing. Luc was our brother. How can we pray for his attacker when we still haven't explained this to his wife? His children?"

"It is our way, Jonah. You know that as well as I."

In lieu of a retort that might have disappointed his father, Jonah picked up a pebble from the road and flung it away. It pinged off a tree across the road with an impact that could be felt by all.

Leaving the photograph-taking and evidence-collecting to his colleagues, Tom headed our way to begin phase two of the investigation.

"I'd like for each of you to sign in with your name, address, and phone number — if applicable," he amended quickly, as though taking note for the first time that the majority of his witnesses were of the Amish persuasion and probably not in possession of a phone. At least, not the traditional kind. I had heard some of them had begun carrying cell phones, acceptable to them since they were not physically linked to the outside world by wires. "I'll need to talk to each of you briefly about what happened here tonight before I can release you."

I watched and listened in silence as Tom began taking down information. Slowly the details I had been waiting to hear began to emerge. The community's weekly Sabbath meeting was to have been hosted at the Ritter farm that evening. Luc's wife, Hester, arrived with their children in tow, and was upset when Luc did not arrive in time for the meeting. When he still had not arrived by the end of the communal meal, the men had decided to go looking for him in the event of an emergency.

Jonah had been the one to come upon the gruesome scene first. The road was dark, the moon fitful behind lacy clouds. He'd been walking past the long stretch of wooded acreage that was known locally as Alden Woods when his German shepherd ran ahead of him, barking like mad.

"I wasn't really paying much attention at first. I thought old Blue here was after a rabbit, or a stray cat or something. I don't even know why I bothered to shine my flashlight over at first."

The first thing the beacon had caught on was the overturned bicycle, its reflectors blinking crazily in the narrow stream of light. Before Jonah had a chance to process the odd image, his dog had started to growl and had gone into a crouch, stalking something only he could see in the trees.

"It made my hair stand on end," Jonah

confessed. "I swung the light beam over farther in that direction . . . and that's when I saw Luc lying huddled on the edge of the road, less than ten feet away." He shook his head, visibly shaken by the memory.

"Did you see anything?" Tom asked him.

"No."

"Hear anything? Think back, son."

"No, nothing. Well, a car or two off in the distance, but when it's dark out here, you can hear a pin drop on the neighbor's kitchen floor. Nothing out of the ordinary."

Tom scratched some more on his notepad, frowning.

The next details were fuzzy. Jonah had hightailed it home and rung the summoning bell, the community's accepted SOS signal. His father took up the tale from that point, explaining how the men had hurried back to the farm and were quickly redirected by Jonah, only to find one of their own in the kind of trouble none of them had ever expected to see.

Luc Metzger, dead.

Tom cleared his throat. "Now, I have to ask this. Did anyone here touch or move the body or anything else out there, even by accident?"

There was a lot of head shaking and mumbled "no"s at the question. Jonah's father spoke up. "We saw the same thing you saw back there. We touched nothing, not even Luc himself, after it was obvious that Luc was gone." After a little pause, he said with some irony, "We may appear to live in another time, Deputy Fielding, but we are not ignorant of the laws."

The cause of death was all too apparent. Luc Metzger had been struck from behind with great force by an unidentified blunt object. His bicycle lay on the side of the road, his body crumpled next to it, half in and half out of the shallow ditch. Had he been on his bike when he was hit? Had death been mercifully instant? He was a simple man. Salt of the earth. Who could have had reason to kill him? Or could it have been an accident after all? Or a case of mistaken identity?

I found myself remembering back to his parting from his wife, Hester. How he'd calmed her fears of the moment. What would his poor wife think when she heard the news? Who would tell her?

So many questions.

Tom snapped his pocket notebook shut. "If no one has anything else to add, then you're free to go. I will ask you all to come down to the station in the morning to file a formal statement."

"Excuse me, Officer." An older gentleman with a full, grizzled beard broke in. "Tomorrow is Sunday."

"Yes?"

"We will be at worship tomorrow morning."

"Oh." Ill-at-ease was a look Tom did not wear well. It clashed with his gunbelt. "Oh, of course. Monday, then."

"Monday we will be hard at work on our farms. Our ways, you see, are very different from the lives you choose. Our families and our farms are our only priorities. That is our way. We do not live in your world, and do not wish to."

Nonplussed, Tom cleared his throat. "Well, I appreciate that, sir, but a crime has been committed. It seems that, whether you wanted it to happen or not, your world and mine have collided. It's not something anyone would have wished to happen, and yet it has. I would think that, under these circumstances, you can see that special sacrifices might be required."

The men muttered together. Finally the older man, acting as spokesman for the lot of them, nodded in acceptance. "We will do as you ask."

Tom's authoritative stance yielded just a notch as he offered, "If it will help, we'd be happy to send an officer out to your farms to take your formal statements."

"Thank you, officer. *Ja,* that would be helpful. You can appreciate that the spring-time is one of our busiest times of year."

"Yes, sir. I can appreciate that."

Tom waited until they had made motions to leave before turning his attention to me. "Maggie."

"Tom." Suddenly nervous beneath the weight of his measuring stare, I lifted my chin, determined to hold my own. False bravado, sure, but it works if you work it.

"I don't suppose you can tell me" — he came a step closer — "why I continuously find you smack dab in the path of danger?"

I opened my mouth to deny it, but with three unexpected deaths in my wholly in-nocent wake, it hardly seemed a debate that was triumph bound. "Well, I'm sure that's an exaggeration."

"Is it, now?"

I cast around for reinforcements, but Mar-cus provided no assistance to that end. He'd melted away as soon as the other men had rounded up their buggies, muttering some-thing unhelpful about leaving the two of us alone. I saw him rummaging through the saddlebag on the back of his bike and pretending not to be paying attention.

"Maybe you want to explain just how you came to be here tonight," he pressed a little harder.

The overbearing tone annoyed me just the teensiest bit. "Liss and I had dinner together, and I was just on my way home when I came upon this." I swept my hand wide to indicate the scene behind us, quiet now that all the buggies had pulled off into the distance.

"Umhmm. And Quinn, he comes into this . . . how?"

That was it? That's all he was concerned about with regard to my presence tonight? All of a sudden, everything clicked. "You're jealous."

His brows pulled together, and he drew his chin in. "What?"

"Of Marcus."

"I am *not* jealous." His voice had risen appreciably with each clipped word. The heads of the two EMTs and the sheriff's deputy swung sharply in our direction. Tom stopped and lowered his voice. "I am not jealous of Quinn. Unless . . ."

"Unless?"

He glanced over at the crime scene again, but the men had gone back to doing their thing. Marcus had taken out a Maglite that he kept in a saddlebag lashed to the back of his motorcycle and was flashing it along the roadside. He was also patently ignoring us. *Traitor!*

Satisfied, Tom edged a fraction closer to me. His eyes softened; he lifted a hand to brush the hair away from my eyes. "Unless you're telling me I have reason."

Drat. That sweet-eyed expression got me every time, but I didn't necessarily want him to know that. "We're just friends, Tom."

His hand fell away, and his brows pinched, ever so slightly. "Yeah, I know. Just friends who relate to each other on a level I'm not comfortable with, and who spend an awful lot of time together."

"I enjoy his company."

"*That* makes me feel better," he said flatly.

"And besides, it's not as though you and I are excl—"

"We could be."

We could be. And that was my fault, I supposed. "Tom . . ."

"Every time I turn around, he's panting at your feet."

And there we were again, circled around back to the Marcus issue when we both knew that wasn't what was holding me back. "He is *not* . . ." I stopped myself just in time. There was something terribly wrong with discussing your love life when a dead man was in the wings. "We can talk about it later, okay?" I said, inclining my head pointedly toward the crime scene.

His mouth opened, then pulled into a rueful grimace. "You're right. I'm sorry."

"Forgiven." I meant it. Ours was a relatively young relationship, and like any other it was not immune from occasional moments of insecurity and doubt.

He cleared his throat. "Right. So, you were visiting your boss, you were driving home, and came upon this."

"Exactly."

"Pass any cars along the way?"

"None that I recall."

"Anyone on foot?"

"No one. Tom . . . this really is unsettling, isn't it?"

"Murder always is."

Tom was a small-town cop — it wasn't every day that we Stony Millers had to deal with something as worldly as murder. And yet, three such tragedies had now befallen Stony Mill in the last seven months. This crash course in murder investigation and helping the victims pick up the broken pieces of their lives . . . well, it was enough to make anyone twitchy. From that perspective, Tom and his cohorts probably deserved medals.

"Any ideas?"

He shook his head. "None that leap immediately to mind. There are too many questions that need to be answered right now." He paused, then said as a gentle admonishment, "You shouldn't be asking, though. You know the rules."

"I know." No fishing for info from the local officers of the law. Even if I did have a semi-close and almost-but-not-quite-personal relationship with one of them.

Which is why his next words took me by surprise . . .

"You don't read the papers much, do you, Maggie?"

Picking up on the undertones I sensed in his words, I gave him a sideways glance. "No. No, I don't."

He measured his words with care. "Two weeks ago, two Amish men were attacked and robbed in two separate incidents. One, just across the county line, in his own barn, and the other not too far from here, actually, out on the road. It's happened before, too, and our area doesn't seem to be the isolated case. Since they don't use the banking system, Amish men are rumored to have sums of cash on their property and on their person. Given the economy, not to mention the drug problems that seem unavoidable nowadays, is it any wonder?"

My mind percolated over all of this information. "Do you think those events and what happened to Luc Metzger tonight might be connected?"

Tom shrugged, leaving the conjecture up to me. "Chief Boggs issued a statement after the one that happened in our county, warning the Amish community to take precautions. We've made visits to as many local hubs as we could . . . but somehow that hasn't been enough. That much is clear."

"Were any of the others killed?" *Surely not, I haven't heard anything, I would have heard, everyone talks, that would be big news . . .*

"No. But that doesn't mean the same people aren't responsible."

I nodded to myself. "So maybe the situation got out of hand, or maybe he recognized the attacker, or maybe drugs were involved and he happened into the wrong place at the wrong time, or . . . Do they have any leads in the other cases, Tom?"

"The only thing I can tell you is what was reported in *The Gazette.* The Amish man who was attacked in our county — he recovered fully, by the way — said his attackers wore masks."

Attackers. As in plural.

Marcus sidled up, his Maglite announcing his presence. "Everything okay over here?"

Tom held up his hand in annoyance as the light accidentally — it *was* accidental, I hoped — caught him in the eyes. "Peachy. I've already talked to Maggie here. She said you both just happened upon this scene tonight. You want to corroborate that statement?"

"It's as she said. I was following her into town on my bike. The buggies were blocking our way. I went up to see if there was anything I could help with, and found this." Marcus shrugged.

Short, sweet, and to the point.

"Kinda cold for a motorcycle, isn't it?"

"I guess, if you're the type to be bothered by something like a little nip in the air. It's no big deal."

Tom stared at him, wanting to say more but holding back. "Maggie said that the men were already gathered around Luc Metzger's body when you arrived."

"Yeah."

"Did you see anyone touch him?"

"No. They were just standing there, around him. One of them, I forget who just now, said no one had touched anything. By the time I got here, it was pretty obvious that the guy was too far gone for help. I imagine they had come to the same conclusion on their own."

His words brought the visual again, thoughts I'd rather not entertain. Violence of any sort makes me cringe. I didn't know what it was, but all it took was a mere mention, and I could feel all sorts of things I'd prefer to be oblivious to: impact, shattering, crushing, grinding, and pain, sometimes unbearable.

If they intended to talk specifics . . . "Would it be all right if I went home now?" I asked.

Tom glanced over at me, and his eyes softened in a way that I knew well from more private moments. "You're tired."

I nodded, even though I knew it was more than that. But for Tom, the too much information rule might be wise to uphold. Given his general suspicion of Liss and her beliefs, I was hesitant to bare my natural inclinations to him, for his approval or rejection. Would he accept my gifts for what they were, or turn away from me in distaste? At this point, I just didn't know what the answer would be, and I wasn't yet ready to risk finding out. And that, my friends, was the rub.

"Let's get you home, then. I'll be here awhile longer, and then more paperwork."

So much for our evening plans. I had come to realize pretty early on in this dating thing that the paperwork associated with Tom's job could be endless, and that was just with the petty stuff he dealt with on a day-to-day basis. With something like this, I'd be lucky to see him before Christmas. "So," I said softly, "I probably won't be seeing you tonight, I'm guessing."

He shook his head. "Sorry."

Not as sorry as I was. What I wanted more than anything just then was to nudge my way into his arms, tuck myself under his chin, and make the events of tonight recede into the darkness from whence they came.

I turned to go, too aware of Marcus's eyes on me, my emotions in turmoil. Tom followed me back to Christine, my Bug, and waited as I started her up. I watched as he gazed cautiously over his left shoulder. Satisfied that no one of importance was watching, he leaned in and gave me a swift kiss that left a lot to the imagination. Too much. I grabbed his collar and pulled him back for one that was a teensy bit more intimate.

Just as the familiar heat was creeping through my veins, he pulled away. "You be careful going home," he said, brushing his thumb along the line of my jaw in a gentle caress.

I nodded. "You, too."

I wanted to say more. I wanted to say that I would miss him, that I wished we had more time together, that sometimes I would be satisfied just to be in the same room with him, each doing our own thing but breathing the same air. It happened all too rarely. But I shouldn't complain. I had no right to complain about something so petty at a time like this.

So instead I closed the door and waved good-bye to him through my window, wearing a brave face.

It was as I put Christine into gear and began to ease into motion that the world around me went dark.

Not dark as in fainting dead away. Nothing so simple as that. Dark as in Christine's headlights completely cutting out . . . as did the engine, the ambulance lights; even the emergency beacons and flashlights blinked away into nothingness.

No power. Anywhere.

"What in the blue blazes — ?"

I unbuckled my seat belt and pulled myself forward in my seat by the steering wheel so that I could peer out. The night was black as pitch — we might have been swallowed alive by a great beast, for all that I could see. I was still peering out the blank canvas of the windshield when a knock at my window nearly sent me straight through.

My heart pumping wildly, I rolled the window down.

"You okay, Mags?" I could tell it was Marcus by his voice, though I couldn't make his face out.

"Yeah. Yeah, I'm fine. What happened?"

"Don't you feel it?"

Of course I did. It was the river of energy I had been feeling, running just below the surface of reality on the underpinnings of the astral tide.

Spirit energy.

I closed my eyes, testing it as it nudged against the outer edges of my personal boundaries. "I feel it. Is it Luc?"

"I'm not sure."

"Maggie! You okay?" Tom came bounding up, his body tense as his gaze searched our surroundings for the cause of the disturbance. "I don't know what the heck is going on. All of a sudden . . . *boom.* Nothing. No lights, no batteries . . . What the hell, even my watch has stopped. I don't get it."

I wasn't in the habit of wearing a watch, but . . . I reached for my purse and dug around in the depths until my fingers

117

bumped against the sleek metallic case of my cell phone. Withdrawing it, I flipped it open. No power there, either.

Without warning, the cell phone flared to life in my hands, so suddenly that I dropped it in my lap. One by one, everything else followed suit. Lights, engines, *aaaction!*

Was Luc trying to tell us that he was still around? Gone, but not about to be forgotten? Or was this a sign of something more?

I was too inexperienced to know for sure.

Maybe I didn't want to know.

CHAPTER 5

By Sunday morning, the whole town seemed to know about Luc Metzger's untimely end. I heard the buzz at the gas station when I stopped in for a cup of bad coffee, and I heard about it in front of the video store drop box. By the time I arrived at Enchantments to play catch-up from Saturday (*yes, it's true — I have no life*) and let myself in the back door, I was pretty sure there were few in town who were still in the dark about Luc Metzger's murder.

Liss was there ahead of me, hunched over some catalogues at the old rolltop desk, a single lamp providing light as she pored through them. She looked up as I closed the door behind me.

"Well, well. Good morning," she said, gazing at me over her half-moon glasses. "*We* had quite the evening, didn't we?"

"I guess you've heard," I said, setting

down my purse and starting to remove my jacket.

"I would guess most everyone has heard by now," Liss said with a rueful smile. She swiveled in her chair to face me and folded her hands in her lap. "Marcus called me last night. How completely awful for you, ducks."

I fell into the chair beside the desk with a sigh. I had slept hardly at all. Every time I did, I dreamed I saw Luc floating and hovering above the crime scene, gazing down on the proceedings. Ultimately my dream perspective morphed and I saw things through his eyes: The circle of his friends and compatriots, heads bowed over his body. The mishmash of buggies. The arrival of the ambulance. I was more than a little disconcerted to see Tom lean in to kiss me. Not Luc me, but Me me. And then I felt my energy withdraw, and I flew straight into the darkness of the wooded plot opposite where Luc was found, dissipating upon . . . impact.

Weird.

I shook the dream images away. "Have you heard from Eli?" I asked Liss. "He wasn't there last night."

Liss shook her head. "I thought I might take a drive out to see him after lunch. If you don't have anything else planned, you're welcome to join me."

And that was how I ended up, for the second time that weekend, bouncing along a narrow county road. Destination? Buggy Central.

Eli Yoder's farm was located on County Road 500 North, on the outer fringes of the close-knit Amish community the Metzger family was also a part of — community in this case meaning not one solid block of Amish families, but an area with a high concentration of Amish families. Eli's farm stood near Joe Aames's place, with the old, dilapidated Rosemont Cemetery situated firmly between the two. Both farms were within two miles of where Luc Metzger had been found, a short distance from his own home.

Liss circled the gravel turnabout, passing the starkly neat white farmhouse with its low-slung front porch, and parked just outside the open door to the barn. From within came the buzzing whine of a saw making contact with wood, countered by the lower rumble of a gas motor. Leaving the Lexus behind, we made our way to the yawning entrance.

It was, in many ways, your typical Hoosier barn. Old school, of course, with weathered wooden planks faded from years of sizzling beneath the hot summer sun, the paint cracked and in places scoured away by wicked winter winds, and inside, cavernous spaces and massive wooden beams high above. The saw cut off as we reached the door. Eli was hunkered down over a group of sawhorses, surrounded by lengths of clean-smelling wood and piles of powdery sawdust on the dirt floor. He raised his head at our approach and lifted a gloved hand.

"I was not expecting company, *ja?*" He pushed his dust-speckled safety goggles up on his forehead, looking at us with a grim smile. "Not on such a day as this."

Liss moved forward to put a comforting hand on Eli's arm. "We wanted to come out and offer you our support, Eli. We just heard about Luc. We're so sorry — it must have been a blow."

"*Ja. Ja,* it was. I was out making deliveries last night after the market closed, and I didn't hear about it until this morning, first thing. It is . . . a tragedy." Sawdust drifted down as he scrubbed a hand over his whiskers, a sure sign that he was under duress, and likely the only clue we would receive. Words came at a premium for our Eli; words conveying emotion even more so. "Luc was . . . a good man. Hester and the children will feel the loss far more than I."

"What will she do?" I asked.

"What she can. It will be difficult, but God will provide."

God will provide. It was a message I had a real problem accepting, but that had more to do with my own private hang-ups than what I saw in the lives of others. But if God could be relied upon to provide, would He have allowed this to happen? Would he have allowed a whole family, assuredly God-fearing, to suffer so terribly? It hardly seemed charitable or loving.

Would a loving God have created darkness at all?

Liss, despite her personal belief system, didn't seem to need to sweat the details. "What will *you* do, Eli?"

Ever the personification of the strong and silent type, Amish edition, Eli turned back to his work and began to clear away the wooden planks he had just finished cutting to size. "I will work. And if God is willing, I will find another to help me in my business. What more is there?"

Well, *I* would have worried and fussed and tried to plan things somehow, knowing all the while that nothing I prepared for would manifest into existence. It was part of my process.

While Eli continued to work and I wondered how to say what was on my mind, Liss wandered around the barn's open center space, drifting toward the Dutch door on the west wall below the depleted haymow. "Have you been having any more trouble out here?" she asked conversationally.

Instantly my radar went on high alert. "Trouble? What sort of trouble?"

Eli had hoisted the planks onto his shoulder. He carried them over to where others just like them were stacked against the wall and began to rearrange them . . . a sure sign that all was not well, because they were already arranged to the point of an obsession with tidiness. "Well, you know, just the usual," he said slowly. "There is the cold spot that follows just behind you. The child spirit. A number of animal spirits."

"How often?"

"It used to be once or twice a month, no more. But lately, it is as it is with every place else we've been investigating. All the time."

"Mmm. Joe mentioned that the spirits on his property have been having regular pow-wows, too."

That would be Joe Aames, a former high school football star who'd given it all up to be a pig farmer. He had a psychology degree from Purdue, but didn't care to use it. He said it was because pigs made a lot more sense than people, and a lot less mess. I guess that didn't apply to Eli — the two were diehard best friends.

"*Ja.* We go out in the fields at night sometimes, just to keep our eyes on things. With my own eyes I saw a fire ring burning that was not there."

Liss came back to stand beside me, oblivious to my sudden skittishness. I knew that Rosemont Cemetery was active — the N.I.G.H.T.S. had done an investigation there in December, my first on-site experience of a ghost-hunting expedition — but somehow I had forgotten that the farms surrounding the cemetery were hotbeds of activity as well. Was no place sacred anymore?

"I don't feel anything negative, though, Eli. There's energy, certainly, but it's all on the neutral side of the wheel. Neither dark nor light."

"For now, *ja.*"

I did what I always did when I got nervous. I changed the subject. "You know, Eli, I had just met Luc Metzger's wife at the farmers market. All I could think of when Marcus and I stumbled across everything yesterday was how awful it would be for her and her children when they found out."

A troubled frown flickered across Eli's normally stoic brow. "Hester is taking it very hard, but she is trying not to show it. It will not be easy for her, that is for sure. The children are young, and she has the farm to run with no man to help her." Most Amish in our area owned their own working farms and also took jobs at the local factories. Even the Amish needed health benefits and steady pay.

I couldn't begin to comprehend being a young single mother responsible for the well-being of four children, let alone four children, a house, and an entire farm — crops, animals, and all. Despite what I wanted my mother to believe, sometimes I could barely take care of myself, let alone anyone else. "Does she have family who will help her?"

"No. No family here. Her people are in Pennsylvania, near Lancaster."

"Pennsylvania? Really? How did she end up here?"

"Luc's people came to this area in the eighteen-hundreds, but some are in Pennsylvania still. He went out to Lancaster to marry Hester and eventually brought her back here."

"Do you think she'll move back there, then?"

He shook his head. "She says not. Jonah Ritter asked her that yesterday. She says her life is here now, and here she will stay."

"But how will she manage?"

"Hester is a good woman. Strong. If anyone can find a way, she will. And the community will make sure she does not want for much. We take care of our own."

It was all well and good to say that, but realistically speaking, platitudes, however well-intended, did not put meat on a kitchen table. "And the children?"

Eli's shrug spoke more of uncertainty than of dismissal. "I hope she will not need to send them away to relatives until she gets her feet on the ground. We will do our best to help."

Poor Hester. She'd seemed like such a nice young woman. To have your whole world destroyed in one fell swoop . . . Poor Luc didn't even have a chance to duck the Great Sucker Punch o' Destiny, and his pretty wife never saw it coming.

"Perhaps . . ." Liss had been quietly attuning herself to the energies of the barn, but now she came forward, a familiar light in her eyes. "Perhaps we could do something for her as well. Take up collections of money and donations of useful items. What do you think, Maggie?"

I nodded, still seeing the strange darkness in Hester's eyes the day before. "My mother might be able to help, too. The Ladies Auxiliary at St. Catherine's often takes on families caught in circumstances beyond their control, with an eye toward helping them through their suffering. I'll talk to her about it. If —" I glanced questioningly at Eli — "if you don't think our efforts would be taken the wrong way."

He gazed at me, then nodded his head. "I will talk with her, *ja?* Anything would help. Luc said often that money was tight. It was why he was working with me. He had been asking for more and more hours. More than I could give. And there is . . . trouble . . . between Hester and the other womenfolk. Some hard feelings, I think. I do not know why, but it is there, unmistakable. She may not accept help from our women."

He gave me a meaningful look, the kind that said *You know how women are.* From anyone else, the look might have annoyed me, but no one could take offense at anything Eli said. Least of all me.

Trouble, he said. Had I witnessed one example of that at the booth, when Hester had gone all strange on me? The ladies staffing the booth with her had seemed down-right hostile. Trouble in noodle territory.

And Eli didn't know why. But then, Eli was a man, and couldn't be expected to understand the complexities of female relationships, if that's what it was. Then again, I didn't get the feeling that the women in the booth had acted out of jealousy. They were reacting out of fear.

Hester had spoken of trouble, too. *We who see . . .*

Was that it? Was Hester an intuitive as well? Had she foreseen her husband's death? Was that why she had been trying so hard to keep him home?

"I took a ride over to where Luc was found," Eli was saying. "Earlier this morning, after I left Hester's. I . . . it was wrong of me, but I took my pendulum with me."

"You did?" Liss's attention sharpened with curiosity. "What did you find?"

"I walked around a little bit, poking around. The police had been out there again at first light. Their searches were very thorough. I did not find anything amiss. I was hoping . . ."

"You were hoping to find something they had overlooked, something that would help them find who did this to Luc."

"*Ja. Ja,* I guess I was. It was wrong of me,

perhaps. We are not meant to judge others — it is not our place — but I cannot help but want them to find the person who did this. Not to punish, of course, it is not our way; but to bring to justice. Such . . . enmity toward the Amish community is . . . unsettling."

Unsettling, to say the least. "This is the third attack in this area alone," I mused by way of agreement, deciding it was okay to repeat what Tom had told me since it had appeared in *The Gazette* and I was probably the last person in Stony Mill to hear of it. "And the second in this county. But it is the first to have gone this far. I wonder why."

Eli shrugged. "Bad luck for Luc. He was in the wrong place at the wrong time. It was after dark; he should have been home with Hester."

"Tom said the police have issued warnings to your community."

"*Ja*. Stay home after dark. Travel with companions. Do not stop for others you do not know. Do not help. Do not trust." He shook his head regretfully. "It is not the Amish way to live in these conditions. It is much to ask of us."

"But it's for your own safety."

"A man cannot live his life in fear."

I've long thought that fear is just a person's safety barometer, a useful tool that serves to remind a person to watch their back, keep their eyes open, stay away from high places, and for God's sake, don't accept candy from strangers. In other words, it is there for a reason. To ignore it is beyond foolhardy.

"Eli . . ." Liss paused expectantly, waiting to be sure she had his attention before continuing. "You didn't say. What did you discover with your dowsing?"

Eli shifted uncomfortably. "Well . . . I didn't use it after all. Things felt too fresh. Too jittery. I knew Luc. I'm not sure that I want to know if he is hanging around."

So much for a man not living life in fear.

"Would you feel better if you had company?" Liss offered.

Whoa, there. "Uh . . ."

"That might be okay. Safety in numbers." Eli fished in his pocket and withdrew his pendulum, a Goddess stone he had found on his property. The doughnut-shaped stone was familiar to me — Eli had introduced me to it during my very first dowsing lesson. Seeing it again, dangling from a leather thong, I felt the throb of energy in my palms, just as I had that first night. The energy pattern of the stone itself, a remembered response.

"Shall we go, then?" Liss asked.

Eli and Liss turned and gazed expectantly at me. As if there was any way I could stop them. They both knew I couldn't bring myself to deny either of them anything. "Ohhhhh . . . all right. Lead on, if you must."

Liss gave me a wink. "It won't be so bad," she reassured me. And then she spoke some familiar words of power, words that many people in this world know, but few use as effectively as my witchy boss: *"Trust me."*

I was a goner.

Eli piled into the back seat of the Lexus while Liss and I took the front.

"Which way?" Liss asked.

I gave her quickie directions. We were there within minutes.

The barricades were down, but the crime scene tape was still up, supported by wooden stakes pounded into the earth at regular intervals. Liss pulled onto the thin strip of shoulder. It was scarcely wide enough for the Lexus's tires. Which meant, of course, that I had to straddle the shallow drainage ditch upon exiting. But hey, it was all in the name of lending support to good friends.

I felt myself pulling back, just a bit, as Liss and Eli headed toward the taped-off area.

Luc had been bludgeoned, hadn't he? Didn't that mean there would be blood, and lots of it? What if they hadn't yet had a chance to clean up the area?

Worse yet . . . what if the energy drain we had experienced last night really was the spirit of Luc Metzger? And what if he had decided to stick around for a while? I knew from my involvement with the N.I.G.H.T.S. that often people who had died suddenly or who felt they had unfinished business remaining in the physical world refrained from crossing over into the Otherworld. Earthbounds, they were called. Murder victims had to be pretty high up on the unfinished business list.

So, to me, the question of the moment was this: If Luc Metzger had indeed stayed in nonphysical form in the physical world, would his misty energy be tied to the place where he had died? Or to the place he loved the most?

Did I get a vote?

Probably not.

I trudged along behind Liss and Eli, quieting my steps as much as possible on the rough chip-and-seal surface of the road. No sense in accidentally awakening . . . *whatever.* But I could delay for only so long. Eli had pulled his stone out by the time I reached the crime scene tape. Liss, on the other hand, stood as still as a stone, her eyes closed and her chin tipped up ever so slightly. Her hands were held out, palms up. Her fingertips fluttered delicately.

"What do you feel?" I found myself asking.

"Chaos energy, very hectic, but nothing specific," she said. She opened one eye to peer at me. "You?"

I didn't want to open myself up to it, so I just shrugged and instead put the whole of my thought processes to work strengthening my personal boundaries against invasion by outward forces. Liss accepted my noncommittal response without comment and went back to putting out feelers. Eli's pendulum, in the meantime, was swinging jerkily back and forth on its leather tether.

"What is it doing?" I asked, frowning.

Eli was frowning, too. I did not find that reassuring. He muttered something under his breath in German and moved away, keeping his eyes on the prize in his hand.

I couldn't bear to stand next to the crime scene tape. Some kind county worker, who probably wasn't being paid nearly enough for the gruesome task, had covered the area with a plastic tarp pinned down at the corners. Whether to preserve the evidence or to protect the delicate sensibilities of passersby, I didn't know, but I was grateful nevertheless.

I turned my face toward the field, clutching my arms protectively over my chest. The dirt had been newly turned, the vestiges of last night's light frost long since melted and absorbed by the clods of musty earth. From somewhere nearby there came the rumble of a big tractor engine, a reminder that spring's labors were in full swing. Living in town, even one as small as Stony Mill, it was easy to lose track of the turn of the seasons. Here on these county roads, far from suburban sprawl, the evidence was everywhere.

"Over here. Here is where the trail of energy ends. Right here."

Eli had paused on the other side of the road, where just a short leap over a narrow ditch, an overgrown trail led into the woods. Yes, that's right, woods. Most people, when they think of Indiana at all, think of cornfields and wheat stretching as far as the eye can see — and granted, we do have a lot of that — but here in the northeast quadrant of the state, we also have quite a lot of wooded expanses. The one that bordered this part of the road was quite thick. Eli stood just within the first row of trees, his feet planted wide in the tangle of long grass. He tucked the Goddess stone into his back pocket, turning his attention to and fro as he did so.

"Right here," he said again. He toed the ground where he was standing for good measure.

Liss opened her eyes, then narrowed them, squinting through her eyelashes at the spot where Eli stood. "Yes, I do think you're right. There is a disturbance in the astral right behind you. I can see it now. A rip or a wrinkle, as it were. You are standing just within it, Eli. It is drawing upon your aura, which I'm sure is why I can see it now . . . but it is not enough to heal."

I did everything I could to see it. Looked out of the corner of my eye. Squinted. Crossed my eyes. Nothing.

"Why don't you step away for a moment?" Liss suggested, holding her position. Eli did as she asked. "Yes, it fades considerably once you're away from there. How are you feeling?"

"Okay, now. When I was standing there, I felt . . . anxious, I guess. It was not comfortable. As though my insides were boiling away, but without the heat. Just the rumbling and churning."

"What are you saying?" I asked. "What

does it mean that the energy trail ends where Eli is standing?"

"Just that, for whatever reason, it doesn't go beyond. Energy imprints generally have a beginning and an ending. Sometimes they are confined to a very finite place, like a cold spot, and other times their boundaries are a bit broader. This imprint is actually quite large; it encompasses the area between where Luc was found and the trees over here," Liss said with the intrigued tone of a scholar examining new evidence on a well-proved theory.

I watched from the distance as she gracefully skipped across the ditch like a woman half her age to join Eli on the other side. She joined hands with him and they closed their eyes, swaying slightly together in the gentle afternoon sunshine. I felt oddly compelled to go to them and offer my energy up . . . but that was crazy. I did *not* want to do that. The nudgings were just going to have to go find themselves another sensitive.

I made myself look away from Liss and Eli, forced myself to break that connection. As I did, a flash of white farther back caught my eye. Probably just a scrap of newspaper or a plastic bag that had been blown into the trees by the winter wind. And yet curiosity burned within me, sudden and sweet. I found my feet moving, propelling me on.

Propelling me on. Toward . . . what?

The answer came a moment later. It wasn't something that could be seen from the road — a pair of big spruce trees nearly obscured it when it was being viewed head-on. I don't know what kind of odds had contributed to my catching a chance glimpse of it from where I stood, and I wasn't about to start ciphering them now.

There was a sign of some sort on the trunk of a big maple tree. A circle of wood, painted in black and white. I made my way toward the tree, rounding the larger spruce until I could see it clearly.

This was no ordinary graffiti, and it was not an identifying mark made by lumbermen to designate which trees were to be culled from the woods this season. This was a sign, almost decorative in nature, that someone had specifically placed there. A stylized drawing of an angry-looking owl with horns for ears, outlined in white paint on a black background. Two axes were clutched in its claws and thorny roses bloomed beneath those clenched talons. Around its head, a circle of something jagged. Above it, what looked like an orange star. I reached out to the tree, hesitating a moment before placing my fingertips against its bark.

Somehow I didn't think it was meant to advertise the Preservation of Owls Society.

Just as quickly, I yanked my fingers away. The tree was buzzing. Like it was full of bees, or . . . like it was alive.

Mother Mary, I thought, gazing up at the tree and the weird sign with a mixture of horror and fascination.

"What is it, Maggie?" Liss called from where she and Eli still stood. "What do you see?"

I couldn't speak. My throat was still full of the strangeness emanating from the tree.

Liss and Eli came up behind me before I found the strength of will to turn away. Liss put her hand on my shoulder as she gazed up.

"Why, what is that doing here?" she asked, her voice full of wonder.

"Any idea what it's for?" I asked through clenched teeth. It was the only way I could keep them from chattering.

Liss squinted at it, considering, then shook her head. "It's interesting, isn't it? I'm afraid I'm not familiar with the symbolism."

"I touched it."

Liss did as well, her fingers twitching as

139

they made contact. "It's magical, that much is sure."

Eli did not reach out. He backed away and said nothing, a frown pinching his brows together.

Someone had placed it here. But why?

CHAPTER 6

"Oh, my God."

Tom's mouth dropped open as he stared at the strange sign, glowing stark white in the waning late afternoon sun. He had finally caught up with me after I picked up Christine from Enchantments and started for home. Although I knew he'd be angry that I had visited the crime scene again, no matter how briefly, I knew I couldn't not tell him about the strange sign we had come across.

"Oh, my God," he repeated. "Was this here last night? What the hell is it supposed to be?"

I shook my head. "I don't know, but I thought I should tell you."

"Damn right, you should." He squeezed my hand to soften the brusqueness of the words. "Listen, Maggie, go back to the road. Carefully. Watch where you step, and don't touch anything."

While he ran back to the squad car, I did as he asked, gladly, taking care with each step to look for footprints impressed upon the ground. Not that that would have meant anything at this late hour — Liss and Eli and I could easily have trampled any evidence in the grass earlier without realizing it.

"You stay there," he said as he passed me, a digital camera in one hand and a messenger-style pouch over his shoulder. "I'm going to take a few pictures."

I wished then that I had thought to do the same, but technology had never been foremost in my mind. I'd forgotten until just that moment about the camera feature on my cell phone. And now, I was standing on the edge of the road, too far away and at too much of an angle to get a clear shot. I took my cell phone from my pocket and looked down at it in my hand, considering. If I waited until Tom was busy taking his own pics, maybe I could slip a teensy bit closer to get one of my own . . .

"Don't even think about it," Tom growled, catching me off guard.

I was getting pretty darned tired of people reading my thoughts. Was I that transparent? Couldn't a girl get a little privacy every once in a while?

In a huff, I tucked the slim phone back in my pocket, but that didn't stop me from gazing back at the symbol and trying to memorize as many details as I could. It also didn't stop me from employing more Stone Age resources. In addition to my phone I had found a scrap of paper and a ballpoint pen in my pocket. With my back toward Tom, I started to sketch the design from memory, pausing for a quick sidelong glance when I needed to fill in bits of detail. When I was satisfied with my artistic endeavors, I tucked the sketch back into my pocket.

Tom was taking longer than I had thought he would, photographing from all angles and scouting the trees. As the sun sank lower in the sky, the chill air was starting to seep through my jeans and creep up under the hem of my leather jacket. Spring was upon us, true, but we were a whole long way from summer. I balled my hands up in my front pockets and began to pace along the crumbling edge of the road in an effort to get my blood flowing again. Back and forth, back and forth.

Finally Tom joined me on the side of the road.

"So, what do you think? Do you have any theories about the symbols on the tree?" I asked him, deciding the direct approach was the only way to go.

He avoided my eyes and shrugged. "Theories, but I'd like to do a bit of research before I lay them out on the table."

"And how do these theories blend with your previous thoughts on the other attacks on Amish?"

He chucked me under the chin and looked me square in the eye. "I'll let you know."

"Come on, Tom."

"You know I really can't tell you."

"But you wouldn't know about any of this without me," I protested, feeling a pout coming on. I hated that. Pouts were for little girls, not grown women trying like hell to believe in themselves. I lifted my chin and summoned my best bid for respect. "I didn't have to tell you, you know. But I thought that perhaps you thought enough of me by now to know that I'm not asking you to betray your police confidences. Generalizations are fine. More than fine; a generalization would be great."

"Maggie."

"Perfect, even."

"Maggie."

"Because the last thing in the world I would want you to do would be to betray —"

My words got caught in the updraft caused

when he seized me by the shoulders and pulled me into a kiss so sudden and hard that my head tipped back beneath the pressure of his lips. My mouth opened in surprise, and immediately he took advantage of the offered opportunity. Our reason for being out there was lost in the intensity of the moment. Heat, pure and primal, poured through my veins. Had I been cold a moment ago? I couldn't remember now. The only thing that was important was this moment, this man, and this wonderful, fluid warmth.

When he lifted his head at last, it was only by increments, as though he, too, was reluctant to break the peace of the moment.

"Not fair," I whispered, not really caring one way or another.

"All is fair in love and war," he whispered back, plucking at my lower lip with his as though playing the strings of a harp. *Oh, yes, he knew how to play me, all right.*

I closed my eyes, fighting against the feelings rushing through me. "What were we talking about?"

"How pretty you look out here, shivering away. You have a really nice —"

"Tom!" I swatted at him, laughing.

"— way of shivering," he finished. "Warmer now?"

145

I smiled. I couldn't help myself. "Infinitely."

"Good." He dropped his arms away from me and stepped back. The loss of his heat made the cool air seem even more chill.

He went silent for a moment as he tucked the bagged evidence more securely into the messenger bag and fastened the flap. "Maggie."

"Hm?"

"I don't know what you were doing out here —"

"Nothing, honest."

"— and I don't want to know. But I was hoping you'd remember your promise to me to stay out of things. We don't know what we're dealing with here, and this" — he waved a hand toward the sign — "makes me even more nervous."

I tried to make light of it. "I'll be sure to watch out for people carrying paint and paintbrushes."

"I'm serious."

"I know. I'm sorry. But I'm not male, I'm not Amish, I have nothing for anyone to take, and I'm not likely to be found alone on a county road. Today notwithstanding. I don't think I'm at that much of a risk."

"I just . . . these things that have been happening lately. All the vandalism, the fights, the domestic shit hitting the fan. The murders. Things are just not right, Maggie. The town's not right."

Tom didn't know the half of it.

"I don't know how to explain it," he went on. "And I don't want you to be . . . I . . . *damn!*" He frowned, clamping his lips together. "Sorry. I'm not very good with words."

He was trying to protect me. The knowledge sparkled in my heart like fairy dust in sunlight, and with it came hope. "I think you're doing fine. Really fine."

He caught my eye, and the corner of his mouth twitched in a wry smile that felt like much more. I was half hoping for another kiss, but he turned away.

"We'd better get going. It'll be getting dark soon."

I started, realizing what he said was true. The sun had been slowly sinking, our shadows stretching long behind us to the east. I wasn't too keen on being caught by the approaching night right smack on top of the place where Luc had lost his life.

"Did you get everything you needed?" I asked him.

Tom nodded. "We'll send a crew out later to expand the search radius. If there's anything more out there, we'll find it. But it will have to wait until tomorrow, when we have light again."

He escorted me back to the squad car, his fingers lightly curved around my upper arm. I paused before getting in. "Do you have to work tonight?"

"Yeah. Grossman called in sick, so I told Chief that I'd fill in." His eyes traveled from my eyes to my mouth, then dipped lower. "But I'm starting to wish I hadn't said yes."

I sighed. Another night alone for me with nothing but Graham Thomas, my worn-out but faithful teddy bear, and maybe a rerun of *Magnum, P.I.* if I was lucky. "Too bad. I guess I'll just have to come up with a way to make you jealous."

He moved in, leaning on the door. "Alone, of course?"

"Story of my life." I smiled to soften the words, but I knew the truth of it. If Tom and I ever did manage to make a real go of things, I would have to come to terms with the fact that I would have a rival for Tom's time and affection, one that claimed so much of him that there was little left over for me. Worse still, it was a rival I had no right to fight. I was the usurper there, the new factor to be shoehorned in. Either I would need to find a way to play nice when it came to the realities of his demanding job, or I was going to have to find another playground.

I would cross that bridge if or when I came to it.

Tom came around and got in the driver's side. I gazed with interest at all of the different appliances and buttons on the console while he set us into motion. How one man, who was also responsible for steering the vehicle, could also be required to run all of these gizmos, widgets, and thingamabobs boggled my mind. "You don't ever have to use these while you're driving, do you?"

"Only during a high-speed chase." He laughed when I stuck out my tongue. "Well, not usually. But you do get used to what you have where." He reached out and turned up the sound on the police scanner. The sound of mechanical voices, squelches, and occasional feedback filled the background.

Tom took my hand and held it, running his thumb in circles against my palm as he drove us back to town. We had just hit the outer limits when a call came for him over the radio. He spoke into the mouthpiece in the terse parlance unique to police officers, then signed off.

"What's up?" I asked when he sighed as he replaced the mouthpiece.

"The usual. Carnage and chaos out near the old juvie home. It's a decent neighborhood — old, but nicely kept — and the little bastards are just taking it over. Rampaging, partying in the woods, vandalizing the neighborhood, petty theft. Drugs are a big reason; they usually are. Most of the kids are in and out of Blackhawk on a regular basis. It's a crying shame, really."

"But if they're there because they've been getting into trouble, don't they have supervision? Curfews? Lockdowns and the like?"

"They're supposed to, but you know how tight funding is for anything and everything these days. The salaries are low, benefits are nonexistent, and it's a high stress, thankless job. The staff turnover rate is astronomical, so guess who ends up running the show."

"The kids. Nice."

"Not. Chief wants more of a presence out that way and at all the other hotspots in town, starting tonight."

"Lucky you."

"Yeah. At least it will keep the residents happy. One of 'em had her yard completely trashed a week or so back. Beer bottles and drug paraphernalia and toilet paper everywhere. Forked her, too, and it's a bitch on the back pulling all of those plastic forks out of your lawn. Poor woman was fit to be tied. Guess she'd ratted 'em out one time too many."

Trial by intimidation.

I was silent a moment, processing everything I'd seen and heard that weekend. Tom had told me to mind my own business, but I couldn't help wondering. "And . . . Tom . . . the other attacks on Amish . . . what happened to Luc . . ."

He gripped my hand a little harder, reassuringly. "Don't worry, Maggie. We'll find out what happened, and we'll make it right. We already have feelers out."

"You said that the other two Amish men who were attacked, were robbed. Was Luc?"

"His wallet was missing."

"So it could have been robbery."

"Or he could have forgotten it. Listen, Maggie, leave it alone. The truth is out there. Someone will crack, eventually. I promise you that. And when they do, we'll have him."

But did we have time to wait? Or was it possible that if we waited too long, another attack could be imminent?

What if we were too late?

CHAPTER 7

Tom received another call as he pulled up outside my apartment in the house on Willow Street. I felt lucky that I got a quick kiss curbside before he took off, leaving me to make my own way through the semidarkness to the sunken entrance. After my break-in scare in December, my father had insisted on installing a security light, complete with motion sensor, above my door. The light blinked on instantly as I began the descent, momentarily blinding me.

Somehow it was almost as creepy to be in the seeing eye of this security light as it was walking down the stairs in the dark.

Yes, I am a coward. Most people are, in the dark of night. I just happen to be one who admits it.

There was a note on my door from Steff, my best friend, who lives on the upper floor of the aging Victorian house-turned-apartment building. I read it beneath the glow of the security light.

Hey, girlfriend!
Won't be able to make it for our usual
tonight — I'm going to have to go in to
work. We've had three people quit in the
last two weeks on my floor alone. Don't
know what's going on in this old place.
Sorry! I left something for you, though,
that I hope will make up for it, just a
little bit. Something to scoop you off to
a faraway land . . . like Hawaii, perhaps?
In the meantime . . . pity me. Pity me.

Lots of love,
Steff

Bemused, I opened the screen door. Just
inside was a sparkly little pink gift bag,
adorned with frothy feathers, fake jewels,
curling ribbons, and misty, ethereal photos
of angels. Girly to the max, just like Steff.

Inside? A bottle of scented shower gel that
was supposed to make a girl's skin gleam
like gold and smell of coconut and hibiscus,
and a blue candle studded with tiny starfish
and shells and rubbed with sand and glitter.

Hmmm . . . it did make a girl think.

*Thomas Magnum, P.I.? Come on down,
honey, and let's test the water.*

I unlocked the door and let myself in, setting my things on the chair inside the door and bending to scoop up the bits of dried leaves that always seemed to swirl in from the sunken entrance. I wasn't particularly hungry, so I grabbed the bag of goodies and made my way to the bedroom. Within minutes my clothes lay flung across the floor with wild abandon, the candle was burning invitingly on the bathroom shelf, and hot, thundering water was steaming the stress from my muscles and the fog from my brain.

That didn't, of course, dislodge tropical island fantasies, complete with a blue-eyed devil with a mustache that teased and tickled as he bent me back over the rushing surf. His arms were strong, his body bronze in the fading sunset, and his kisses as intoxicating as the fantasy itself. Dreamtime Tom (Fielding, that is) butted in, and I even let him, so long as he promised to go with the fantasy flow and appear in either a swimsuit or a birthday suit, and not a police uniform.

Hey, it was my fantasy. I could switch guys mid-surf if I wanted to.

Except once Tom appeared on my fantasy island, I couldn't help wishing he was here for real. About that time the island drifted away like so many bubbles down the drain.

Another good fantasy wasted.

Sighing with disappointment and wistfulness, I turned off the water, bent at the waist to wrap a towel turban-style around my hair, and another around my body. Since the fantasy was pretty much a loss, I decided a little bit of self-indulgence might be called for. Some scented body oil, a pumice stone, and a pedicure later, I was feeling sparefreshed and ready for a little bit of surfing. TV surfing, that is. I slipped on an extra-long T-shirt, a robe, and my fuzzy bunny slippers, grabbed a fleece throw blanket to cover my legs beneath my robe, and settled into my favorite wingback chair with a cold Diet Coke in one hand and the remote in the other.

Time for a little bit of Magnum ogling. Maybe I could get that daydream back . . .

I barely had a chance to enjoy the theme music when my cell phone began blaring again. "I have *got* to remember to program in another ring tone," I grumbled as I struggled out from under the blanket over to my purse.

"Hello?"

"Hello, beautiful."

"Marcus!" My heart thumped wickedly. I bit my lip, but it didn't stop the happy glow from spreading through my veins. "What a surprise. What are you up to this weekend?"

"Well, I was thinking about going down to the library to do a little ghostly surveillance for Aunt Marion."

I raised my eyebrows. "Tonight? It's awfully late, isn't it?"

"Maggie, it's seven o'clock."

"My point exactly. The library is closed."

"Well, it does make it easier to do an investigation without mundanes to get in the way. And you know spirit activity is higher after sundown. No time like the present." Until six months ago, *I* had been what he called a mundane, a person oblivious to the spirit world around her. "I, ahem, was hoping to convince you to join me."

I glanced down at myself. I was dressed for comfort, not company. "Um —"

"Come on, Maggie . . . it won't take long. I just wanted to check Marion's camera setup and do a walk-through. Maybe take an EVP or two while we're there. Nothing in an official capacity. Just you, me, and old Bertie. And Aunt Marion, of course. What do you say?"

You, me, and old Bertie. Old Bertie being Boiler Room Bertie, the nebulous spirit resident who liked to dart around the library's antiquated boiler room as a glowing blue ball of light. Marcus had let me in on Bertie's existence last December. I

156

couldn't say I'd been champing at the bit for a personal introduction.

"Ohhh . . . Are you sure that you wouldn't rather have Devon or Joe? Or Liss? Liss would probably be your best bet."

"Maybe so. But I asked you."

It was the soft tone that got me. That and the implied preference for my company. Even though I knew he was probably just trying to reassure me, help me to feel comfortable with all the spooky stuff. "All right," I said, reluctant but not wanting to hurt his feelings by refusing him when he was trying so hard to help. "I guess it wouldn't hurt for a little while. You said mostly Bertie just shows up as bright blue orbs, right?"

Orbs were okay. Nonthreatening. Benign, even. Orbs I could handle . . . so long as they didn't follow me around. No stalking of the N.I.G.H.T.S. fraidy cat allowed.

"Right. So you're in?"

I laughed. "Yeah, I'm in. I've always liked the color blue."

"Bertie will be glad to hear it."

"What time do you want to go?"

"How does now sound?"

Another glance down at my less-than-appropriate ensemble. "Um —"

The knock at my door nearly sent me into spasms.

"Marcus?"

"Maggie?"

I clutched the phone tighter to my ear. "Is that you out there?"

"You were expecting John Wayne, maybe?"

"Well, I wasn't expecting anyone yet!"

His laugh crackled through the earpiece. "Knowing your feelings toward spirit activity lately, I didn't want to give you the opportunity to duck out the back before I could get here."

"Marcus, I live in a basement apartment. There is no back door."

"And that makes it sooo much easier to find you," he drawled in a voice as smooth and sweet as honey.

I opened the door without a thought, giggling despite myself. Marcus stood on the doorstep, mirroring me perfectly with his phone at his ear. We stood for a moment on either side of the threshold, grinning at each other.

"You are a nut," I told him, swinging the door wider.

"And you are a closet exhibitionist. That's quite the getup you've got going on."

I looked down at myself, bare legs, frowzy robe, bunny slippers, and all. "Whoops, sorry!" I backed toward my bedroom, all kinds of embarrassed. "I'll just go change now."

A smile played about the corners of his mouth. "No need to apologize, sweetness. You've got great legs. In fact," he called after me as I closed the bedroom door, "if you'd like to go like that, I'm all for it. Don't think you have to change for me."

Margaret Mary-Catherine O'Neill, what do you think you're doing, girl? I heard the chiding tones of my conscience inside my head, as I so often did, speaking in the voice of my late grandmother. *Your boyfriend goes off to do his civic-minded duty, and you take up with the first man who sweet-talks you? You should go to confession.*

Later, Grandma, I answered as I dug through my dresser drawers for a pair of jeans and a T-shirt, *I have things to do. Besides, I wouldn't really call Tom my boyfriend. Prospective boyfriend, maybe. And I'm not taking up with Marcus. He's just a friend.*

A man who looks at you that way? That's no friend. Didn't your mother tell you to watch out for men like that? All long legs and soft eyes and sweet nothings. What are you going to do with a man like that?

It was probably better not to answer a question like that, even to a girl's own conscience. Some things are better left unsaid. And besides, I wasn't going to do anything with a man like Marcus. He was a friend. F-R-I-E-N-D. And he was taken, and so was I. I just felt comfortable with him, that's all. He had somehow managed to get me to open up to him in a way I didn't with many people until I had known them for a very long while. Besides, even if he was free, and I was, too, I wouldn't be so stupid as to risk something special like that.

Not me.

Just to reassert with my overactive worry-wart of a conscience that I was not trying to be anything more than reasonably put together, I dug out my oldest and most shapeless oversized sweater to wear over my tee and surveyed the results in the mirror over my dresser. My hair was a bit unruly after the shower (definitely not enough frizz serum!), so I dragged a comb through it, then twisted the lot of it and pinned it up on the back of my head with a few hair clips. As usual, the finer pieces at the front slipped from their moorings, but I was satisfied with the result. At least I didn't look like I'd just rolled out of bed.

Marcus was standing in the middle of my living room when I came out of the bedroom. My remote was in his hand, pointed

at the TV, which he was watching with interest. I glanced at the screen and froze.

"So. I take it you're a big Magnum buff."

Busted! "Um, why do you say that?"

He slanted a knowing glance my way.
"Because you have at least fifteen other
VCR tapes labeled *Magnum, P.I.* in addition
to this one."

I made a face at him. "All right, you
caught me. Yes, I like *Magnum, P.I.* He's
funny. I like Hawaii. Higgins is hilarious.
Great characters. Lots of action. What more
can you ask for in a TV show?"

He sauntered over to the rest of the tapes
stacked on my bookshelves and squinted at
the labels with great interest. "Yeah, I can
see there's lots of action and great characters. 'Hot Hot Hot Magnum.' 'OMG
Magnum.' 'Dear God in Heaven Magnum.'
'Ha-cha-cha Magnum.' 'Sigh-worthy
Magnum.' 'Be Still My Heart Magnum.' "

Flushed with embarrassment, I gave him
a cool stare. "And your point is?"

He smirked. "That's kind of like a guy saying he reads *Playboy* for the articles, isn't
it?"

"Very funny." I decided changing the
subject was probably the best approach.
"So, does Marion know we're stopping in
tonight?"

"Nice save, Mags. Yes, Aunt Marion knows. She'll be there to unlock the doors for us."

Marcus drove us over in his old beat-up pickup truck — much warmer than the back of his motorcycle. The springs on the bench seat were going out, giving me a faint bobble-head feeling, but his radio worked a lot better than Christine's, which made it all worthwhile. We spent the short ride listening to the musical stylings of the latest British import — my kind of music, all soft rock, sensitive imagery, and driving drum-beats — until we pulled up beneath the tree canopy in front of the library. Marion's old VW Rabbit was already there in its usual reserved spot. Marcus parked directly behind her and switched off the ignition.

"Ready?"

I nodded.

He grabbed his backpack out of the back seat and hurried around to my side to hold the door, which I'd already flung open.

"Hello, you two!" Marion greeted us at the double doors, holding them open while Marcus shouldered his way through with his hands full. "Good Lord a' Livin', you're packing for bear. What all did you bring?"

"What, this? Oh, most of this isn't for ghost-hunting. It's my knife stuff. My truck doesn't lock up too tight, and I've been hit by teenagers once too often. If I have it with me, it goes where I go."

Ooooh. Knives. Hoping to ward off another lengthy monologue, I reached around Marcus and gave Marion a warm hug. "Hello, Marion."

"Hey there, girl. Marcus told me you'd be coming."

"Oh, he did, did he?" I asked, giving Marcus a sidelong glance.

Marcus grinned. "I said I *thought* you'd be coming with me."

"So he's been hustling you, hey?" Marion chuckled and shook her head. "My pit bull of a nephew. Marcus has a way of getting what he puts his mind to."

"Mind over matter, Auntie. Mind over matter." He threw his left arm around his aunt and his right arm around me, and escorted us into the library.

The Stony Mill Carnegie Public Library was one of my favorite places in the whole world. A unique, bell-shaped brick building that had been updated over the years with a nonmatching glassed-in portico that housed the entryway, the library had been an important part of Stony Mill's downtown area since its inception in 1907. The only full-time librarian, Marion ran the library with a deft and capable hand, not to mention a near photographic memory when it came to a given patron's reading tastes. She still remembered the time I took out Judy Blume's *Forever* without my mother's permission — and she had kept my secret all these years. There was something unapologetically subversive about her at times, despite the fact that she was a regular at St. Catherine's. Maybe that was why I liked her so much.

"So, Aunt Marion, what do you have for us?"

Marion led us through the library, back toward her office. Our footsteps echoed across the hardwood floors, which gleamed beneath the dim glow of the security lights. I'd never been in the library after hours before, but I was discovering that the building held much less attraction for me without the lights on. The tall shelves, the many aisles that ended in pools of darkness, the strange sounds coming from unknown sources . . .

I heaved a sigh of relief once we were safely within the four walls of Marion's comfortable office, a place that called up images of books, tea, and cozy sweaters. Ah, sanctuary.

"Sit down, you two. I just brewed a fresh

pot of coffee. Anyone up for a cup?"

"Love one," Marcus said as he slouched down in a chair, all jutting knees, lanky legs, and big boots.

Marion handed me a cup before I had a chance to say anything. The heat from the drink burned its way through me, steadying my hands and fortifying my nerves.

"All righty, then." Marion opened up her laptop, clicked through the opening screens, and then turned it toward us. "Remember, Marcus, that I told you I was working on some new and improved ways to try to draw in donations for the library?"

"The website and webcam?" Marcus nodded as he took a sip from a heavy-duty mug with the words Book Fiend emblazoned on one side in fancy script. "Yeah. Great idea, considering the library's history."

"Right. Well, ever since the webcam was installed, Bertie the Ghost has been making himself known even more often. It's almost as though he knows the camera is there, and is acting up accordingly."

I'd heard of spotlight hogs, but that was ridiculous. "What is *your* take on Bertie?" I asked Marion.

Marion poured herself the last cup of coffee from the pot and carried her delicate porcelain teacup and saucer to her desk. I was surprised it wasn't leopard print.

"Bertie," she said, "isn't something that I believed in at first. The librarian who left her post to me, lo, these many years ago, asked me if I had a strong constitution. 'Why?' I asked her. 'Because we have a presence in the basement.' Well, of course I thought she was just trying to scare me. You know, to leave her mark on the place. And for a while it was easy for me to pass off the things we and many library patrons were experiencing. You know. The cold spots. The uneasiness. The sounds. The feeling that someone was there, even when we were the only ones in the building. All of that can be passed off as overactive imaginations getting away from us."

"What changed your mind?" I asked.

She set her cup down and looked me square in the eye. "Because I saw him. What is it they say in *Ghostbusters*? 'A full-torso vaporous apparition'? Only once, after all these years. I was sitting here at my desk one night four months ago, filling out federal grant paperwork for the upgrades to the multimedia room. It was getting late; I didn't want to advertise the fact that I was here alone, so the only lights I had on were the one at my desk and the security light at the end of the hall facing me." She nodded toward the open door to her office.

I followed the line of her gaze and shivered. The security light was on at the end of the hall, just like that night she was describing. "Go on."

"Not much more to tell, really. I was just sitting here, scratching away on the papers, and I happened to look up." Her eyes grew distant, remembering. "He was standing right there, just behind the water cooler. He was dark, but not a shadow. Definitely human in shape. And I could have sworn . . ." She took a deep breath. "I could have sworn that I saw eyes. Red eyes. Glowing eyes."

At this Marcus sat up straighter. "Red?" he said, a frown pinching his brow. "You didn't tell me that."

Marion cocked her head to one side. "Does that make a difference?"

He didn't say anything for a moment. "I'm not sure."

And if Marcus wasn't sure . . . I shuddered involuntarily.

One thing I had always admired about Marion was that, like Liss, she was absolutely unflappable, and this situation was no different. "Well, as soon as you know something, you just let me know whether I should worry or not. Otherwise, I'll trust that I'm in capable hands."

167

Marcus scratched something down on a notepad he had pulled from his backpack. "Aunt Marion, think back to that moment. I want you to close your eyes and picture it in your mind."

Marion did as he asked, leaning her head against the back of her chair.

"Now, can you remember what made you look up?"

"I guess . . . a sense of movement, and when I turned my head, I saw a dark shape. A three-dimensional . . . *something.* Something with both depth and dimension, but not bulk or heft. I don't know how else to describe it. I'm not a fanciful kind of woman. I've lived long enough and seen enough that not much scares me. And this didn't really scare me, as such, but there was a difference to this shadow. It had substance, and something more."

"What, Aunt Marion?" Marcus prodded. "What did it have?"

She was quiet a moment, trying to gather her thoughts. "Awareness," she said at last. "And, maybe, intelligence."

Holy Mary, Mother of God.

I watched, mouth hanging open, as Marcus shot to his feet and went to the end of the hall. He crouched down behind the water cooler. "Like this?"

Marion squinted at him. "Hmm. Taller than that. But not quite as tall as you."

That was a comfort. Marcus clocked in at over six feet. Six feet of attractive and intelligent male was enough to make most women go weak in the knees. Six feet of intelligent shadow with glowing eyes? *Yeesh.*

"Did it do anything else?"

"No. He just looked at me. And I stared at him for a good long while. I couldn't seem to get a really good fix on him. Every time I thought I saw a bit of detail, the shape shifted and I lost it."

The lights in the office flickered, once, twice, then caught and held.

The security light in the hallway glared brighter.

"Marcus?" I said nervously.

He rose to his feet, as nonchalant and at ease as ever, and held his hands out, palms down, beneath the extra-bright light. "Electric," he said.

Marion started. "Well, it had better not be, if that clown at Burlington Electric knows what's good for him," she said in a huff. "He's checked our system three times, up, down, and sideways, and swears there is absolutely nothing wrong."

Marcus shook his head. "Not electric that way. Just energy. The hairs on the backs of my hands are standing on end."

"Oh." Mollified, Marion's prickle un-pricked. "Oh, well, that's all right, then."

"All right?" I echoed, standing up. "Why is that all right? How can that be all right? How can any of this be all right? Geez, Marion, it's not all right. You have a ghost in the library! Not balls of light or spooky noises, but an all-out, actual ghost!"

"Yes, but we knew that, dear."

"But I thought you said he was in the boiler room!"

My outburst had the desired effect of shocking some sense into them. Marion fell silent. Marcus's brows drew together.

"You know . . ."

"She's right," Marion finished for him. "I hadn't even considered that. We'd always seen the evidence in the basement."

"Which means he's either on the move, or —"

"Or there's something else here. Which the webcams I installed also seem to suggest. I just didn't realize it." Marion shook her head, frowning slightly. "Why didn't that occur to me?"

"You mean the shadow and Bertie aren't one and the same? That maybe there's more than one spirit at work here?" I asked, deflated by the very possibility.

170

"Perhaps."

I was okay when I thought we might be reviewing a bit of tape from a webcam, or even setting up recording equipment to log hours of silence for possible EVPs from the ghost world. But this . . .

The power spike in the hall drained away as though it had never happened. I nudged Marcus, but he was already watching the security light fade back to normal with interest.

"Aunt Marion, you did say you thought your webcams had picked up something. Can you show us?"

Marion eagerly complied, pulling her laptop over to herself and powering it up. "Most of the footage is nothing, of course. But take a look at this."

She opened a file from within her video playback software and pressed Play. Marcus leaned closer to the screen. I had to make myself look.

The image on screen showed the children's area, made plain by the reading posters, the tot-sized tables and chairs, and the proliferation of stuffed animals in evidence. Much of the room was in darkness, except for a security light near the lighted Exit sign.

"Whoa." Marcus reached a hand toward the screen. "Play that back. Just back it up thirty seconds."

Marion clicked as directed. The video played back, reviewing what we'd just seen. God help me, I couldn't keep myself from watching this time.

I saw it, just as Marcus said, "There. By the door. Did you see?"

Something was forming in midair, or at least trying to. There was a shimmer in the space next to the door, mirage-like in appearance.

"Look at that," Marcus said, awed.

I was looking. It made me as nervous as hell. First Marion's dark Something, then the flickering electricity. And now, seeing the disturbance firsthand, even in digital form, was just taking me a step too far onto the path toward the Otherworld. I grabbed my cup and took a big gulp of coffee. It was blissfully, shockingly hot, but it was very real and very normal, and it reminded me that I was, too. I took another gulp, grimacing as the nerves in my tongue sizzled.

Marion, on the other hand, looked as pleased as punch. "I knew it was something! I knew I wasn't just reading too much into things."

"Oh, it's something, all right. Aunt Marion, I can't believe you have this on file. It's amazing. Listen, I'd like to show it to some of the other N.I.G.H.T.S. Can you make a copy of it for me?"

"Of course I can. Well, I could if my DVD drive hadn't gone down. We've had a rash of computer equipment malfunctions of late. Things melting down left and right. That wouldn't have anything to do with this, would it?"

"It's possible," Marcus told her. "Electronics are notoriously unreliable around active locations. Battery-powered items are even worse. E-mail?"

"I'll e-mail it off to you right now." Marion's fingers clicked across the keys. She paused a moment, gazing at her beloved nephew. "You know, dear heart, there's something I've been meaning to ask you."

"Sure, Auntie. Anything, you know that."

She nodded, taking her time to sort through her thoughts. "Well, since you don't seem to mind, I don't see any point in beating around the bush. Marcus, honey, are you a Christian?"

CHAPTER 8

The unexpected question made me splutter into my coffee.

Marcus, however, proved as unflappable as his aunt. It must be in the genes. "What makes you ask that?" he said, keeping his eyes on the laptop screen.

"Well, I don't know, exactly. Intuition, maybe. Are you?"

He sighed and squatted down next to her, taking her hands in his. "No, Aunt Marion. I would say I'm not what you or most people would consider a Christian."

"Ah. I didn't think so."

"Does that bother you?"

A smile played about her generous mouth, and she patted his cheek. "No, honey, it doesn't bother me. I know your heart, remember? You do what feels right to you. The rest generally takes care of itself, doesn't it?"

Marcus grinned up at her. "Aunt Marion,

I have to say your view of the universe is very progressive."

"Thank you. I like to think I'm a pretty hip chick."

Much hipper than me, apparently. I was still stuck in the mire somewhere, trying to decide what was right and wrong. But maybe that was the problem. Maybe I was thinking too much. Maybe I just needed to trust myself. To trust what felt right.

"Besides," Marion continued, "I have a feeling your alternative viewpoint is going to come in very handy here."

"You know I live to serve."

"What should I do now?" Marion asked as the computer windows closed down, one by one. "I mean about the library, of course."

"Do you feel comfortable carrying on?" Marcus asked her.

"Do I feel comfortable?" Marion looked as though the contrary had never occurred to her. "Of course I feel comfortable. The library is my home."

"And you feel safe despite what's been happening?"

She shrugged. "I'm not going to be intimidated by a little air disturbance," she said matter-of-factly. "I've been living with him, or whatever it is, for twenty-five years now.

If it's not going away, it has to accept that neither am I. I'll be fine." She lit up all of a sudden, excitement making her seem suddenly years younger. "I'll tell you what. One happy by-product of all of this is that I have really found the most intriguing little tidbits in the course of my research, about the library and Stony Mill in general. I've made copies of everything I've found and I've just started cataloguing it, trying to make sense of it all as I go. Fascinating stuff. Fascinating." She looked at both of us. "I don't know if you've noticed or not, but things seem to keep happening in Stony Mill."

"Trust me," I said, thinking of my own sense of impending calamity, "we've noticed."

"And I'm not just talking about the murders. Are you aware that the county has had a rash of petty social disorder? Drugs, domestic problems, vandalism, aggression . . . it's been happening left and right. *The Gazette*'s police report column is overflowing with it."

Well, I had to admit I hadn't noticed that. I tended to avoid news reports when at all possible. I had found that the pain and suffering that was often conveyed in the reports was hurting me physically, and stayed with me far too long. It was better that I avoided

176

it entirely. I figured if anything big happened, someone would tell me about it. Everything else was beyond my control.

But it did echo what Tom had said in passing.

"It's affecting everyone. Good, churchgoing people. Why, just yesterday I saw Louisa Murray — you remember that she won that big armoire in the crafters' auction? Anyhoo, Louisa told me that someone had chopped her beautiful roses down to the nubs, presumably out of spite or mischief. Years and years of tending and of growth gone, just like that. And after losing her husband early last year to the cancer, well, it's just inconceivable to me. Why would anyone want to pick on a widow woman like that? I just don't know what this world is coming to." She shook her head, tsk-tsking away.

Neither did I. And wasn't that the trouble? Our world was going crazy, and our town was, unfortunately, displaying all the symptoms.

Marcus and I were silent as he drove me back to my apartment, each of us absorbed in our own thoughts. As for mine, they weren't pretty. Stony Mill was sick, that much was clear. The town had come down with the Big City Crazies, and we didn't have the resources to combat it. Which didn't seem too important right now. The big question was, what were we as a community going to do about it?

Combine that with my earlier discovery that the world I knew was a far more complex and shadow-ridden place than I had ever dreamed, and it left me feeling more than a little vulnerable. Fear could be crippling, or it could motivate a person to fight back. I was straddling the fence between the two options, and I knew it. Could I find the strength within myself to make a stand with the forces of Light before the darkness took over my town completely?

"Maggie."

"Hmm?" I pulled myself away from the worries that were eating at my composure.

Marcus was gazing at me, his angular cheekbones and lean jaw highlighted by the dim glow from the dash. "We're here," he said in a quiet voice that harmonized with the stillness in the truck cab.

I looked up to see the familiar outlines of the aging Victorian house against the backlight of the town glow reflected in the sky. Home, sweet home.

The streetlamp in the back alley blinked out as we entered the pea-gravel drive.

"Damn," I said, staring up at it. "I hate it

when that happens."

"Want me to walk you to the door?"

I gave him a grateful glance. "Would you mind? I still get a little creeped out going into a dark apartment after the break-in. I mean, I know it had little to do with me personally, but still . . ."

"Happy to. You know that."

He left the pickup running, its headlights providing ample light as we walked companionably up the drive.

"Marcus," I said when we reached the recessed entrance to my pseudo dungeon, "do you ever wonder about what's been going on around here? In Stony Mill, I mean."

"Yeah. I have to admit I have."

"It doesn't feel right."

"No. I'm not sure what we can do about it, though."

"I know," I said as I started down the stairs. "But sometimes I get the feeling that we're supposed to do something. I just don't know what that is."

In the puddle of illumination from the security light over my door, I dug for my keys. "Aha, there you are. Pesky little things, always hiding on me. Or maybe it's gremlins."

"Or fairies. They can be very sneaky."

I laughed in spite of myself. "A man who

believes in fairies. I would never have guessed."

"I believe in lots of things."

Typical Marcus. As mysterious as ever. "Seeing is believing?"

"Sometimes, believing means seeing. And not only in the gullible sense." Marcus took the keys from my hand and opened the door for me, reaching within for the light switch. Taking me by the hand, he led the way in, giving the room a quick but thorough once-over before stepping aside. "Everything looks okay, I guess."

"Thanks, Marcus."

"I haven't checked your bedroom, of course," he said, grinning at me and waggling his eyebrows.

I laughed in spite of myself. "Well, now, did you think you were going to?"

"Just thought I'd make the offer."

The tone was light, but I'd glimpsed a flicker of something in his eyes before he looked away, and it was anything but teasing. And in that moment I knew that the subtle shift I was feeling in the air at that moment had nothing to do with gremlins, fairies, ghosts, or even a malfunctioning power supply. It was him. And, God help me, it came from me as well.

"Yeah. Thanks. Well, goodnight, then," I

said, edging toward the door. I grabbed hold of the knob and pulled the door open, leaning on it for support with my heart yammering away in my chest as Marcus moved silently toward the only exit . . . and me.

For a moment I thought I was safe. That the heightened awareness I was feeling around him was nothing more than a by-product of the weirdness in the library following on the heels of the tragic events of the weekend. Survivor syndrome, nothing more. And then he leaned in to give me the usual friendly parting peck on the cheek.

Something shifted in the air again, and before I knew it, so had we.

"Maggie," he breathed, dangerously close to my mouth.

I couldn't make myself move. I was lost to this one space in time, incapable of conscious thought or action. My eyes drifted closed of their own accord, and I had the sense, briefly, that this had happened between us before. Seconds ticked by unnoticed before his hand came up under my jaw to tilt my head back. My chin fit neatly into his palm, and his thumb tested the very corner of my lips. Gently. Sweetly.

And then slowly, irrevocably, he lowered his mouth to mine.

Attraction is a funny thing. Sometimes it

comes at you like a randy bull in mating season — ready, raring to go, and unwilling to admit defeat. Other times it sneaks in like a cat through the back door, peeping around corners, skulking behind the furniture, until the singularly perfect moment of its choice when it decides to pounce on your chest, sink in its claws, and Make Itself Known. And then, sometimes, it's a force of nature, like spring rain or summer sunshine or the sweeping winds of winter scraping over the frozen earth. It just *is.*

I didn't have the time or presence of mind to decide which of these applied in this case. I was too busy enjoying the feel of Marcus's body crushing mine against the door. His hands were splayed on either side of me, flat against the planes of the door itself, as though he didn't trust himself to let them roam free. It didn't seem to matter, though — he was more than making up for it with the rest of him. As for me, at some point in time I'd wound my arms tight around his neck, and I was clinging to him like a drowning soul. And maybe I was, just a little. Maybe I needed a bit of earth to hold on to.

I don't know how long it was before we came up for air. Long enough for the door panels to be imprinted into my shoulder blades, and more than long enough for my body to be singing his praises. That he was feeling the same way was perfectly, deliciously obvious, and yet we both pulled back at the same moment.

Only a hairbreadth, but it was enough.

"Sorry," he whispered, his breath warm against my lips. "That was out of line —"

"No, don't," I whispered back, trying to rein in the physical reactions that were demanding further action. "You wouldn't have if I hadn't —"

He hadn't stepped back, and I hadn't let go. I think I was afraid to. That would mean moving, which was risky, risky, risky.

It took supreme strength of will to push sensation away and replace it with reason. Somehow, we both managed.

My breath rushed out, in relief, in disappointment, in acceptance. I'd get over it, just as soon as my hormones stopped clamoring. That's all this was. Hormones.

The guilt, I knew, would come later. Just as soon as the sexual fog had cleared from my brain. That was pretty much a guarantee.

I couldn't immediately look him in the eye. I locked my gaze on his Adam's apple instead, and swallowed hard.

"I, uh, guess I'd better go," he said, beating me to the punch. He pushed off the door, and me, a few inches.

All I could do was nod and try not to feel the pain of the loss too much.

"Okay. Well, if you're sure," he hedged.

"Marcus." I risked a glance up at him. "I . . . I just can't. Tom —"

He pushed the rest of the way off and turned his face aside. A muscle in his jaw gripped and flexed with the effort. "Hey, it's no big deal. No problem. I understand."

"I just —"

"Yeah, I know. Tom."

And Liss. I couldn't do this. It was wrong.

Aaaand there was the guilt. Right on schedule.

What in heaven's name was I thinking?

On second thought, that had been part of the problem. I hadn't been thinking. I hadn't been capable of it. Once I'd thought of Marcus as a dark and dangerous kind of guy. I just didn't realize how susceptible I was to that kind of danger.

Good to know.

"Okay. Well, thanks for taking me tonight. It was . . . an illuminating evening." In more ways than one.

He glanced my way at last, just a flash, but to me it was a sign that maybe he wasn't so pissed at me that he wouldn't get over it. "Yeah. See ya later."

He touched my cheek before he left, his thumb grazing lightly over my cheekbone, but that was the end of it, and then he walked out the door. I closed it quietly behind him, still breathless and feeling as though I'd just rumbled with Don Juan and somehow come away with my panties still on. A nicer Don Juan, but a master seducer nonetheless. From the first moment I saw him, Marcus had exuded a deliciously sinuous male grace that was mesmerizing in action. I suppose I had Tom to thank that I'd withstood the call of this dark angel of temptation for as long as I had.

I would have said "Small favors," but I really didn't think Tom would appreciate it.

CHAPTER 9

By morning, the guilt that had settled in the night before had managed to magnify tenfold. I was pond scum. Worse than pond scum. I was the reek that resulted when pond scum had been baking under the hot summer sun. No one was lower than me. I had nearly betrayed the trust of a most beloved friend, and had no one to blame for it but myself. Pond scum that I was.

Liss and Tom both deserved better.

I forced myself out of bed, determined to face the day and face up to the consequences of my betrayal, whatever they might be, like a man. Well, woman. Whatever.

A shower seemed a good start. Hot, soapy, nonscummy water to wash away the lingering press of Marcus's body . . . to clear the scent of leather and man from my nostrils . . . to strip the brush of his fingertips from my hair . . .

My eyes flared open under the torrent of

hot water.

Oh, boy. I was in trouble. Big. Trouble. Huge.

No wisecracks from the peanut gallery.

I jumped from the shower as though the hounds of hell were nipping at my nethers, and scrubbed myself dry. The clothes went on just as quickly: a rough wool sweater, trouser-style jeans, and pinch-toed boots. My hair I drew back in a severe mass of bun at the nape of my neck — nothing soft and yielding about it. Today I was all about self-punishment and contrition. The bathroom lightbulb popped out of commission as I was leaving the room, but I paid no heed to this particular metaphysical raspberry other than to flip the power off. Even Christine's determined radio static did not filter through the cloud of misery laying claim to my psyche. I punched the button to another station, but Christine has a way of doing what she wants. Pretty soon the radio was tuned to the oldies station again, with the warbling strains of that 1970s classic "Torn Between Two Lovers" grating on my nerves. I turned off the radio altogether, but it was too late. The song was stuck in my head on repeat.

I let myself in the back door of Enchantments as always, calling "Hello" to Liss, whose car was parked in its usual space.

"Out here, luv!" Liss called from beyond the purple velvet dividing curtains.

I set my purse down with a sigh and parted the curtains to go up and help myself to some of the coffee I could smell brewing. Liss was there, behind the counter, her glasses perched on the end of her nose while she studied the screen of her PDA.

And at the end of the counter . . .

"Marcus," I gulped as my heart came to a screeching halt.

He glanced up at me. "Oh, hey. Mornin', Maggie."

Good morning, Maggie? That was civil. Blasé, even.

I cleared my throat. "Good morning."

"Here, ducks, let me pour you a cuppa," Liss said, slipping from her stool and pulling a cup from the shelf. "You look as though you could use something to get you going."

I'd had quite enough to get me going last night.

I cleared my throat again.

"Are you coming down with something?" she asked, casting a narrowed glance in my direction. "I have just the thing. I'll mix a bit of honey in. You don't mind it sweet, do you? Do be careful, though, it's a bit hot."

This conversation was going from bad to worse with its unintended innuendo. "I'm all right, really. I'll just take it plain, Liss."

She set the steaming cup down before me. "Marcus and I were just going over some of the data from the library digital."

I raised my brows and chanced a glance at Marcus. "That was fast. Marion just sent the file over last night."

He smiled, meeting my gaze. "Well, I didn't have anything better to do, so I stayed up late analyzing it."

Ooh. Ouch. I cleared my throat a third time for good measure, avoiding Liss's concerned gaze. "So, what do you have?"

It wasn't in Marcus to hold a grudge. He slid his PDA over to me. "You saw the digital yourself. But take a look at this."

The screen displayed a zoom-in on the wavering image in the children's section of the library that Marion had captured with her webcam. The screen was smallish, but the picture quality was good enough to show what appeared to be a face forming in the midst of the air distortion and shimmer. A face with full lips, fine bone structure, and arching brows.

A woman's face.

I frowned. "But I thought that Bertie was a male spirit."

Marcus nodded, his gaze never leaving my face.

"But if he's male . . . and he exists . . ."

"Oh, he exists, all right," Marcus assured me. You saw the blue glow yourself, remember?"

How could I forget? It was back in December. I'd never even heard of Boiler Room Bertie until then. Leave it to Marcus to introduce me to the creepy blue fella. "But if he's male, and he exists . . . who the heck is this?"

"Don't know. But it's definitely a female face, isn't it?"

I nodded. "Did you tell Liss what Marion said about the shadow?"

He hadn't; he'd only just arrived. Briefly he described Marion's experience with the dark spirit with red eyes.

"It almost sounds like an imp," Liss mused. "Or I suppose it could be what they call a shadow man. I'm not convinced the two are separate issues, myself. Just different in size. And it appears this was a fairly strong entity, based on its interference with the electrical power sources."

An imp or a shadow man. Was either better than your garden variety ghost? I couldn't be sure. Neither one sounded all that promising to me. "Is that in addition to

Bertie?" I asked, frowning.

"It appears so, yes. Unless it's just another way for Bertie to materialize."

"So the library could have not one entity attached to it, but three?"

"Well . . ." Liss looked at me. "The number of spirits who visit a given location is limitless," she said quietly. "Spirits — in this case meaning souls who have crossed over — have the ability to pop in from time to time, at their discretion, to look in on those they were close to, or places they loved particularly well or had some affinity for during their lifetimes. They're not tied to linear travel or linear time lines, as we who are on this side are. But, though people often mistake those visitations for hauntings, they are quite different. Generally speaking, a true haunting occurs when a place or a person has attracted a spirit who neglected to cross over due to confusion or fear . . . or a spirit who *refused* to cross over for whatever reason. Both can be problematic, given the right circumstances. Especially if they conflict somehow with current residents."

"Which is not the case here, right?" I said, looking at the two of them for confirmation. "Marion looks fairly comfortable with the notion of living with a resident spirit.

191

The website, the webcams, her research . . . she almost seems to revel in it."

"Aye, that's true," Liss said, a little too thoughtfully. "Unless . . ."

I raised my brows at her, waiting for her to continue.

"Unless the imp-slash-shadow creature is a dark entity. In which case, all bets are off."

A dark entity. That made absolutely no sense to me. "How could the library attract a dark entity? I thought they rallied around people with dark intentions, dark natures. Dark practices. The library and Marion definitely don't fit that scenario at all. She's one of the sweetest, nicest, most giving people I know."

"Most of the time they do, but not always. Unless . . ." She paused. "Unless Bertie or the unknown entity with the female aspect has opened the door to others."

"What, you mean a portal of some kind?" Marcus asked.

Liss inclined her head, as contemplative as ever. "It's possible, I think."

"Aunt Marion said that she has been researching the town and the library itself," Marcus told her.

"Brava. Forewarned is forearmed. Your aunt's propensity toward scholarly endeavors could be very valuable to us all."

We fell silent a moment, each absorbed in thought. Liss rose to unlock the front door and switch on all the lights. I glanced at Marcus, but he was avoiding my gaze again.

Probably for the better. For both of us.

"Did Maggie tell you, Marcus," Liss said as she returned to the counter, "about our visit with Eli yesterday?"

I shook my head. "I, uh, didn't mention it."

"No time," Marcus added helpfully, fiddling with the buttons on his PDA.

Hm, maybe he was feeling a little guilty by now, too.

Liss poured herself a fresh cup of tea, adding as an afterthought a splash of cream and a sprinkling of sugar. "Maggie and I went out to Eli's place yesterday afternoon, to see how he's doing. It must have been a wrench, Luc's passing. Eli is holding up well, but he's torn, I think, between his ways and convictions and the very human desire to see justice done for his friend."

"That's understandable. Eli is very big on honor."

"And on friends." Liss smiled. "We went out to the place where Luc was found, you know. The three of us."

"Miss Maggie included?" Marcus quirked a brow at me. "Wow."

193

I stuck my tongue out at him, but nearly bit it when his gaze lowered to my mouth and his brow rose even farther.

"Miss Maggie was indeed included. In fact, Maggie was the one who found the symbol on the tree."

"What symbol?" Marcus asked, all seriousness again.

"A sign on a tree, just off the road. Definitely magical in nature."

"Light or dark?"

Liss hesitated, picturing the scene in her mind. "Light, I think. Though it was difficult to know that for certain. The energies of the place were all mixed up. Pure bedlam."

"Did Eli use his pendulum to try to sort things out?"

Liss and I both nodded. "It wouldn't work right," I supplied. "The pendulum just swung wildly. Erratically." I paused, wondering whether I should say more. I had carried the piece of paper in my pocket ever since finding the sign; I didn't know why. Maybe in hopes that the opportunity to understand would present itself to me when I least expected it, and thus I needed to be prepared. "I, uh, did make a drawing of it."

"Oh, that's brilliant, Maggie!" Liss proclaimed. "And here I was thinking I was going to have to go back out and take a picture of it myself."

If it had been just Liss, I might have admitted my own reasons for not taking a photograph, but there was no way I was going to confess to Marcus that the reason I hadn't snapped a pic rather than make a drawing was because Tom told me not to.

Liss furrowed her brow as she puzzled over the drawing, tracing the outlines with her finger. She leapt up and headed for the stairs. "Back in a mo'."

"You okay?"

I looked up in surprise at the unexpected question from Marcus. "Yeah, I'm okay. You?"

He smiled at me, managing somehow to look mischievous and confident and brazen all at the same time. "Yeah. Not mad?"

I smiled back at him. "Nope. Not mad. Definitely not mad."

"Good. Because I would hate to lose you as a friend over something as trivial as a kiss."

"Oh . . ." Somehow I wasn't quite sure I liked how that sounded. "Um . . ."

My cell phone blared trumpets from my front pocket. "Remind me to change this, would you?" I said as I flipped the case open. "It's driving me crazy. Hello?"

195

"And how are you this morning?"

It was my mother's voice, surprisingly cheerful, given that it was Monday morning and I had been too busy to call or visit over the weekend. "Hi, Mom. I'm good, good. How is everything?"

"The same, of course. Your father has been grinding his teeth at night. I don't know what is going on with that company, but they really need to hire some help. He can't go on putting in all of the hours that he does. He never has any free time, and his 'Honey Do' list never gets any shorter. You should see the state of things around here."

My mother was big on Honey Do's. When we kids had lived at home, most of our weekends were filled with the minutiae Mom hadn't gotten around to during the week. Much of it had been necessary, but a good bit of it felt more like busywork meant to fill our hours and days — idle hands are the devil's playthings, as Grandma Cora had been fond of saying. But mostly I think Mom relished directing traffic. So to speak.

"I don't know, Mom. I think what Dad really needs is a vacation." Either that or an intervention.

"What he needs is to find his backbone," Mom said, as sympathetic as usual. "Things will never change if he continues fulfilling that company's whims on his own. Why should they? They have a willing victim right there in front of them. He just needs to tell them no every once in a while."

It was easy for Mom to say. She didn't have the responsibility of supporting the family in an uncertain business world resting on her shoulders.

"Aw, Mom. You know, I think the house looked fine when I dropped by yesterday. I think Dad's getting more done than you're giving him credit for."

"Grandpa said you'd stopped in for a quick visit while I was out." There was an undertone there, unmistakable, that made it sound as though I had purposely timed the visit to coincide with her absence. Which, this time, was patently untrue. "But . . . cookies, Margaret?"

Whoops. Busted! How did she manage to ferret that out of him so quickly? "Sorry. I thought he'd like them."

"He does; only too well. When he wouldn't eat his rice pudding last night, I knew something was up. He'd eaten the whole dozen you'd bought him!"

It was probably because she kept him deprived of his creature comforts 95 percent of the time, but now was not the time to say so. "Sorry about that."

"You know your grandpa," she continued, on a roll now. "An ornerier man you'll be hard pressed to find. You give him a yard, and he'll go for the touchdown before anyone else even gets into position. Honestly, I think I'm going to have to take his battery pack away. As soon as the snow melted, he started going out and about on his Hoverchair, sniffing after the widows in the neighborhood. One morning last week he went out and forgot that he hadn't put his teeth in. I ask you, how do you forget your teeth? That's what I want to know. Apparently he thought the ladies were all smiles that morning because of his abundant charm."

I laughed at the visual. "He *is* a handful, that's for sure."

"He is, and your Grandma Cora must have been a saint for putting up with him all those years."

Saint Cora. Now *that* was funny. I wondered if Grandma filled Mom's head with random thoughts of conscience, the way she had commandeered mine.

"Hey, Mom," I said, with my eye on Marcus, "I'd better get back to work. Did you want anything in particular, or were you just calling to chat?"

"Actually, I did," she said, and the tone of

her voice made me suddenly wary. "It's about time that you brought your young man home to meet your family, don't you think? You've been ducking us long enough, and God help me, I've let you. But I'm starting to get the feeling that you're ashamed of us, Margaret. You've been seeing him since October . . . things must be going well, hmm?"

Oy.

I had almost forgotten that I'd somehow, kinda, sorta given my mom the impression that Tom and I were indeed in a committed relationship, and that we had been seeing each other since October. It had seemed such an innocent little lie, but that one little fib had been giving me grief ever since because my mom had real issues with letting go of things once she sank her claws in. Case in point. It would never occur to her that she might be the reason for my reluctance to bring a guy home. That it might be easier to forge a relationship without fending off the well-meaning intrusions of a mother who was a matrimonial force of nature and who would not rest until she saw her oldest daughter married, with a mortgage, children, a cat, and a dog. And the sooner, the better.

Besides, she had powers of perception that

could sniff out Tom's not-quite-divorced status in a heartbeat. Any such dinner would require a rigorous premeal briefing with Tom — not to mention Dad and Grandpa, who were both in the know — and I wasn't quite convinced that any of them were up to the face-off.

"Well . . . Mom, Tom has been really busy with everything that's been happening around town."

"He has to take time to eat, doesn't he? An hour, that's all I'm asking, Margaret. Just long enough to shake hands with your father and get acclimated to Grandpa on his best behavior, before he has a chance to tell too many of his awful jokes."

I smothered a sigh and stared at the ceiling. "When are you thinking about doing this smorgasbord of fun?"

I could hear the triumph in her voice before she uttered a word. "I'll tell your dad that we'll be expecting you for lunch this Sunday after church. Easter Sunday is so important. And you won't forget to go to Reconciliation beforehand and receive Communion, of course? Does Tom go to church? Maybe he'd like to be our guest for that as well."

"I'll let you know about that later."

"Don't wait too long. You know I like to

be able to plan ahead."

"Yes, Mom, I know." Boy, did I ever!

"Oh, there's another call coming in; I'd better go. You have a good day, now."

" 'Bye, Mom."

I glanced up. Marcus was watching me with an amused twinkling in his eyes. "Mommy trouble?"

I shrugged. "Typical mother stuff. Dinner with the family, and she wants me to bring Tom. You know."

He grimaced. "Ooof. Prospective husband meet-and-greet. Better Tom than me."

I had no doubts my mother would concur. Marcus, with his shoulder-length hair and Goth-punk-rock-star clothes preferences, was not quite her idea of husband material.

"I think I found it!" Liss called from the door to the loft. She came toward us waving a book. With both hands. The thing was huge.

I turned my head sideways to see the title. *"The Lightworker's Complete Encyclopedia of Magical Symbols?"*

"Mm," she enthused, plopping the thing down on the counter and flipping to the table of contents. "There has to be something in here to help us. And if there is," she said, sliding her half-moon reading glasses into place, "I will find it."

Marcus threw back his head to down the last of his coffee, then set his cup down on the scarred antique countertop with a very male kind of clatter. "Well, ladies, it's been fun, but I have to get going. Places to go, people to see, magic to make. The usual." He blew a kiss to Liss, then with a wink at me, he was gone.

Marcus's leaving was like the opening of floodgates as far as Enchantments was concerned. All morning long, the shop had a steady stream of customers, most of whom seemed to be in a buying mood. I spent most of my time zipping back and forth assisting in the trenches, while Liss rang up the purchases with her usual style and grace. The hours sped by. When my cell rang again and I opened it to see Tom's number on my Caller ID, I could scarcely believe it was already twelve thirty.

"I don't suppose I could entice you to have lunch with me?" he asked by way of a greeting.

"Hmmm, you're singing my favorite tune. Where and when?"

"Now, and Annie-Thing Good?"

"You got it. I'll be there in five."

"Don't you stand me up and break my heart."

Liss looked up expectantly as I ended the

call and approached the counter. "Lunchtime beckons?"

I nodded. "And so does Tom. Do you mind?"

"Of course not. You go on, we've hit a lull."

"I'll bring you back some soup."

"Annie's? You're on."

The lunch crowd had thinned out somewhat by the time I pulled Christine up in a parking spot across the street from Annie's always bustling café. In the seven months since Annie Miller, N.I.G.H.T.S. member and chef extraordinaire, had opened her doors, she had quickly claimed her space in the upper echelon of Stony Mill eats. I loved the ambiance of her place, a mix of old Midwestern comfort food combined with modern health-nut sophistication, where you could get your soup and eat it, too (not to mention your gourmet sandwiches). But the things Annie was especially known for were her desserts. Cheesecakes, pies, and brownies of all types and textures, including my favorite: a double fudge turtle brownie with the meltingest caramel swirling in and out of layers of brownie and fudge and pecan. It was out-of-this-world heavenly.

Come to think of it, I had not had a truly cosmic experience in way too long.

Tom waved at me from a table in the front window as soon as I walked through the door, my entrance accompanied by the chiming of a dozen brass feng shui bells. Not seeing Annie immediately, I headed over to join him.

"I've already ordered for you," he told me. "Barley vegetable beef, baguette, and raspberry iced tea. I hope that's okay."

The soup was still steaming in the bowl. "Yum, thanks. This will be great."

He smiled at me as I sat down, his gray eyes soft with affection. "I'm glad you could get away. I missed seeing you last night."

I felt a pang of guilt, wicked sharp. "I missed you, too. You've been so busy."

"And I'm about to get busier," he said, avoiding my gaze.

"What do you mean?"

He stirred his soup around and around in the bowl. "I spoke to Chief yesterday. I've been promoted. Kind of."

"Oh, wow, that's great! I mean, well, isn't it?" I frowned, confused.

"Chief has named me the SMPD's Special Task Force Investigator, to work in conjunction with all other agencies in the investigation and resolution of the problems facing Stony Mill, including the recent murder but not exclusively that. What this really means is, anything beyond the scope of traffic tickets, family disturbances, and general peacekeeping falls to me and my team." My gaze fell to his hands, which were making a shredded mess of his baguette. "It also means whatever hours are needed to see it done, will be done."

It didn't take a lot of imagination to see what might be required. It sure didn't leave much room for deepening the connection between us, should we — *I* — so choose. "I see."

"It's important, Maggie."

But I wanted to be important, too. Was that too selfish of me? I supposed it probably was, but knowing that didn't seem to change the wanting inside of me. "I know. It has to be done."

He nodded, absentmindedly stirring the bread crumbs that had fallen from his baguette into the lower reaches of his soup. "Did you know . . . one of my cop buddies said his pastor has been preaching that the devil has descended upon Stony Mill? That the Old Deceiver is the reason behind the craziness we're experiencing? The violence? The unrest?" He paused a moment to add emphasis to his main point. "The murders."

I shrugged. "Everybody is entitled to an opinion. What church does he go to?"

"It's a newish church that started up just a few months ago. First Evangelical Church of Light."

The name of the church rang a bell, and I knew why. It was Reverend Baxter Martin's baby. "Ah. I've heard of Reverend Martin. From what I understand, that seems to be par for the course. He sees devils in everyone."

"Yeah, but . . . as far as theories go, that one seems just as good as any other I've heard lately. You have to admit it, Maggie. The weird sign thing that you found out at the crime scene could just corroborate that."

"The sign," I echoed. It flashed before my eyes again, black and white and somehow menacing. Liss thought it was magical in nature. I didn't know much about the symbolism used in the various traditions of magical practice, but based on the amount of energy emanating from and surrounding it, I would have to say I agreed. But to what purpose? "How could it possibly —"

"Be satanic?"

My brows shot up, and I gaped up at him. "Beg pardon?"

"There's a theory being bandied about at the station that this symbol, and other things that have been found around the county, all point to satanic worship."

I choked down the bread that had gotten stuck in my throat. "You don't really believe that, do you?"

"Honestly? I don't know what to believe right now. Three murders in this town in the last six months. *Three.* That's not right. That's not normal. You yourself have said something is going on, Maggie. There has to be an explanation."

Yes, but one not rooted in superstition and fear, I was about to say, then realized that my own experiences in the months just behind us hadn't been above what most would label as rooted in superstition and fear. Even I was having difficulty coming to terms with it, thanks to all that I had been taught as truth when I was growing up.

"Tom, just because something is a part of a ritual used for magic doesn't make it satanic. Nor does it make it dark. Or black. Or whatever you want to call it."

He looked out the window, his expression closed and unreadable. "You know, I have to say this. I don't want to hurt your feelings, but . . . I think you're a little biased when it comes to this subject."

My mouth fell open. "Biased? How can you say that?"

"Biased because of your boss and . . . some of your friends. I'm trying to be nice about this, Maggie. Because even you have to admit, things started happening about the time they came to town."

CHAPTER 10

For heaven's sake, he made it sound like a conspiracy come to life. Which was ridiculous. I might be a trusting soul at times, but I was not blind. Unlike Tom, apparently. It was not the first time he had been in danger of allowing his prejudices to get in the way. "Well, you seem to be full of answers," I said, trying my best to keep my tone level, even if the words themselves were not. "I hope this doesn't mean that you're jumping to conclusions again. Because I have to tell you, the tendency to jump to conclusions isn't exactly conducive to impartial investigative techniques." Or to potential relationships.

His eyes snapped in annoyance, and he clamped his lips together. "Maybe it was a mistake to talk about this."

"Good."

"Because you're obviously not in the mood to listen to me, even though I say it because I worry about you."

"You don't have to worry about me. I can take care of myself."

"Yes, I know. I've seen the results first-hand. Jesus, Maggie, I don't see why you can't see that weird things happen when your friends are around."

"Amanda Roberson didn't have anything to do with my friends," I retorted, referring to the teenager who'd been murdered in December. "If you're going to bring up ancient history. And neither did Luc."

He exhaled loudly, heavily. "I hope you're right. I really hope you're right."

We both dipped into our soup, which was cooling, to alleviate our tempers, which were not. But even after a few bites filled with nothing but stilted silence, I could not let it go completely. "I do hope you realize that Liss was actually a Stony Mill resident for years before any of this started."

"Maybe so. But you know, I'm having a hard time believing that Luc Metzger was a simple mugging gone terribly awry. I want to believe that, I really do. More than you can know. But something — call it that sixth sense that you want so much to believe in, if you like — something has got my radar up big time. Now, I don't have any proof to that end. But if it's out there, I'll find it."

It worried me that he could be so closed-minded, that he could not see the good in people as easily as he could see the potential bad. That he could not believe in the things he could not see unless he imagined evil incarnate right there with them, orchestrating all. Truth be told, this was the main reason I was hesitant to move forward into a genuine committed relationship, and I had to admit it was a biggie. All I could do was hope that he might come around eventually.

Our edgy silence was interrupted when Annie Miller came bustling up to our table. "Maggie!" she said, wiping her hands on her apron. "Hey, girl! I didn't see you come in."

I smiled up at my N.I.G.H.T.S. friend, happy for the interruption. "Hey, Annie! Long time no see. How's that godbaby doing?"

Proud godmother that she was, Annie rolled her eyes heavenward in pure joy. "I have never seen such a little angel. Have I shown you a picture?"

She had, but I let her have her fun, even when she snapped out a fat wallet-sized bundle that would have been excessive from any new mother. I oohed and aahed over them appropriately. "Aw, she's beautiful. You have every right to be proud."

"You know, I've been a little worried about you," Annie admitted, giving me a maternal little pat on the shoulder. "You haven't been in here much, and with you missing the meetings . . . well, I've been meaning to call. Sorry I've been so tied up."

I wrinkled my nose in embarrassment. "No worries. I just . . . I've been busy, that's all."

"So I see," she said, darting a meaningful glance at Tom. "Well, if there's a good reason for a girl to miss seeing her friends, a handsome guy has got to be it. How are you, Deputy Fielding?"

He held out his hand to her. "Tom, please."

"Been keeping our girl busy, have you?"

Tom and I looked at each other, our gazes bouncing away as soon as they met.

"Annie," I said, changing the subject, "I think I'm in the mood for dessert today. What've you got?"

Food was Annie's favorite subject. It was her life, but it was also the way that she communicated with the world: Everything under the sun could be fixed by a good meal. With her fuzzy red hair drawn back into matching Pippi Longstocking braids, her open face, and her lighthearted approach to life, she was one of the most feel-good people I knew. Especially when combined with her killer desserts.

"Hmm," Annie said, pretending to think. "Are you in the mood for chocolate? Because if so, I have just the thing to tempt your tastebuds: a Black Forest torte with eight layers and a goodly helping of whipped cream. Not to mention the raspberry filling."

"We'll take two," Tom said before I had a chance. I looked at him. He shrugged. "They say chocolate is good for you."

Annie laughed. "Chocolate is *always* good for you. Trust me on this."

When Annie had moved away, Tom shrugged again. "I just thought we could both use something to sweeten our dispositions."

I made a face at him, but the interruption had diffused the tension between us, and my face metamorphosed into a smile. He grinned back at me. We were both relieved, so much so that when Annie returned with two huge slices of the torte, we pushed aside our uneaten soup simultaneously and tucked into our cake.

Annie surveyed our faces with immense satisfaction. "See? What did I tell you? Works every time."

"She's right," I said, licking the frosting

and raspberry preserves off the tines of my fork. "God, this is good."

"Mmph" was all Tom could get out.

I was willing to make the first move. Somehow it was easier over chocolate. "I'm sorry. I didn't mean to ruin our lunch date."

He reached out and took my hand. "You didn't. I could have been more sensitive. I guess I've been hanging around the guys for too long."

My lips quirked; I couldn't stop them. "You were a little . . . heavy-handed."

His right eyebrow followed my lead. "And you were a little . . ."

"Overbearing?" I supplied.

"Too forgiving, I was going to say."

He squeezed my fingers, and my stomach went all squishy and warm. Even warmer and squishier when he lifted my fingertips to his lips and brushed a soft kiss on them.

"So," I said, trying to find balance in a topsy-turvy world, "how is the investigation going, if you don't mind my asking?"

He gave me a look.

"What? I'm just making conversation." I couldn't help it. It was curiosity, mostly. Morbid? Probably. The curse of small-town life? Definitely. "I mean, I'm not asking for specifics."

"It's going fine. We're waiting for results

to come back from the coroner's office right now."

"Mm. Have any witnesses come forward?"

"None whatsoever. Just now we're trying to put together the time line of where Luc Metzger might have gone after leaving Heritage Park. There seems to be some discrepancy between where Metzger was supposed to have gone and where he actually did go."

I couldn't help wondering what that might mean, but I couldn't ask it. Not without him thinking I was dipping my tippy-toes where I had no business interfering. "That makes it a bit difficult."

"Potentially. We'll get it, though."

I nodded, content to leave the investigation to the professionals. Namely, Tom, Special Investigator Extraordinaire.

I glanced at my watch. "I'd better be getting back."

"I'll walk you to your car, just as soon as I take care of the bill."

I waited with him, remembering to ask for a serving of the vegetable barley for Liss at the last minute. Annie handed the cup of soup over, neatly packaged within a paper sack.

"You tell Liss I said hello, okay? And tell her I'll call her about the May Day celebration. Just as soon as I'm done with Easter prep for the Latter-Day Saints."

"Sure, no problem," I told her.

Tom held my hand as we headed for my car, wrapping his fingers tightly around mine. "So, what's on your plate this afternoon?" I asked him.

"I have to respond to a call from the director of Blackhawk Juvenile Hall, for one. He thinks a few of the boys have been involved in a theft and wants me to take a look at the evidence. What about you?"

"Just work. Call me when you get off tonight?"

"I'll try."

The kiss he gave me left me a little wistful, because I didn't know when I'd be seeing him next. And while I understood, it didn't make me any less lonely. Good boyfriend material was hard to find. And apparently even harder to find regularly.

Liss was just finishing up with a customer when I walked in the store. "Here you are, a nice cup of vegetable barley soup, and I think Annie threw in an oatmeal scone," I told her, jiggling the bag enticingly before me.

"Wonderful! I'm famished," Liss said, holding her hand to her stomach. "How was your lunch date?"

I smiled. "It was nice."

"Nice?"

Her eyes searched mine. I scratched the bridge of my nose in embarrassment. "Yes, nice. It was good. Tom has been promoted."

"Oh?"

"His new title is Special Task Force Investigator. He's been put in charge of the investigations of all things unusual that happen around Stony Mill."

"Well, well. He's going to be busy."

Her British sense of irony might have struck me as funny if I hadn't been the unintentional butt of the joke. As it was, I had a hard time keeping the disappointment from settling in my throat.

Self-pity serves no woman, Margaret. The words rang through my brain as surely as though I'd heard them spoken aloud. But then, if there was anything to be learned from growing up in a rural working-class society, that was number one, and it was a lesson my Grandma Cora had drummed into my head whenever the opportunity presented itself. I busied myself straightening the piles of old linens that had been rummaged through during the course of the morning while Liss tucked into her soup.

"Mmm! Excellent, as per usual."

"Annie says hello, and she'll call you about

the May Day celebration. She has a job she needs to finish first." I paused. "Um, what May Day celebration?"

"Oh, my dear, haven't I told you? No, of course I haven't. I mentioned it at the meetings, but with you being busy . . . Well, May Day — Beltane — is very important to my beliefs, and I hold a gathering to celebrate it every year, just as I do the end of the harvest. And of course you're welcome to come. In fact, I had hoped I could ask you to play a part, if you're willing."

"Play a part?"

"A simple part. Important, but simple. I think you'd enjoy it. But of course, if you're not comfortable . . ."

I didn't know what I thought, or what I was or wasn't comfortable with, anymore. "And when will this be?"

"The first of May, of course. It's a Saturday this year, which is perfect for an evening ritual. We have a couple more weeks in which to square away the plans. It's a very special day to me, and if you're at all interested in taking part, it would make it that much more rewarding. Think about it?"

I nodded, not certain what my decision would be in the end. It looked like I might need to do a little quiet research into what comprised a May Day celebration, just to set my mind at ease.

"Have you given any more thought to what we could do for the Metzger family?" I asked. "I know my mother has done things like that before. Maybe the Ladies Auxiliary from St. Catherine's would like to work with us."

"I think that's a fine idea. Why don't you give her a call?"

I should have thought to mention it to my mother this morning. Phone call number two, coming right up.

While Liss began to straighten the counter from the lunch rush, I dialed my mom. The phone rang in my ear, once, twice.

"Hello, Margaret."

Caller ID, of course. "I have a favor to ask, Mom."

"Well, considering that you've finally agreed to bring your new friend to lunch with us, I'm feeling generous. So, what do you need help with?"

Oops, I had forgotten to mention that to Tom. *Mental note: Must call Tom later.* I cleared my throat. "You've heard about the Amish man who was found on the side of the road this weekend?"

"Of course. The whole town is buzzing about it."

No doubt all of her friends were as well.

"Liss and I want to do something for the Metzger family. One of our friends is Amish, and he said that it would be helpful and welcome. I was wondering whether your Ladies Auxiliary might want to join forces with us. Kind of give the effort more bang for the buck. What do you think?"

She was silent a moment. "I think my daughter is growing up at last. Of course the ladies would love to help. This is just the sort of project we should be undertaking." I could see the proverbial lightbulb turning on in her head. "In fact, I think I know just the person who can help us most. Why don't I give her a call and set up a meeting of like minds?"

"Sure, that would be great. I'll tell Liss. Thanks, Mom."

I pressed End. "My mom is certain her friends would like to be involved," I told Liss. "She's going to make some calls and set up a meeting. I told her that would be okay."

"Perfect." Liss beamed. "I've already been mentioning it to our regular customers. I think we'll find a lot of help coming in from all circles. Stony Mill has a very giving nature when the going gets tough."

It did, at that. It was the main thing that the town had going for it. If a family found themselves on hard times, everyone stepped up to give what they could to get them back on their feet. Unless the hard times were due to stupidity or self-destructive tendencies in the hearts of the "victims." In that case, the idjits were on their own.

We mapped out our plans in between customers, and then Liss retired to the office to send e-mail announcements to all of her friends. I remained up front, taking care of business.

Afternoons at Enchantments are typically slower until after four o'clock, so I found myself with plenty of free time on my hands. I ran the dust mop over the antique floorboards, polished an entire display of Irish crystal, and plotted out a new display for our front window. Eventually everything was done that could be done, so I sat down on the tall stool behind the counter and waited, trying not to twiddle my thumbs.

My gaze fell on the fat magical encyclopedia of symbols that Liss had left under the counter. I pulled it out, grunting at the weight of the tome as I hefted it to the countertop. Good grief, it was heavy. Must be a thousand pages in this thing. I flipped through some of the pages. Image after image in photographs and pen-and-ink representations of symbols leapt out at me,

221

categorized by chapter headings that were organized by country and region. Looking at it, seeing the names of magical traditions that crisscrossed the world over, absorbing the relevance of it all . . .

Sweet Mother Mary. So many.

I didn't know whether to be impressed or unnerved. Because where there was a tradition of magic, there was also a tradition of need for it. A need to exert some control in an out-of-control world.

Frowning, I flipped the book over and opened the back cover with its loose flyleaf. The author's photo leapt out at me — I don't know why. I held the cover open with the flat of my hand and gazed down into eyes that seemed so familiar to me, even though I knew I had not seen this man before. They were kind eyes, gentle, alive with a light of deep intelligence and, I felt sure, filled with good humor. But more than anything, I felt a calling as I gazed into them. A tugging from spirit to spirit. A whispering on the winds of the astral tide. *Can you hear me . . . Do you see . . .*

Hear what? See what?

The photo was black and white, no more than a head-and-shoulders shot. I could tell that he was trying to look academic, but he resembled a stuffy old professor about as much as I did. Dark hair, longish, with curls that were swept back and a little mussed, as though he'd just pushed his fingers through it. A broad forehead, the lines across it showing both concern and expression as well as the advancing of years toward middle age. Strong features. And eyes that were both blue and green, a mix of colors as quixotic as the man himself.

The photo was black and white, but I knew I was right about their color.

The eyes are the windows of the soul . . .

Dr. Merrick C. Butler, M.A., Ph.D., I read, *is a lecturer at the University of Edinburgh's Parapsychology Unit, and has been recognized worldwide for his contributions to the emerging field of parapsychology. Years of fieldwork and scholarly endeavors have contributed to the massive undertaking of this encyclopedic work, which is meant to provide a deeper understanding of the symbology used in magical practices of all traditions.*

I traced my thumb over the photo, wondering why I kept seeing a winding stone staircase in my mind's eye.

"What do you think of it?"

I jumped guiltily. Liss was standing on the other side of the counter, watching me. I hadn't heard her come through from the back. "Wh-what?"

She nodded toward the book on the counter. "What do you think of the book?"

"Oh, this?" Relieved that she had not picked up on more than I was willing to surrender for now, I patted the oversized volume. "It's amazing. Quite scholarly. I was dumbfounded by the sheer number of entries. That there are so many different magical traditions across the world. Well, it's amazing," I said, knowing I was repeating myself but unable to think of a better word with my bum sizzling away on the hot seat.

She came forward and pressed the back cover open so that she could see. "Did you find anything of interest?"

Instantly my cheeks flamed, and I was a stumbling fool. "Oh, lots! Loads. So many interesting . . . drawings and symbols. Just . . . amazing."

Liss nodded, a smile tilting up the corners of her mouth. "I'll be sure to pass on your compliments to my nephew."

"Nephew?" My ears perked up. "Your nephew is a professor of metaphysical subjects?"

"Among other things," she acknowledged. "He has a degree in sociology, and a doctorate in metaphysics. I guess you might call his specialty parasociology. The effects of the paranormal on a society at large."

I didn't even know there were such fields of study. I had an idea it might have been considered little better than snake-handling in some intellectual circles, though.

So Dr. Butler was an academic pariah of sorts.

"As you can see, it runs in the family. The interest in all things Otherworldly, I mean. It's a part of our heritage. Although, I must say, he does an admirable job of keeping a scientific view of all of his theories."

A scientific view of the mysteries of the paranormal world. Oil and water, in most people's eyes. Liss's nephew, I decided, was either a man with an iron constitution and diehard self-confidence, or he was too far gone to realize how close to reputation ruination he actually was.

I might have asked Liss more about her nephew, but our chat was interrupted by the yammering arrival of Evie and Tara.

"Liss! Maggie! You'll never guess what happened today!" Evie breezed her way toward the counter, her blond hair shifting in the air currents caused by her passing.

"Yeah. You'll never guess." Tara came at a much more sedate and dignified pace, slinking in like a salamander. As dark as Evie was light, she was her friend's antithesis and foil in every other way as well. And yet the two girls had found enough common ground to form a friendship so tight in the last few months that I could easily envision it lasting well into adulthood. In them, I saw myself and my best friend, Steff, a few years ago. Best friends forever.

"All right, then," Liss said, smiling with a motherly pride at her two youngest protégées. "Tell us."

"Guess," Tara replied with a self-satisfaction that left no doubts as to her preference for having the upper hand. She shrugged out from under her backpack and dropped it to the countertop with a muffled thud.

Obviously not one for guessing games, Evie blurted out, "The police came to the high school!" Her china blue eyes flashed with excitement and concern.

My eyebrows rose, but I waited for one or both of them to continue. Liss was less patient. "What happened?"

Now it was Tara's turn to provide information. "Cops came and took away three boys. Snagged 'em right out of Mr. Grant's Industrial Tech class, from what I heard."

"Industrial Tech?" Liss echoed, looking to me for clarification.

"Shop class," I explained quickly. "So,

what's the deal? What did the boys do?"

"No one knows for sure," Evie explained breathlessly.

"But I heard it had something to do with that Amish guy's murder," Tara inserted quickly, not to be trumped.

From the depths of my memory I dredged for what Tom had told me about the previous attacks on Amish men. Hadn't he said that the only other victim from our county had said there were multiple attackers?

High school boys responsible for the death of Luc Metzger? Could it be?

"Who were they?" I asked.

"Tony Perez, Jeremy Connor, and Joel Kelly, I heard," Tara provided.

"Blackhawk boys," Evie added with a meaningful lift of her brows.

Liss looked at me again. "Blackhawk Juvenile Hall," I translated. "It's where they send minors who have been in trouble with the law. Repeat offenders, mostly."

And hadn't Tom said that he was heading out to Blackhawk after lunch? It couldn't be coincidence. Frankly, I didn't believe in coincidence anymore.

But what could the connection be? Tom had mentioned that the director had found evidence relating to a possible burglary. Perhaps Tom hadn't realized the full import of the evidence at the time, because I was pretty certain that if he had, he would never have mentioned it to me. And then there was the small matter of the sign on the tree.

"Do either of you know if these boys have a background in magic? Even if it was only playing around with it?" I asked them.

Evie looked puzzled. Tara shrugged.

Liss met my gaze. "You're thinking about the symbol we found?"

I nodded. "It has to be tied to Luc's murder, doesn't it? There's no other reason for it to be there that I can see. I mean, it's not exactly in a well-traveled area, is it?"

"What symbol?" Tara pressed.

I looked at Liss, silently questioning.

"Stop doing that!" Tara waved her hands at us as though warding off a cloud of bees. "Geez, just say what you mean. We're not children, you know."

Liss shrugged as though to say *It can't hurt.*

I pulled the encyclopedia out and opened to the page that Liss had left off on, where my chicken-scratched drawing was serving as bookmark. Silently, I held the scrap of paper out to them. Evie looked but didn't touch it, her frown evidence enough that our theory about the symbol was right on the money — Evie had a psychic radar that was stronger than my wildest dreams. Tara, on the other hand, demonstrated her usual full-speed-ahead lack of restraint — she snatched the paper out of my hand and began to examine it. It wasn't that Tara didn't have gifts of her own, but unfortunately psychic precaution didn't seem to be one of them.

"Tom thinks — well, someone on the force does, anyway — that the symbol is a sign of satanic worship."

Tara made a face. "It figures. Cops are always looking for the worst in people."

"Tara!"

She held up her hands, her expression a well-honed smirk. "Hey! I call 'em as I see 'em. But this isn't satanic. It's hoodoo."

"It's what?"

"You know. Hoodoo."

Something was getting lost in translation. "You mean voodoo?"

Tara rolled her eyes with a green flash of impatience and impertinence combined. "No. Hoodoo. Like, you know, folk magick."

I stared at her, open-mouthed with surprise. "How do you know that?"

She shrugged her slender shoulders. "You have your secrets. I have mine."

I asked Liss, "Will that information help us find the symbol in your nephew's book?"

"Well, it can't hurt," Liss replied. "But it may in fact do us little good unless we can discover who made the sign on the tree. The trouble is, folk magick is so very customized. Symbolism is often specific to a region, a family, even one person, depending on what is meaningful to them."

So we would be barking up a very large and convoluted tree. But what choice did we have? Someone, somewhere in the area, had a history of magick.

My cell phone rang again, with my mother's number showing on my Caller ID. I excused myself and turned away. "Hi, Mom."

"I have the Metzger relief meeting all arranged, dear. Can you get away around six thirty? It would be nice to get this thing going."

I glanced at my watch. Three forty-five. "Sure, that should be okay, I guess. Tonight is one of my early nights."

"Ah, good. That worked out nicely, then. You can meet me here and we can ride together."

As soon as I hung up, I turned back to Liss. "My mom has arranged a meeting to get things started with donations for the Metzger family. Can you get away at six thirty tonight?"

Liss looked stricken. "Oh, my dear, I'm afraid I can't. I have an appointment that I just can't get out of."

"We could reschedule."

"No, that's fine. Better to get things started. You can always ring me on my cell if you need my input on anything specific."

I would have loved her help, but I had no doubt that my mother would have more than enough input for all of us.

CHAPTER 11

Mom was waiting for me when I pulled up in front of Ye Olde Homestead. An old-style farmhouse adrift in a sea of nondescript suburban modernity, it was as warm and comfortable as a slouchy knit sweater. I wouldn't have minded the chance to pop in and say a quick hello to my dad and Grandpa Gordon, but my mom immediately jumped in the car and nodded toward the road. Between that, her fussy wool jacket-and-skirt combo that might have been in style in the early Eighties, and her purposeful expression, it was pretty obvious she wasn't in the mood for delays.

"What's wrong with your heater?" she asked as she fiddled with the limited number of knobs, levers, and buttons on Christine's dash.

"Oh, you know. Old vehicles. Sometimes they get a little testy."

Her mouth made a little moue of distaste.

"You might think about getting yourself a more reliable vehicle, you know. Reliability, that's the ticket. A young woman needs dependable transportation. You can't afford to be breaking down on the side of the road in this day and age. There's just too much . . . too much . . . Well, a young woman can't be too careful."

That was as close as she would come to saying that recent events had rocked her world. And my mom wasn't exactly a rockin' 'n' rollin' kind of girl. More like stallin' 'n' stoppin'.

"I *am* careful, Mom," I said as I steered Christine down the road, full speed ahead. "And besides, I have a cell phone now, in case I do break down on the side of the road. It's the next best thing to a spanking new ride."

"Hmm," she mumbled, unconvinced.

"Where are we going?" I asked, hoping to distract her.

"We're meeting at Louisa Murray's house over in the Woodhaven subdivision on Alden Road. Just a small crew this evening on such short notice, but that will do for planning purposes, I should think. You remember Louisa, she was your Sunday school teacher when you were little."

I didn't, not really, but because it was

easier, I said, "Um, yes. Sunday school. Right."

"Louisa was very keen to head this up when I talked with her," Mom said conversationally. "It was a brain wave on my part to call her, you know. She was the one who fell in love with that armoire that Luc Metzger and your Amish friend made. I knew she'd want to help, and of course she has so much experience, I was inclined to let her organize the whole thing. All the better for poor Mrs. Metzger, and that's what's important, after all. Besides, it gives Louisa a sense of purpose. After her husband died a couple years back, she foundered a bit, as though she didn't quite know what to do with her time. She needed something to draw that eagle eye focus of hers, and the Ladies Auxiliary has helped."

I listened to her chatter on about her friend, the other ladies in her group, and the various projects they'd tackled, but only with half an ear. As I zigzagged across town, Mom eventually fell silent. It might have been the car that blazed through the stop sign on Wabash, a near miss, or maybe it was just my driving in general that made her nervous. Whatever the cause, conversation ceased but for the occasional muffled groan and wild grab for the door handle whenever I rounded a corner a little too fast for her liking. Funny how she had a way of still making me feel all of sixteen and newly licensed, with all of the driving uncertainty that entailed.

The Woodhaven subdivision rested on the very northwest edge of town. Not too terribly long ago, this had been a middle-class neighborhood, fashionably hugged by old and sprawling Alden Woods. In recent years it had begun to show its age, but while peeling paint and sagging fences were often the name of the game, the meticulously maintained lawns had the mark of undivided attention. I had a feeling many of the homeowners were aging as well.

"There it is. Number five-oh-two," Mom said. "The last house on the left."

Compared to some of the neighboring properties, Louisa Murray's home was almost kingly. Not new enough to be considered a hot property, but kept up sufficiently to keep it from being written off as undesirable, the house was a large cottage style, complete with deep front porch and porch swing, and fronted by a pretty white picket fence that looked fairly solid. Set back from the house, an old carriage barn had never been replaced by a more modern garage. Only the advancing sprawl of the woods detracted from the simple beauty of the property — surrounded on the right and from behind, the place had a strangely hemmed-in feel from the overhanging trees and encroaching underbrush, as though the woods were trying to reclaim some of the space that the subdivision had carved out of them.

The driveway was blocked by a nondescript sedan, so I made a neat three-point turn and pulled up to the curb in front of the house. As I did so, a woman rounded the corner of the house from the back yard. Louisa Murray, I would assume. Mom was right, I did sort of remember her from Sunday lessons of half a lifetime ago. She wore, incongruously enough, a trim calf-length skirt, a frilly blouse that tied at the neck, and a sturdy canvas apron that fronted her from sternum to knee. In one hand she carried a steaming bucket; in the other, a shovel. Following on her heels like a pair of nipping puppies were two just as fussily garbed ladies. The first I recognized as an Enchantments regular, and I was also pretty sure I remembered both of them from the farmers market the other day: Ladies Pink and Periwinkle. What a surprise that my mother knew all of them.

Not.

We got out of the car and waved a greeting as the women registered our arrival.

"I'll be with you in just a minute or three," Louisa called to us with a tight smile of welcome.

Perhaps because she dressed a lot like my mother, my first impression was that of an older woman. But beneath the Church Lady threads it was obvious she had a good figure still, and when she turned to face us, I could see that Mom had a good ten years on her.

"Sorry to have to keep you girls waiting," she apologized as we approached, "but I just found this here. As you can see, it's not the kind of mess you can put off cleaning until later."

My eyebrows rose as we drew nearer. The mess that Louisa referred to turned out to be a sizable pile of manure on her front doorstep. It was also swiped across the front door in big, malignant smears.

"Well, good heavens! What in the world is this town coming to?" my mom exclaimed, her gaze sweeping the scene as she took it all in.

"We just found it this way," Pink Lady said, breathless and quivering. Her eyes were bright with excitement. "Frannie and Louisa and me, we just got here after the weekly soup kitchen planning meeting up at the church."

Frannie nodded vigorously. "We were only gone the afternoon, but I suppose that's long enough if someone's got mischief on their mind. You need to get yourself one of those motion detector cameras, Louisa. Get yourself set right up and catch those little rascals red-handed."

My mom arrowed in on that. "You know who did this?"

Louisa plunked the bucket down, sloshing steaming water over the edge and wetting her rubber Wellington boots. "I have my suspicions, but of course I don't like to say anything without proof."

"Well, it doesn't bother me to say," Pink Lady jumped in. "Of course it was those boys. The same ones who have been giving you so much trouble for calling the police on 'em. Don't you think, Frannie?"

"I'd bet my bottom dollar on it."

"The little bastards —"

"Grace!" Frannie said on an intake of breath.

"Sorry, *brats* — have been wreaking havoc on Louisa and others out this way for weeks, and the police just let them run roughshod over the entire neighborhood."

Defensive words leapt to the tip of my tongue, but I bit them back. It wouldn't do

Tom any good for me to protect his civic honor. My mom took one look at my face and stepped in.

"You remember my daughter Maggie, don't you, Louisa?"

I would have shaken Mrs. Murray's hand, but she was busy drawing on blue latex gloves and barely noticed me. Gloves in place, she took the spade in hand and began to wield it like a pro. My nose twitched as the tip of the blade disturbed the pile of manure. Its drying surface broken, it let loose an odor that was unmistakable.

"Here, now," my mom said, placing a staying hand on Louisa's arm. "Why don't you let us help you with this? The five of us will have this taken care of in a jiffy."

I couldn't help wondering what Grace and Frannie thought of being included in the venture, but it was far too late for any of us now. My mother had already removed her wool jacket and was rolling up the sleeves on her silky blouse, despite the cooling evening temps.

"I couldn't —" Louisa protested.

"Piffle. You just hand that spade over to Maggie, she's better dressed for that sort of thing. Do you have any other scrub brushes?"

I knew it was the nice thing to do — it

wouldn't be neighborly to let one of my mother's friends, and a widow to boot, suffer through the cleanup from this mean-spirited attack on her property while we stood by and watched. But geez, was it too much to ask to be consulted before Mom went about offering my services for things? And exactly what was wrong with the way I was dressed, anyway?

I know, I know. I grabbed the shovel anyway. "Um, where would you like this?"

Louisa turned and fluttered her hand toward the flower border that rimmed the picket fence along the front walk. "In the roses is fine."

I took a hearty scoopful, swallowing the gorge that rose as the blade sank into the stinking mess. *Eeeeeh.* I lifted the shovel with both hands and turned in the direction she'd indicated, took a few steps down the walk, and paused. "Roses?" All I saw was mounded hillocks with oddly shaped and gnarly lumps emerging at semiregular intervals.

Her back to me, Louisa paused. She took a deep breath, held it a moment, then let it out in a rush. Toward the end, the sigh broke into a thousand pieces. I watched in horror as her shoulders began to quiver.

Oh, my God, was she crying?

240

Frannie and Grace sent me withering stares as they and my mother put down their brushes and sponges and hovered over their weeping friend. I tightened my grip on the smooth wooden handle, feeling ineffectual as my mother began to pat her friend on the back. "There, now," she crooned. "It's all right. The police will find out who did this. Maggie's boyfriend is on the police department" — I cringed at that — "and she'll be sure to put a bug in his ear about this. Just don't you worry anymore."

But Louisa seemed more angry than sad or worried. Or was it just resignation? She jerked away from my mother's hands, and thrust her scrub brush into the bucket of soapy water, applying it fiercely to her door. "It doesn't matter anymore, does it? You can't even tell the damned roses were there. Years I spent, tending them. Slaving over them. Years. And now they're gone, in the blink of an eye. Not even worth a good layer of crap that some vicious little . . ."

She clamped her lips to stop the diatribe and swished the brush in the bucket again. Frannie and Grace exchanged a look.

Unexpectedly, Louisa dropped everything and rose to her feet, regaining at once the poise and quiet demeanor that had slipped momentarily. "On second thought, let's just leave this. It's not going anywhere, and I wouldn't be much of a hostess not to recognize that we could all use a cup of coffee."

She wouldn't take no for an answer, and shooed my mom and the older ladies inside as though guiding hens toward their roosts for the night, arms outspread, manner purposeful. I, on the other hand, still had a loaded shovel in my hands, and it was getting heavy. Couldn't exactly drop it. I turned and walked the pungent scoopful down the path to where the roses used to reside. They really were pitiful, these ravaged root-balls. Whoever had cut them down had done a wickedly effective job. The cuts (hacks?) had bitten ruthlessly into the root-balls. I let the stuff slide off the end of the spade into the compost, covering the one with the most obvious damage, and then followed everyone into the house.

My mom was waiting for me at the door. "Thank you, Maggie," she said in an undertone. "Louisa has been having a hard time of things lately, as you saw."

I felt instantly guilty. "I live to serve," I said lightly, just in case she looked close enough to notice.

"The rest of the girls are in the living

room," she said as she took my jacket from me.

"I was just looking at what's left of her roses, Mom. Not much, unfortunately. Who could have done that?"

"I don't know. Maybe those boys she was talking about. Anyone who knows Louisa at all knows how much those roses meant to her. She was always out there, spraying, deadheading, tending. Even talking to them. She used to tell me that was her secret, talking to them. It's a shame. A crying shame."

We made our way into the living room, just in time to catch the tail end of a similar discussion.

"You should report it."

"No. No more reporting," Louisa said, leaning forward in her chair to fuss with a coffee tray on the table before her. "I'm done with that. What has being a good neighbor and concerned citizen gotten me except a lot of grief? No, I've made my last police report. The police can do nothing to help me."

Grace made a *harrumph* of displeasure. "Well, in my opinion, you need a man, Louisa Murray. How long has it been now since Frank died? Two years? Time for you to move on and get yourself hitched to that wagon again."

Mom and I slipped into the room, taking seats on a loveseat as unobtrusively as possible. This was one discussion neither of us would dare take part in. More power to Grace.

"Men aren't immune to violence, you know," Louisa said, unperturbed by Grace's forward remark. She picked up the coffee pot and began to pour the steaming liquid into the cups before continuing. "Just think of the reason we're here today. Luc Metzger was a man in his prime, I think we'll all agree, and someone found a way to dispatch him." She set the cups in front of each of us.

"Shocking," Frannie agreed. "And unnerving, if a girl thinks about it too much." She gave an overly dramatic shiver.

"Imagine, winning that auction on the day of that poor man's precipitous death. Now that's what I call unnerving. Doesn't it make you feel just a little off, having that cabinet in your house, Louisa?" Grace asked. "Makes me go all goose pimply, just thinking about it."

The armoire . . . I had almost forgotten. I glanced around surreptitiously, wondering where it was. A bedroom, perhaps. I wouldn't mind taking another look at it.

Louisa didn't seem to take offense. "Just

bad luck, I guess. If you believe in that sort of thing. Now ladies, why don't we get started?"

"Oh, yes, of course."

"Why don't you lead us through, Louisa?" my mom suggested.

Louisa took a spiral-bound notebook from the table and opened it. She took a deep breath. But before she could say anything, Grace cut in again. "That Luc Metzger, though. *Hooeee.* Now *that* was a looker. That man could have trimmed my bushes any time."

Frannie looked confused. "I don't think he did gardening, Grace."

Grace rolled her eyes. "Frannie, dear, has it really been that long for you?"

"For what?"

"For sex, dear heart. You know. A tasty tumble on the kitchen table. A hearty roll in the haymow. Rocking the old porch swing. Good gracious, dear, have you forgotten already?"

"For your information, Grace Mansfield, my memory serves me perfectly well. You needn't act so high and mighty about it. I've done my share of rolling in the haymow, if you must know. I just choose to be a lady and not discuss it, that's all," she said with a haughty sniff.

"Good. Then you'll agree with me that Luc Metzger was one hot bit of honey who looked like sugar wouldn't melt on his tongue, but a woman certainly would."

"I will not."

"You didn't think so?"

"I didn't say that."

Louisa heaved a long-suffering sigh. "Ladies, please. Must we discuss that man in this way?"

"What way?"

"It isn't right to discuss him like a piece of meat."

"Well, lah-dee-dah. Aren't we the pious one today?"

A flush crept up Louisa's neck. "Isn't it enough that he's dead? It isn't right to speculate on his . . . his . . ."

"Virility?" Frannie supplied helpfully.

Through gritted teeth, Louisa said, "Precisely."

"Oh, pooh. You're no fun." Grace's mouth, carefully drawn in crimson, puckered in disapproval.

Louisa leapt to her feet and with a jerky movement removed the tray from the coffee table. "We'll be needing more refreshments, I think," she said stiffly before turning on her heel and heading toward the kitchen.

My mom leaned back in the loveseat with

a sigh. "Well, now you two have done it. She's wound up like a cuckoo clock. And is it any wonder, given what she came home to this afternoon?"

Grace's mouth twisted up like a corkscrew. "You haven't seen the half of it. Wait 'til you see the backyard."

Mom and I looked up in surprise. "What's wrong with the back —"

Before we could finish, Louisa came sailing back into the room like an avenging angel, seized her notebook, and took her seat before fixing us with a baleful stare. "If you all are done gossiping, perhaps we could get back to the business at hand, hmm?"

The meeting of minds proved short and sweet. Where I had no experience to back up my wishes to be helpful to Mrs. Metzger and her family, Louisa, Mom, Frannie, and Grace had boatloads, and I deferred to them on every point. Together they made up for my lack a dozen times over, with ideas and plans flying back and forth while I took notes. My only real contribution was to suggest that we use Enchantments as a drop point for donations in order to ease the burden on St. Catherine's. Mom and Louisa took care of the rest, bless their civic-minded hearts.

Finally, Louisa closed her notebook.

"How's the new hobby going, Louisa?" my mom asked.

"The scrapbooking? It passes the time. Amazing how many pictures one accumulates throughout one's lifetime, isn't it? A habit learned from my mother, I suppose, snapping pictures of everything and everyone. And now, sorting through them, cataloguing them, finding just the right memories . . . it's like recording the story of one's life for posterity, isn't it? A little daunting, when you think about it that way. How do you want people to remember you when you're gone? Do you show everything? Or do you pick and choose, to remember your life in the most positive way possible?"

"Well, I, for one, would prefer they remember me young and beautiful," Grace declared. "They can do wonders with computers these days. They can fix up wrinkles, nip in waists, perk up the boobs, the whole works."

"Isn't that a bit like lying?" Frannie asked owlishly.

"Oh, pshaw. What's a little lie among family and friends? And besides, I'll be gone then. It'll be too late to matter to anyone then."

"You know, I've been thinking about taking up scrapbooking," my mom mused aloud. "But I'm afraid I don't even know where to start."

Louisa rose to her feet. "Come into my project room. I have a couple of books I'd be happy to lend you that might give you a few ideas."

We all obediently filed along behind her to a room just off the short hall. A long table, set up along the wall to the right, was loaded with an extraordinary number of frilly pink photo boxes, numerous organizer trays filled with papers of all colors, boxes of ribbons, cups of pens and scissors and punches. A smaller table rested beneath the windows that overlooked the back yard. On it rested a digital camera at the ready, a laptop, and a photo printer. And to the left — voilà — the armoire I had been looking for. Louisa had covered it with a white sheet, a corner of which had fallen away, revealing the carvings on one door frame.

Louisa led the way to the table, where her most recent pages were spread out. While Mom and the girls were oohing and aahing over the pictures of roses Louisa had taken last summer, lovingly rendered in Louisa's scrapbooking vision, I backed away slowly to take another look at the armoire. It really was beautifully done, the carving heavy but not overbearingly masculine. In fact, the motifs — woven braids, trailing vines, stunning sunbursts — were quite graceful when taken one by one.

"That's the cabinet, isn't it, Louisa? The one from the market."

I didn't have to turn around to know that they'd all gathered behind me.

"Yes, that's it."

I smiled at her. "You were lucky to get it — my boss, Felicity Dow, was especially keen to have it at the store."

"Ugghh." Grace gave an exaggerated and noisy shudder. "Gives me the willies just looking at it now. I don't know how you can have it in your home, Louisa. You know what they say about people who die unexpectedly — their restless spirits are doomed to walk the earth, and they attach themselves to things that were important to them."

You could have heard a pin drop as the five of us stared at the massive piece of furniture.

"Don't be so dramatic, Grace," my mom said in a voice like the crack of a whip. "You know there's no such thing."

I didn't want to be the one to burst my mom's bubble, so I kept my mouth shut, even though I knew differently.

"Well, if there was such a thing," Louisa

said mildly as she swept us from the room, "the man wouldn't be here. You can be sure of that."

I was the last to follow her through the door. As I reached for the light switch, I heard the low click of a latch. From the corner of my eye, in that second between the flip of the switch and the anticipated darkness, I saw the door to the armoire drift open. I hightailed it out of the room, but not before I glimpsed more pink photo boxes ensconced within the armoire.

Was the spirit of Luc Metzger attached to the armoire? I couldn't help wondering as I helped Louisa carry the cups and tray to the kitchen sink while the others fetched their coats. I didn't see why or how. And then I remembered the way the power had drained at the murder site as I had prepared to leave. That had been spirit, too. Luc's spirit? I had worried so at the time. Maybe he wasn't attached to the armoire. Maybe he was making himself known to anyone who could "see." And since I had been there that night . . .

Was he making himself known to me in particular?

It was not a thought that sat well with me. I'd never wanted to be a guru to the tenants of the Otherworld. And really, if he knew how little control I had over my abilities, Luc would definitely have chosen another ground control.

As I reentered the living room, my mother's gaze followed me, a quiet watchfulness on her face. Then, frowning, she let her gaze drift over my shoulder, toward the hall.

In the blink of an eye she resumed her usual staid demeanor. "Good-bye, Louisa, dear," she said, taking her friend gently by the shoulder and leaning in for the air kiss. "You take care of yourself, and you call if you hear anything that makes you nervous. I can always send Glen out to check up on you at the very least, if need be."

Louisa cupped Mom's elbows and air kissed her back. "Thank you, Pat. You're very kind."

Grace and Fannie said their good-byes, too, before Louisa led us out through the kitchen to the back door, instead of the front. "I apologize in advance for the state of the yard," she said, "but I did manage to get the walk and porch swept off. Don't mind the —"

Eggs. A single bulb shone pitifully from the old fixture beside the door, not enough to cut through the gloom of the backyard but more than enough for us to see the remains of a large number of eggs splashed, dashed, and smashed against the back of the house.

"Jesus, Mary, and Joseph," my mom said, crossing herself.

"Didn't I tell you so?" Grace said with just a touch of one-upsmanship.

Mom turned to Louisa. "Would you like me to send someone out to help with this? Really, it would be no trouble."

I hoped she didn't mean me. There was something I didn't like about Louisa's backyard. Something . . . predatory. Maybe it would be different if I saw it during daylight hours, but now, in the full swing of darkness, the trees hanging over us seemed like the clutch of a great black beast. The wind rustled through the woods as though whispering secrets. Grace and Frannie didn't seem to notice. They turned to wave as they hustled down to the nondescript sedan and were gone before Mom had finished her offer of help.

"No, really. I'll be fine. It will clean up fast." Louisa gave a small, tight smile. "I've done it before.

The boys that she was afraid of could be out there, right now. Watching us.

What was the world coming to when Sunday school teachers and charity mavens were attacked, and when peace-loving

Amish were struck down in their prime? Was anyone safe anymore?

I could hear my mom's heartbeat in my ears, and felt the fear radiating from her, so I knew she was not immune. She grabbed my arm as we felt our way down the steps. I closed her hand within my own to reassure her, and together we made our way step by step toward the corner of the house and the driveway, beyond the protective circle of the weak porch light.

Off to my left I heard a sharp crack, followed by a shuffling sound that left me cold. I whipped my head toward the noise, my eyes huge as I willed myself the ability to see through the night. A huge, pale shape loomed in the corner of the yard. Vaguely I remembered the old, ramshackle carriage barn huddled there against the trees that seemed to want to swallow it whole. Was there something out there? Hiding behind, or even within, the barn? Or were the sounds coming from the woods?

My mom's fingers clenched my own. Her face glowed as pale as the moon in the darkness next to mine. "What was that?" she whispered. Scarcely a breath.

"I can't see a thing," I whispered back. "Probably just a raccoon or a possum or something."

A sad attempt at reassurance, granted, but when your mom has you in a death grip, what else are you gonna do?

I fished in my coat pocket for my car keys. Attached to the key ring was a handy-dandy little LED flashlight. I pressed my thumb against the concave plastic casing and shone the light toward the direction the sound had come from.

Eyes.

CHAPTER 12

"Holy Christ!" I exclaimed, dropping my keys, flashlight, and everything else to the ground.

My mom sucked her breath in through her teeth. "Margaret!"

My swearing had momentarily shocked her out of her fear, but under the circumstances it was the least of my worries. Apparently she'd not seen what I'd seen. On the other hand, she hadn't stopped squeezing my hand to a pulp, so maybe she'd just managed to retain her motherly wits about her. Keeping my eyes locked on the place where I had seen the glow of phantom eyes, I swallowed my fear and stooped down slowly. I patted the ground around me. Eggshells. Sticky eggshells. *Ick.* Where the heck were my keys? *There.* I snagged them and stood up.

Before I could move, something rushed past my ankles.

I let out an involuntary yip. Mom's grip tightened to near cosmic force.

"Light, light, light!" she yelped, hopping from one foot to the other as though someone had lit matchsticks between her toes.

In any other circumstances, this might have been funny. As it was, I was having a hard time restraining myself from doing much the same thing.

Whoosh.

We were rushed again, and we both screamed. Inside the house, lights went on where before there had been none, making stark rectangles of light on the ground to our left and right. Mom and I froze, clutching each other as we waited for whatever was terrorizing us to make itself known.

There was power in knowing. Power we needed.

A big and furry something made a tight circle around us. I heard it panting, but we were huddled together between golden rectangles, and it was keeping to the darkness. Was it animal or something more mysterious?

Something inside me snapped. I let go of my mother and stood up straight, putting my hands on my hips.

"All right. Whatever you are, you'd better just stop it. Right! Now!"

In the next instant, it launched itself straight at me. It was too late for regret — I saw the dark shape beating a path across the yard, heard the pounding of padded feet against the cold earth. *Ummmm* . . . The thing reared up on its hind legs and opened its white-toothed maw in my general direction. My heart leapt to my throat and I forgot how to breathe. It pawed at the air with its front feet, once, twice. And then it leaned/aimed/fell forward toward me, the snarling, gaping mouth opened, and . . .

It licked my chin.

Floodlights snapped on from the heights of the carriage barn, and suddenly the backyard was ablaze with enough light to chase the shadows away. I had a quick vision of what had terrorized me so completely: a dog, pale in color like a yellow lab, but with a narrower, shepherdlike muzzle that was a dark, chocolatey brown. Behind me the door opened suddenly, ferociously, and Louisa rushed out with a broom in hand. She swung it about toward the dog, wielding it like a warrior might swing a mace. "Scat, you mangy, ugly cur! Get out of here! Scat! Scat!"

The dog winced and skittered away, galloping about on thin gazelle legs to keep just beyond the long reach of the menacing broom.

"Get out of here! Go on! You don't belong here! Go on before I go get something that'll knock you clear to the moon!"

Its black button eyes glittering, it sat down on its haunches and cocked its head to the right, as though bewildered by her outburst. Fortified by her weapon, Louisa advanced. The dog waited until she was nearly upon it before it dashed out of the way of her swing. It danced there, back and forth, long tail wagging, as it awaited her next move.

It thought she was playing.

"Uh, Mrs. Murray —"

"Just leave" — *swing* — "me" — *whoosh* — "alone!"

She almost caught the dog in the hind-quarters on the last attempt. It danced around some more before shooting off toward the looming shape of the barn. Back and forth it zigzagged, finally circling wide and coming around to hide behind my legs. My mom hotfooted it back on the porch steps, looking on with astonishment.

Louisa turned on me, her eyes blazing. "You just step on out of the way, Maggie, and I'll take care of that flea-ridden menace."

The dog whined and nudged my fingertips, huddling the bulk of its body against the backs of my legs. That's what did it. This poor little guy didn't need to be gotten rid of. It needed shelter. It needed food. It needed a soft rub around its floppy ears. I bent down and reached behind myself to do just that. The dog nudged me again, and I felt something hard bump against my hand.

"What's this?" I shifted slightly to allow some of the dim light to fall on the dog's head. In its mouth was a tool of some sort. Using my fingers I prised it away from the dog, who instantly went into a crouch, hind end up and wagging, as though it thought I wanted to play. I looked at what I'd taken from it. "It's a hammer. Yours?" I held it out to Louisa.

Louisa frowned down at it and shook her head. "I don't have many. That must belong to the roofers I had put on my new barn roof last year."

"Yours now." In exchange for the hammer, I reached for her broom. "Here, why don't you give me that? I'll take care of the little guy for you."

She considered only a moment before releasing the broom to me. The dog skittered sideways. Exit, stage right. You take the high road, and I'll take the low road, and I'll get out of the way of the crazy lady with the broom afore ye.

As soon as the door closed behind Louisa, I turned to my mother. "Mom, we've got to get this guy out of here before she accidentally hurts him."

My mother opened her mouth. "But —"

"He doesn't mean any harm, Mom. He thinks she's playing with him. Look at him. Flea-bitten he may be, but he's not going to hurt anyone unless he knocks you over trying to get out of the way of the broom."

As if to prove my point, the dog approached my mom, then sat down at her feet, head cocked as he gazed up at her with his mouth open in a half pant, half smile.

Mom looked down at the dog, looked up at me, looked down at the dog again, then rolled her gaze heavenward. "Oh, all right," she said finally in exasperation. "What do you want me to do?"

"Get the car door open. We'll have to entice him inside."

To my mom's credit, once she made her mind up, she didn't mess around. She scurried around the house. The dog proved smarter than I thought — he trotted along behind her, nibbling and licking at her swinging fingertips as if to say, *Hey, wait for me!*

I stepped up to the screen door. Through

the open inner door I could hear shuffling sounds coming from within. "Uh, Mrs. Murray? Mrs. Murray, the dog's gone — nothing to be afraid of now. My mom and I are going to go, okay? If you need anything, just let us know."

The shuffling, searching sounds ceased. Mrs. Murray came to the screen door, frowning as she gazed out into the night. "It's gone?"

"Yes, ma'am."

"I have a feeling it'll be back. It always comes back."

I bit my tongue. Obviously she had been bothered by the dog's presence for a while. I didn't know why she didn't just call for someone to come out to pick it up. "Yes, ma'am. Well, good night, and thanks again for all of your help."

I hurried toward the curb, where Christine awaited my return with my mother and the dog safely ensconced within. I got in quickly and shut the door behind me. The dog had settled down on the tiny back seat, taking up much of the space. I gave it a little reassuring pat and a ruffle of the ears, wondering what it thought of the situation it found itself in. Did it see me as its protector? Savior? Or just a dry bunk away from the crazy lady with the broom, until the next bunk came along?

"I feel bad for her, you know."

I blinked at my mom, still in doggie mode. "Louisa, you mean?"

My mom had been staring at the house, her expression pensive. "Life seems to have abandoned her, doesn't it? Even this house seems to be on permanent hold, somehow. Of course she's always been cool as a cucumber, ready for any situation. She was a good match for her husband in that respect. Despite the fact that her mother didn't want her to marry him. I guess it goes to show that mothers don't always know best."

Mom didn't believe that for a minute, and I knew it. It didn't matter; she still amazed me with the amount of information she carried in her head about people within her sphere. Miss Marple and her afternoon teas had nothing on my mom.

Sucked into my mother's ruminations, I glanced at the house. "Why didn't her mom want her to marry her husband?"

"He was nearly fifteen years her senior. Her mother didn't approve. Wanted her to wait and find someone her own age. And, well, John was always such a cold fish. But Louisa knew he'd take care of her, and he had standing with the church, and that's what she wanted back then. To have a standing that would rival her mother's." Mom shook her head, remembering. "I wonder. If given a second chance, would she do it all over again, knowing that he'd leave her behind at such a young age?"

"Maybe she'll find someone else, then," I suggested, turning the key in the ignition. "Start a new life with someone. It's happened before."

My mom shook her head. "I don't see it. She was completely devoted to John."

"I would suggest that she get a dog, but under the circumstances . . ."

Right on cue a great fuzzy head inserted itself between us. It gave me a wet snoot in my ear, then turned to do the same to my mom, knocking her glasses askew. I laughed; I couldn't help it.

"I think I'd better take you home," I told her, "while I figure out what to do with Junior, here."

"Junior Here" didn't have a collar, so I stopped at the hardware store and had my mom wait with the dog while I ran inside for a collar and leash combo. While I was at it, I grabbed a squeaky bone. The lot of it would have been cheaper at Wal-Mart, but the parking lot at the discount giant was always a waking nightmare, and I wasn't in the mood for risking my life.

"Thank the Lord," Mom said when I got in again. The dog was sitting on her lap, all fifty-plus pounds of it, steaming up the windows. I took the chew toy out and handed it to my mom. Despite her grumpy words, she had her arm around the dog's chest and was stroking its velvety ears, so I knew she wasn't too put out. Still, I made sure no further stops were on the menu before I got her home.

"What will you do with it?" she asked me as I pulled into the drive.

I shrugged. "I guess I'll talk to Tom to see what the options are."

"I don't suppose there are many. The county doesn't have an animal shelter, you know. I suppose the next county over might be a possibility."

"Okay. Thanks for your help today, Mom. Say hi to Dad and Grandpa for me."

She reached out and patted me on the cheek in one of her rare displays of affection. "Take care of yourself, Margaret. Don't forget about Sunday."

Oh. Sunday. I had forgotten to mention that to Tom, hadn't I?

Next on the agenda? The Stony Mill Police Department. Maybe Tom hadn't left yet. Considering his new role within the department, I was willing to bet he was behind a desk somewhere, taking care of business. His little Subaru pickup truck was parked in the lot behind the station, confirming my theory.

"Ready, Junior?" He just looked at me, his tongue hanging out. "Come here and let me get this collar on you."

My size estimations were a little off, but I made it work. And Junior didn't seem to care. He cocked his head this way and that while I fastened the collar, then hooked the leash to the loop. He seemed pretty taken with the fuzzy bone, because he insisted on carrying it with him while we made our way inside.

I nodded toward the door. "Come on, then."

Little blonde Jeannette was behind the safety glass in Dispatch this evening. She smiled and waved before reaching out and unlocking the sliding window.

"Hey, Jeannette. Is Tom still here?"

"You betcha. I'll just get him."

"Thanks."

Junior decided to investigate the ficus tree in the corner while we waited. I hated to tell him it was fake; far be it from me to burst his little doggie bubble.

The door to the back buzzed as it unlocked, and Tom appeared behind it. "Hey!" He smiled. "I wasn't expecting to see you here."

Behind the window, Jeannette waved at me with a wink and said, "I'll be right back. Gonna go get some coffee."

Grateful for her discretion, I turned back to Tom. "I wasn't expecting to be here." By way of explanation, I held up the leash.

Tom's eyebrows lifted. "Well, well. Who do we have here?"

Briefly I explained how I had come into possession of Junior. "I couldn't leave him there. Mrs. Murray was so nervy about everything that's been going on out there, she might have ended up hurting him." I looked down at the big furry face and the trusting eyes, and my heart tugged. Especially when he wagged his tail in a big, happy, sweeping motion and quirked his eyebrows at me, then cocked his head.

"Her."

I looked up at him, lost. "What?"

"Might have ended up hurting her."

"Junior's a her?"

"Let me guess. I take it you didn't notice the lack of plumbing. You see, there's one key difference between the male and the female of any species, Maggie." His lips quirked.

"Ha ha."

"I'd be happy to give you a demonstration —"

"Never you mind. So, what should I do with her?"

"Depends. We don't really have the facilities to keep her here, but I could make a call to the next county in the morning."

"Morning?" I looked down at Junior, then back at Tom. "What do you usually do with them until then?"

He grinned. "I usually summon all my powers of persuasion to appeal to the charitable impulses of whoever picked up the stray to take the dog home and settle in for the evening."

I looked down at Junior, who had sat back on his, I mean *her,* haunches and was now scratching her right ear with the kind of dedication and attention that only a dog could manage. "I wonder if she's potty trained."

Well, I didn't have much of a choice. I couldn't just let her roam the streets, and I couldn't exactly leave her at Mrs. Murray's house. "Well, Junior, it's just you and me, kiddo. Unless . . ." I gazed at Tom, as appealingly as possible.

He held up his hands. "Don't look at me. My landlord doesn't allow pets."

I sighed. "Like I said, Junior, it's just you and me." I paused a moment. "So, are you almost done here?"

He shook his head. "Sorry, no. We had some stuff go down this afternoon, and it's going to take me a while to get through the paperwork."

I knew it was a long shot anyway. "I guess I'd better go, then, and let you get back to it."

"I'll walk you out."

At least it was something. Even better, Tom caught hold of my hand as we left the building. Pleased by the attentions, I let Junior (and it was obvious I was going to have to come up with a better name, considering Junior wasn't exactly the most feminine of monikers) tug on the end of the leash, sniffing at the concrete, the grass, the bushes, as we made our way back to Christine in companionable silence.

"What will you do tonight, then?" he asked me, stroking my fingertips with his.

I stroked back, wishing for more. "I guess I'll go home. Have wild and crazy sex with the first man who asks. You know. The usual."

"Hmm. Maybe I should stop by."

I cozied up to him and toyed with the insignia over his left breast. "Maybe you should. Besides, then I could ask you about what I heard today about the inquiries made at the high school."

"Oh, you heard about that, did you?"

"Mmm. And I also heard that it had something to do with the Metzger investigation."

He had the mask on again. "You hear an awful lot for someone who isn't paying attention to things they're supposed to be staying out of, for their own good."

"I don't ask to hear things, you know. People just tend to confide in me. I can't help it." I paused, looking deep into his eyes in an attempt to see what he didn't want me to see. "So, is it true? Did you arrest those boys? Come on, you know I'm probably the last person in town to know anyway."

Tom heaved a long-suffering sigh. "That's because this town has more busybodies per capita than any other town I know."

"It's a typical small town."

"Don't I know it. Well, in the attempt to dispel some of the rumors grinding out of the grist mill right now, no. No arrests have been made. Jesus, we're doing our best to try to put things together. The biddies in this town will have these boys tried, found guilty, and convicted before breakfast tomorrow morning."

"And you don't think they are."

"Of theft, yeah, sure. I have a feeling it wouldn't be the first time. Maybe even assault. But murder? I don't know what to believe."

I was beginning to think that confusion was the natural state of things. "Ohhh," I breathed as I remembered something that he'd told me in passing. "The previous attack on the Amish. You think they might have been involved?"

He shrugged.

"You went out to Blackhawk because the director had found something he wanted you to see. What was it?"

Tom pulled away from me and leaned his hip against Christine's rounded hood. "A wallet and ID from the man who was attacked a few weeks back here in this county, buried in their footlockers with some contraband drugs they'd bought. Some cash. Surprised me. I would have thought they'd burn through all of that right away."

"But nothing from Luc?"

He shook his head slowly. "No. Nothing."

"Still, it doesn't mean —"

"You know how you're always talking about intuition and all that psychic mumbo jumbo? Well, cops have their own version of

271

that. It's nothing you can put your finger on, just a gut instinct that tells you when someone is trying to put one over on you. We've got them running scared — make no bones about that — but did they kill Luc? I just don't know."

"In spite of the other attack."

"Yeah."

Which left the investigation exactly where?, I wondered. If the boys were responsible for the other attacks but they didn't attack Luc . . . who did?

"Your Mrs. Murray should rest easier now, though," he commented offhandedly. "I have it on good authority these same boys were the ringleaders of the group who have been making trouble in the woods out by the Woodhaven addition."

"Two birds with one stone. Well done."

"Well, not quite. But at least it's a start."

"Well." Junior was tugging, trying to reach a bush for a good, hearty sniff. I shifted the leash to my other hand. "I suppose I'd better let you go, since you have work to do. You won't forget to call in the morning?"

"I won't forget."

"Okay. Oh, by the way, there's something quick that I forgot about earlier."

His eyes lit up with good humor. "Hm. Sounds interesting. Not quite sure about logistics, but —"

I pretended I didn't know what he was implying. He knew as well as I did that teasing wouldn't lead anywhere tonight. "The truth is, my mom is insisting that I bring you to lunch to meet the family. In fact, she's asking about after church on Sunday."

"Sunday? This Sunday?"

"I know it's short notice, but she's been after me for a while now, and I keep putting her off."

"Now?" He didn't look pleased. "I mean, I just got this promotion, and we're right in the middle of a murder investigation. It's just not a good time."

"I know, I know. But you know how moms are — and my mom has it down to a science. Maybe I could convince her to bring Dad down to Annie's after church and we could meet them there. That way you wouldn't have to worry about changing or driving across town or anything. Oh, and one more thing. If she asks how long we've been seeing each other —" He narrowed his eyes, so I pressed on before I lost my nerve. "Well, could you just go along with whatever time line she puts before you?"

"Why would there be a problem with that?"

"Well, maybe because she thinks we've

been seeing each other for longer than . . . well. And one last thing —"

"You already asked one last thing."

"This is really the last one. Mom doesn't know that you're only separated from your wife, and . . ."

"You want me to lie to her about that, too."

When he put it that way, I winced. "Yes." When he still resisted, I cajoled, "Please, Tom. I don't want to, either. Trust me on this, I know exactly how my mother is — but that's the point. I'll never hear the end of it if we miss it this time. If you like, we can have dinner with your parents sometime, to make up for it."

He didn't say anything.

"Okay, well, think about it at least." I reached up and gave him a quick kiss on the cheek. "Talk to you later."

Somehow I managed to coerce Junior into the car, despite her clearly communicated preference for staying at the station to wind around Tom's legs. (I knew I should have tried harder to get him to keep her.) She sat in the passenger seat, her nose smearing the glass, and whined pitifully as we pulled away.

"Well, Junior my girl, I guess it's just you and me, babe."

She turned her head to look at me, her ears lowered dejectedly.

I had to admit it felt good to take her home with me, to not greet the darkness of my apartment by myself for once (because whatever lights I left on would not *stay* on, darn it). As soon as I had unlocked the door and twisted the knob, Junior barged through the door and spent the next twenty minutes sniffing out and exploring every inch of the small apartment. When she was done, she loped across the floor and took a flying leap into the middle of my bed, quickly turning herself around on her tummy and issuing me a mischievous appeal, quirky ears, glittering eyes, and all.

"Well," I said, leaning my shoulder against the door frame. "I guess this means you don't want to *eat*. Well, that's fine, that's fine. I'll just have a hamburger all by myself, then. With cheese. Maybe even bacon. And I'm going to *eat* it, too. All. By. Myself."

Whistling nonchalantly, I headed toward the galley-style kitchen. I didn't even get a chance to bang a couple of pots and pans together before I turned around and she was there, looking up at me. Mouth open, tongue hanging at the ready.

"I thought that might tempt you. Subtlety isn't really your forte, is it?"

Junior wagged her tail expectantly.

I fixed three hamburgers, one for me, two for the pooch, and set the plate on the floor before her. Junior had hers gone in seconds, then immediately laid her chin on my leg and tried to look appealing.

"Hey," I told her. "You had yours. Let me have mine in peace, huh?"

I was about to take a bite of my hamburger when it occurred to me.

Wow. There I was, talking to a dog, and I was liking it. How sad was my life?

Hello, Universe? Girl needing a life down here. Ya got one in mind for me?

I heaved a sigh and stared at the hamburger on my plate with little interest.

Everyone else seemed to have a life. Even my little sister, who had been surprisingly quiet of late, probably due to the whole gestation process. My life depended all too much on the schedules of others, which I definitely needed to do something about. Not that I could do anything about anyone else's schedule, but I could do something about forging a life that didn't depend on anyone but myself.

Junior nudged my hand with her snoot as if to say, *Hey, what about me?*

I fluffed her ears for her. "Aw, poor girl. Don't worry, we'll find a nice home for you.

You just have to show everyone how sweet you are, and you'll charm them all. Won't you? Yes. Pretty girl. Aren't you? Yes, you are."

So I was talking to a dog. Big deal. At least she was putting in face time with me. That made her all right in my book.

I was about to settle in for a night of TV when there was a knock at my door.

"Hey, Mags! Are you home?"

Steff!

Steff, my best friend, had been a little tied up for the last several months. Okay, so she has a boyfriend and a life. The truth was, I had been missing her like crazy, so tonight's knock at the door was just what the doctor ordered.

I hurried to the door, Junior nipping at my heels, turned the locks, and swung it wide. "Hey!" I practically launched myself at her. "Oh, I'm so glad to see you!"

Steff laughed and hugged me back. She smelled like citrus and white flowers, happiness and sunshine. "Wow! What a welcome! Let me guess, you really wanted a shared Magnum moment tonight."

I felt like Snoopy dancing, and it was only at that moment that I fully realized how much I'd been missing her company. "Magnum, Schmagnum. I'm just happy to see you. How have you been?"

She came in and closed the door behind her. "Tired. And who do we have here?" she asked, her auburn curls falling softly against her cheeks as she bent over to give Junior a double cheek rub and an ear ruffle. Junior basked in the extra attention, tongue lolling happily.

"This is Junior. She's just spending the night."

"Junior, huh? Aw, you're a cutie. Um, did you say she?"

"Long story. Come on in, put up your feet. Don't mind Junior, she's obviously a people doggie. You don't mind a little drool, do you? Want a pop?"

"Sure."

I handed her a Diet Coke from the fridge and dropped down on the sofa beside her. "You've been working a lot lately. How're things with Dr. Danny?"

The smile that curved her lips lit up her whole face. "Good. Very good, actually. He's really special."

"I know. I can tell. You've been with him for, what, six months now? Seven? That's like forever for you."

"I know! Isn't it wonderful?"

It was, at that. "I'm happy for you. I won't lie and say I don't miss you, but I'm happy for you. *So.* Is it True Love, do you think?"

She shrugged, but I saw the truth of it in her eyes. Junior had climbed on the sofa between us and rolled onto her back. Steff reached over and played with one of her paws. "How are things progressing with you and Tom?"

I shrugged. "Okay, I guess."

"Any new developments?"

"Well, because of everything that's been going on in town, he's been promoted to Special Task Force Investigator."

"What does that mean?"

"It means he has a lot more responsibility, for one thing. Which kind of goes along with more hours, unfortunately."

"Oh. I'm sorry."

I nodded. "It comes with the territory, and it's important to him. To the whole town, really."

"Mm. How is he doing with the whole, you know, woo-woo thing? Any better?"

"He thinks Satan is responsible."

"Ah. Pretty much the same, then. I'm sorry for that, too. But maybe he'll surprise you, Mags. You never know."

"Maybe."

She lifted her Diet Coke and waited for me to meet it with my own. "Well, here's to our guys, long hours and quirks and all. And

279

here's to us, for having the patience to deal with it."

I laughed. "Hear, hear."

Steff and I had been in and out of each other's lives so often since we were ten years old that catching up never took long. She was the sister of my soul — how many times had we looked into each other's eyes and known what the other was thinking? Too many to count. And as we talked and giggled and shared tonight, I kept getting the feeling that she was going to have an announcement to make someday very soon. I wondered if she realized that. Was it something I was picking up from her, or from the universe itself?

"Mags! Check this out." She was holding Junior's paw in her hand, running her thumb over the pooch's paw pads.

"What?"

"This. Junior is polydactyl."

"Polywhat?"

"Polydactyl. She has six toes. I don't think I've ever seen a dog with six toes. How cool is that? Junior, you're special!"

Junior, who had made herself right at home, lifted her head about two inches and blinked sleepily as if to say, *Well, of course. What else would I be?*

Really, it must be nice being a dog, I

thought as I marveled over her unusual feet. They are so secure in themselves. You never find a dog staring at its reflection in a mirror, wondering whether it looks fat, or turning up its nose at food because it'd eaten a little too much the day before. They don't obsess over boyfriends, or wonder what they are going to do with their lives. And when they're feeling blue, all they have to do is turn on the puppy dog look, and no one can keep their hands off 'em. What a life.

I wanted one. A life, that is.

"You heard about what happened the other night?" Steff asked.

"You mean Luc Metzger? Yeah. I was there, actually. Marcus and I happened to come across the scene just before the cops got there."

Steff sat up straighter. "You didn't tell me that!"

"I just did! Besides, I was going to, but you had to work last night, and, well, yesterday was a bit busy."

She sighed. "You're right. I guess I've just been really missing our talks lately. Life, the universe, and everything has been getting in the way."

I was so relieved to know I wasn't the only one. "I've missed you, too."

Junior blinked herself awake — kind of —

281

and stretched her body across the two of us.

Steff laughed. "Wow, it must be nice to be a dog. Have you ever seen anything as relaxed as this? Goofy thing." Turning back to the subject at hand, she said, "So, you were there. How creepy is that? And what, exactly, were you doing with Marcus, pray tell?"

"Yes, very, and it was totally innocent." Well, nearly innocent. The kiss, as blazing as it was, didn't count. Much.

"Hmm."

"Honestly. Marcus and I . . . we're just good friends."

"I've always enjoyed being friends with hot guys."

"Hot guys who are taken," I reminded her. "He's seeing Liss, remember?"

Steff smiled, taking a delicate sip of her Diet Coke before licking her upper lip the way she always did right before divulging a particularly juicy bit of info. "Right. So that would be why I saw your boss with a really nice-looking older gentleman at La Chanteuse, that French restaurant on the north side of Fort Wayne, looking absolutely *chummy*."

My mouth fell open. "Liss wouldn't do that to Marcus."

Steff looked me pointedly in the eyes. "Are you very sure that the two are an item?"

"Well, of course, I . . . they . . ." Confused now, I thought back to when I had first met Marcus through Liss. Even though it felt as though I had known both of them for years, in actuality it had been less than seven months. Liss had introduced me to Marcus the morning her sister had died. But had she introduced him to me as anything in particular? Or was that a case of my perception coloring my reality again?

Had either of them actually said that they were together in anything other than a magical partnership sense?

"I'm not sure," I admitted, as much to myself as to Steff.

"Mmhmm. The only reason I ask is because, well, I get this feeling . . ."

Far be it from me to discount feelings.

Oh, this was so not helping. I shook myself mentally, determined not to let myself get that far off track. "Anyway, Saturday night, Marcus and I were visiting with Liss, and he was following me back to town. Luc Metzger had already been found at that point."

If Steff noticed the slight change of subject, she allowed it to pass without mention. "Did you see anything?"

I shook my head. "Marcus wouldn't let me. Not that I wanted to. I don't think it was pretty."

She took a sip of her pop. "I heard about it at the hospital, of course. Nurses talk shop from floor to floor, you know. Whoever it was did a number on his head — there's no way he survived more than a few minutes."

"There's more," I told her, knowing I could trust her with anything without fear of judgment. "A lot more, actually. I met Luc Metzger the day he was killed. I saw him at the farmers market, and I can honestly say I don't think I've ever seen another Amish man like him. He was . . . beautiful. Truly. Half the women around the auction area were too busy staring at him to even think to bid on anything." And I had the oddest feeling that he had known that. Maybe he wasn't as immune to the tuggings of earthly pleasures as a man of peace should be. Maybe that was the cause of the discussion between him and his wife. Maybe it was him and women in general.

Hmm.

"I've never thought of Amish men as beautiful. Solid and quiet and solemn, yes. Almost asexual in a way, although I know they're not. No one who's ever seen their large families could truly believe them that,"

Steff said with a twinkle in her eye.

I laughed, too. "No, I suppose not. Maybe we've just been blind all this time, eh? Anyway, after that happened on Saturday, Liss and I kinda sorta ventured out to the crime scene area late Sunday afternoon with Eli Yoder. You know, from the N.I.G.H.T.S.? Luc worked with him, and I think he was kind of torn up about the whole thing, even if he wouldn't directly admit it."

"What is it with men not wanting to admit when they're hurting or confused? Honestly! So, what did you pick up at the crime scene? I assume you felt something."

I shook my head. "I was trying not to."

"Why?"

"I don't know. I guess it makes me nervous. This whole empath thing. I mean, you know my mom. And the Church. It's not like this kind of thing was ever encouraged. And while I know in my heart that it's not something that comes from the Devil — and I'm not even convinced the Devil exists anyway — it still makes me feel a little . . ."

"You're scared."

"Yeah." I met her gaze. "I am."

"Maggie." She took my hand in both of hers. "You're one of the best people I've ever known. Nothing you could do would convince me otherwise. Regardless of what the Church says, this 'whole empath thing,' as you put it, is a gift. From God, from the universe, from whatever you want to call it. And I think that by not using it in the way it was meant to be used, by running scared . . . well, aren't you really turning your back on what was meant to be? On who *you* are meant to be?"

I bit my lip. "Maybe. Oh, great, yet another thing to feel guilty about."

She laughed at me. "So, what did you turn away from at the crime scene?"

"Well, it wasn't just me. Liss gets feelings about things, too, and Eli is a master dowser for spirit energy. There's a lot of energy out there. Chaos energy, Eli called it. And we found something. A sign on a tree. Liss said it was a symbol used in some magical circles. We haven't figured out what it means yet, but she thinks her nephew might be able to help in that regard."

"Should I assume Tom knows all of this?"

"Yeah, and he was none too happy. The magical symbol really creeped him out. Some of the guys on the force are the ones pushing the satanic worship theory."

"It doesn't surprise me. So many people seem happy to look for evil in everything. What does puzzle me is how they can be surprised when that's exactly what they find."

"Well, I won't deny that there's something bad going on in town." I looked at her as a sudden notion struck me. "You feel it, too."

She shrugged. "Maybe. Yeah, I guess I do. Maybe that explains why the hospital has been so wacky lately. Honestly, I don't think any of the patients really sleep anymore."

As if to prove her point, Junior suddenly sat bolt upright, ears perked and whiskers twitching.

"What's the matter, girl?" I asked her, feeling the hairs on the back of my neck stand on end. Uh-oh.

"Maggie," Steff whispered, her eyes like saucers. She pointed to the door to my bedroom. It was swinging inward, creaking on its hinges as it went.

Junior leapt to her feet, her fur standing at attention from head to tail. Growling, she advanced on the opening door, creeping step by step as hackles traveled like the vibrations of a Magic Fingers mattress up my spine.

The bedroom door slammed in the dog's face.

Steff and I jumped to our feet at the same time, staring in shock at the closed door. Junior abandoned all pretense of bravery.

Whining now, she backed away from the door, a frown worrying her doggie brow as she came to rest with her rump leaning against our legs. My hand reached down to her, to give and to receive reassurance in kind.

"Does it do that often?" Steff asked, a little shakily.

I shook my head.

"That's good. Wow, I wasn't expecting that."

I shook my head again.

"What is that, exactly?"

"I don't know. I don't know if it's attached to the house, or to me, or what. Maybe it just wants to remind us that it's there." I thought back to the armoire cabinet door at Louisa's, and shivered.

"Wow. I mean, I've seen a ghost before — remember I told you about the one that used to sit on the end of my bed back in Massachusetts? — but he was fairly quiet and mostly reserved himself for odd moments in the middle of the night. Yours is, uh, pretty bold, isn't it?"

Leave it to me to have attracted a poltergeist. I mean, I had a possessed car, a conscience that had adopted the voice of my Grandma Cora as its mouthpiece, and my apartment housed little black shadow goblins, so why not one more?

Or were they all one and the same?

Actually, so long as it wasn't Luc Metzger hanging around . . .

Maybe it was time to stop being afraid all the time. Maybe it was time to work to understand.

Everything. And that meant the chaos energy, too.

CHAPTER 13

Junior had a surprise for me the next morning. More than one, actually. First thing, I awoke to hot breath washing over my face. Blearily I opened my eyes and in the gray half-light of dawn I saw a dark face hovering over my own.

Gaaaaaah.

I half-scrambled, half-rolled out from under my bedcovers, scrabbling instinctively for the baseball bat I'd taken to sleeping with. It took me a moment to remember Junior, and a little longer to remember the reason for her presence.

Junior, undeterred, pranced playfully across the bed and launched herself at me. My breath left me as her feet hit my shoulders. "I guess you need to go outside, huh?"

She licked my face. Repeatedly.

Now, far be it from me to refuse kisses from anyone, even slobbery ones, but when you're still blinking the sleep out of your eyes and trying to find your bearings, such exuberance can be a bit off-putting. Gently I took her paws in hand and lowered them to the bed, stepping backward as I did so.

My bare foot met with something cold and revolting on the carpet.

Oh. My. God.

"Junior!" I screeched. "What have you done?"

Junior leaned her front paws down and her rear up on the bed in a combined full body stretch/tailwagging extravaganza. Obviously she didn't realize how close to an untimely demise she really was.

Simultaneously gagging and cringing in horror, I pulled my foot out of the pile of muck and, lifting it off the floor, I hopped to the bedside table in order to switch on the lamp, hoping and praying I didn't encounter any other, um, deposits of any kind. With the lamp on, I twisted and fell to the bed, careful to keep my foot from coming into contact with anything important while I surveyed the damage.

Sweet Mother Mary! Did the animal not sleep at all? A minefield of shredded newspaper studded the carpet, toilet paper stretched from the bathroom to the bedroom and back again, and then of course there was the dreaded spot, which was now mashed into the carpet. Not to mention the socks and other sundries that had been dragged from the laundry hamper, which *someone* had knocked over on the bathroom floor.

What I couldn't figure out was how she had done all of this without waking me.

Somehow, all of this seemed even harder to deal with than the spooky stuff the night before.

Junior snuffled my ear, then rolled around on the bed, kicking her feet joyously in the air. Completely unconcerned that her character was being maligned due to her involvement in World War Three.

I sniffed as tears sprang inexplicably to my eyes. "Junior, I don't like you." Sniffle. "I really don't. No, don't you dare try to apologize. Just let me sit here a moment and wallow in my misery."

There was only one thing to do that didn't involve PETA jumping down my throat. "Well, come on, then, you six-toed goober. Let's get this cleaned up."

It took me nearly an hour to get the bedroom put back to rights, mostly because every time I turned my back on Junior, she tried to undo everything I was working so hard to accomplish.

"What am I going to do with you?" I asked

her, facing her down with my hands on my hips.

There was only one thing for it. She was going to have to go with me. Hopefully Tom would have heard from the shelter in the next county by the time I got to Enchantments.

Junior enjoyed the car ride, but between the wet nose prints, dog slobber, and shedding, Christine was never going to recover. It was with some relief that I led her into the back office at Enchantments and fastened her leash to the doorknob.

"Well, well, what have we here?"

Liss had poked her head through the curtains when she heard the sounds of my arrival, and was now gazing upon my unlikely friend with some amusement.

I cleared my throat. "It's a long story. Suffice it to say, Junior either had to go with me yesterday evening or face certain extinction. And now I need to call Tom, because if Junior goes home with me, she is going to face certain extinction all over again."

Liss's eyebrows lifted. "Long night?"

"An even longer morning cleaning up after a busy night."

"Ah. Did you say *she?*"

"Don't ask."

"Consider that a nonquestion," she said,

293

trying to hide her smile.

I picked up the phone. It was a little early still, but if I knew Tom . . .

"Stony Mill Police Department, Sergeant Howard speaking. Is this an emergency?"

"No, no emergency. Hi, Jim, this is Maggie O'Neill. Is Tom there?"

"Oh, hey, Maggie. Yeah, he just stepped in the door. Let me get him for you."

I heard a click as he put me on hold. A moment later, I heard Tom pick up.

"Your dog left her bone here at the station," he said by way of greeting.

"Good morning to you, too. She did? Good. She'll have something to chew on while waiting for the shelter people to come get her."

There was a pause, the kind that gave me a sinking feeling in the pit of my stomach. Behind me, Junior pulled on the end of her leash and whined. "Um, there might be a bit of a problem with that," Tom said.

"What kind of problem?"

"Well, you see, there's no room at the inn. The shelter is full up, Maggie. And since they're a no-kill shelter, well, they have to have room before they can accept any more."

I absorbed all of this, trying to decide what it meant to me. And what I was coming up with was a whole lot of doggie messes.

"Now, if you want me to, I could have a go at some of the other shelters we have access to, but none of the others are no-kill."

I shook my head. "I can't have rescued Junior from certain injury only to give her up to a shelter that can't even guarantee her prolonged good health. I'm just going to have to come up with an alternative."

"I'm sorry, Maggie. I wish the news was better. But hey, it's not the end of the world. She's a cute little thing, right?"

Yeah. This cute little thing — who currently had her teeth sunk into the tail of a coat that was hanging from the coat rack, and was now pulling with all of her might — was a furry-faced menace in the making. It wasn't her fault — I knew it was because she must have been raised in a barn, or a garage, or something. But that didn't help when I was the one stuck with cleaning up her messes.

I hung up feeling more than a little bit desperate. What on earth was I going to do with a sixty-pound tornado with a poop and paper fetish?

Liss came up and put her hand on my shoulder. "Bad news?"

I sighed. "You could say that. I'm not sure

what I'm going to do with Junior here. I thought I was helping matters by taking her home, but now I'm not so sure."

"Hmm. With all the farms out here, I'm sure someone could use a good dog."

"They'd have to be special, though. Junior is a sweetheart, even if she is a little on the excitable side. I couldn't let her go to just anyone."

Liss thought a moment. "What about Eli? Perhaps he'd know someone."

Good idea! "Would you mind if I pay him a visit?"

"Of course not! We have to take care of our animal friends."

"It'll only take a little while," I said, grabbing hold of the leash and giving Junior a solid chin scratching before either of us changed our minds. "I'll be back before the store's official opening."

"Take your time, no need to hurry. I'll be here when you get back."

I left Liss there, sorting through a box of new tarot card designs that had just arrived from the U.K., and headed out toward County Road 500 North. It occurred to me, not for the first time, how lucky I was to have found Liss and my job at Enchantments. I had never belonged in the corporate world, even such as it was in a small town like Stony Mill, Indiana. I wasn't cut-throat, I didn't care about moving up the corporate ladder one vicious rung at a time, and it annoyed the heck out of me that it wasn't intelligence and proven ability that moved you up that ladder, but rather a total lack of regard for your fellow man. Enchantments suited me. At the store I got to know our regulars but didn't have to spend time with them after hours. I was surrounded by beauty and music and things that made my soul come alive. I had a steady supply of all the best teas and coffees Stony Mill had to offer. I had a boss who understood my every sensitive/intuitive personality quirk, and didn't seem to mind a single one of them. Not to mention there was a freedom attached to the job that I had experienced nowhere else. I was lucky, lucky, lucky, and I knew it. Someone was definitely watching out for me that day I spilled through the door. Someone knew what they were doing. I was just the blessed beneficiary. In my heart I knew that Liss had been sent to me for a reason. Perhaps in time I would fully understand what that meant.

Eli was just coming out of his barn when I crossed into his driveway. I pulled up next to him and rolled down my window to talk.

"Liss said you were on your way," he said

with a nod by way of greeting.

"How — ?"

He patted his breast pocket. "I have a cell phone for business purposes."

"Oh. Oh, I didn't even think about that."

I must have looked embarrassed, because he laughed at me. "This is the twenty-first century, *ja?*"

Was I being lectured about the need for technology by an Amish man? What was this world coming to?

"So, what can I do for you, Miss Maggie?" he asked. He bent down and looked into the car, his big square face as kind as ever beneath his flat-brimmed hat. "Who do you have here?"

Junior pushed her way between me and the steering wheel so that she could stick her head and half her body out to meet Eli's hand. "This," I said as I dodged her sweeping club of a tail, "is a friend of mine. I picked her up last night — the poor thing was terrorizing an older woman in town who knows my mother, and I was afraid she was going to take her frustrations and fear out on the dog."

"That was kind of you."

"Yes, well, it was supposed to be a temporary fix, but the only no-kill shelter in the area is full up, and Junior here is better

298

suited to being an outdoor dog, I'm afraid. It took me an hour this morning to clean up the havoc she'd wreaked overnight."

He held the dog's face between his massive hands and gazed into her eyes. Junior melted into a puddle at the attention, right before my eyes. Amazing. "She was excited. New surroundings. She wanted to, how do you say? Make her mark? Mark her territory? She meant no harm."

As if to confirm this, Junior pulled her head back inside just long enough to lick my cheek, then went back to Eli's gentle ministrations.

"How do you know that?" I asked, curious at the certainty of his assessment.

He shrugged.

"Well," I said, willing to give him and his insight the benefit of the doubt, "she may have meant no harm, but she was just a bit destructive, and she doesn't appear to be house-trained. I think she's probably been an outdoor dog, which makes keeping her in my little apartment problematic."

He nodded in understanding. "Some spirits are more suited to the wide-open spaces."

"Exactly." Now, that was what I liked about Eli. He had an innate understanding of what made people — and spirits — tick, and he expressed it with such steadiness and wisdom that a girl couldn't help but feel reassured by his very presence. But that didn't make the next part any easier. "Liss suggested I ask you . . . I mean, I was hoping . . . Would you possibly know . . ." I wasn't usually this tongue-tied, but it was a big request to make of anyone, and I wasn't sure how to proceed.

"You say you picked her up in town?" he asked, seemingly oblivious to my discomfort.

Distracted, I nodded. "Yes."

"You know, she has the look of . . ." His voice trailed off as he picked up the dog's foot. "*Ja,* that's it. This is Luc Metzger's dog."

I stared at him while an uneasy ripple traveled up my spine. Yet another connection to Luc. Following on the heels of the armoire "spirit," it did not make me feel at all comfortable. It was almost creepy, the idea that a spirit could be facilitating from beyond the grave for his own purposes.

Eli didn't notice. "*Ja,* see here? Her feet? Dead giveaway, those toes. If you don't mind driving, we could take her over there right now and make sure I'm right. It's only a mile or so."

"Sure," I found myself murmuring, still

boggled over the latest in life's little synchronicities. "Hop in."

Within minutes we were bumping into the driveway of another Amish home, its identity obvious due to its lack of electrical wires leading from the poles to the large white farmhouse. Not to mention the plain exterior, horses in the pasture, and laundry hanging on the line, all in shades of blue, black, and white. The property had several fenced-in areas of pasture, some with horses, some with milk cows, one with goats. Relegated to the back seat when Eli had taken over the passenger side, Junior seemed to perk up the farther we traveled up the lane. By the time I pulled to a halt, her entire body was quivering with readiness, and her tail was swishing nonstop. I felt sure that Eli must be right. "Is this home, girl?" I asked her, patting her on the head.

A young woman had stepped onto the porch when she heard us pull up. Garbed in the traditional Amish garb of a dark blue dress, ugly black shoes, and white apron and head cap, with a black wool sweater thrown on for warmth against the spring breezes, Hester Metzger set down the little girl she'd held supported on her hip and came down the steps to meet us.

"Eli, what a pleasant surprise. I wasn't expecting you." Her gaze flicked to me as I rose from behind the wheel, and her brows drew together slightly as she tried to place me. "And — I have met you before, I think, but you must forgive me, I do not remember where."

"You have met before?" Eli asked, looking at me for confirmation. "I did not know that."

"It was at the farmers market," I said, dipping my chin in a respectful hello to Hester. "I bought noodles from you. They were very good, by the way. I can't remember when I've had better."

"Thank you. Yes, that's right. The farmers market." She nodded to herself, but her eyes never left me. "I remember you."

"The cookies were very good as well," I added, to fill the silence that seemed determined to settle in. "My grandfather loved them."

"Thank you." She folded her hands over her tidy apron front, waiting. "What can I do for you, Eli?"

"We were wanting to check in with you, Hester. See how you were faring."

Her face remained noncommittal. "I am fine, as you can see."

"No more . . . troubles?"

Trouble? What trouble?

Hester shrugged, her pink cheeks going even pinker. "People will believe what they wish to believe. It is not my concern."

"It should be. You will need help."

"Not from them."

"Ah, Hester, a place like this does not run itself. The community is important."

"What they think is not important. I have done nothing wrong."

Whoa, whoa, whoa. What was going on?

Hester must have noted my curiosity, because she threw a glance my way and clammed up, at least on that subject. "As you can see, Eli, I'm doing fine. Things are fine here." Her daughter, a sweet-faced little thing in a dark-hued pinafore, tugged on her skirt. Hester picked up her daughter and held her, hugging her close. Cheek to cheek they stared at us, a united front. "We're all fine."

So, basically, everything was fine. That was reassuring. Too bad repeated assertions generally proved the opposite when all was said and done.

Eli met my gaze. I knew he was thinking the same thing.

But Eli was a gentleman in Amish clothing, and if Hester didn't want to talk about her troubles, he would respect her wishes.

"That is good. But if you need anything, you will send someone over, *ja?*"

She didn't look at him, but she nodded. "Is there anything else that you needed, Eli? It was too far to have come just to check up on me."

The Amish concept of too far I found more than a little amusing. It couldn't have been more than two miles. "It was because of me, actually," I said to get Eli off the hook.

"You?"

"Well, me, and Junior here. Eli thought she might belong to you." I stepped aside and opened the car door. Junior bounded out, all sixty pounds of exuberance and energetic doggie joy. She danced around us all, ears bouncing, tail wagging, rump shaking.

"Peaches!" the little girl cried out, and reached both arms toward the dog. "Peaches, Peaches!"

She wouldn't stay in her mother's arms any longer, so Hester set her down on her feet. The dog immediately bowled her over as she bumped against the child in her efforts to lick every inch of the girl's plump cheeks, much to her giggling delight. The girl couldn't have been more than four years old. To see her joy, the sparkle in her eyes, the way that she threw her arms around the dog's neck and clung as though she would never let go . . .

I knelt down as well, smiling through the tears that clouded my vision. "Peaches, huh? I didn't know what to call her. I'm glad she's yours. I don't think she liked being called Junior much."

"Thank you for bringing her back to us," Hester said, an honest smile touching her lips for the first time since we'd arrived. "She often followed Luc if he would let her. We thought she was lost for good after she did not come home the day that . . . We thought . . . The children were frantic. Where on earth did you find her?"

"Actually, she was terrorizing a woman on the edge of town. I took her in because I was a little afraid the woman might freak out and hurt her or something," I told her. "She was holed up in the woman's barn, I guess, and she seemed to be afraid of her."

"Peaches doesn't bite!" the little girl piped up in defense of her pet. "Peaches is a good doggie!"

As though to prove her point, Peaches reached back toward me and snuffled my hand, rolling her head into the attention with slobbering adulation.

"Yes, honey, Peaches is a good doggie.

Some people are just afraid of doggies," I told her.

"Why?"

"I don't know. They just are. Peaches is a special doggie, did you know that? She has six toes on her feet."

"Of course she does. Did you know I can count to six? I can count to six *hundred*. But my brother Jude can't, and he *is* six. I'm only almost five."

"Hannah," her mother admonished. "You're bragging."

Little girls were so funny. I leaned down to her and said, "Wow, that's really smart of you. Did you know most doggies don't have that many toes?"

"All our doggies do. They're really special. Mama says they came with her from Pen — Pen —" She pursed her mouth in a thoughtful corkscrew. "Where was that again, Mama?"

"Never mind, Hannah," Hester said, giving her daughter a motherly pat on the rump. "Why don't you go out to the barn and get Peaches some of her food? She might be hungry."

"Okay, Mama," the little girl said. "Come on, Peaches! Come on!"

A happy girl, a happy dog, a happy mother. My work here was done.

306

I watched Hannah head toward the big red barn, the dog trailing along behind her. It was an idyllic scene — a beautiful child, adoring dog trotting at her heels, the tidy house and yard, the lovely old-style barn. Not some modern sheet metal monstrosity, this barn was made from wood — solid, adorned with white paint and . . .

Round signs over its big doors.

The red paint on the barn was older and peeling, but the white signs were painted with great care with designs in bright colors. They reminded me a little of quilt patterns, many-pointed stars and pinwheels. But they also reminded me of the sign we'd found in the woods.

"Pretty," I said, indicating them with a nod of my head.

"Thank you. The others in the *Ordnung,* they do not like them much, but they bring me peace. Luc always liked them."

Luc. I offered Hester my hand. "I was so sorry to hear about your husband. It must be terrible, to lose him so young."

Her lips quirked in a tight smile. The strain of the last days was taking its toll. I couldn't help remembering how pretty she'd looked that day at the market. How much older she looked today. "Thank you. I appreciate the sentiment, but I assure you, we'll be —"

"Fine." I nodded. "Yes, I know. Listen, I have no right to say this, but something is compelling me to ask you. At the market that day, you said something to me. At the time it just seemed a little odd, but meeting you again today and looking back, well, it has gotten me to thinking, so I hope you'll forgive me. That day, you mentioned something about 'those who see.' What did you mean?"

She looked over her shoulder to see how closely Eli was paying attention. "I think you know exactly what I meant."

"You see things — feel things — too?"

She shrugged, but to me the answer was clear.

"You don't have to worry about Eli," I told her, smiling. "I don't think he would see it as unusual at all. You see, he's a bit of a sensitive as well."

"My mother was a seer," she whispered. "And I have seen things as well, ever since I was a little girl. And — with Luc — I saw it coming — I knew —"

"You knew he was going to die?"

"I knew something bad was going to happen. That's all."

But was it? Or did she know more? Because I couldn't help remembering that day, picturing it in my mind's eye. And the more I did, the more feelings I was starting to get. Maybe, had I not been so dead set against "feeling" and "experiencing," had I not been quite so skittish about my abilities, maybe I would have picked up on things sooner.

I thought about it as I got in the car, and I was still thinking about it when I pulled up to Eli's home ten minutes later.

"You've been quiet," Eli remarked, his hand on the door handle.

I nodded. "Sorry about that. I was just thinking . . ."

"About Luc."

A statement, not a question. Yes, without a doubt, Eli was one who saw. "Eli, you knew him better than most people, I would guess."

"*Ja,* I would guess I knew him well enough."

"What was he like, as a person?"

Eli half smiled, half frowned. "Luc was Luc. A man. Not without sin — we none of us are without sin, especially not men. Luc and Hester . . . well, I don't think he knew what he had in Hester. She was a good wife to him. A good mother. Luc wasn't always . . . a good husband. But he was trying to be, I think."

Did that mean the same thing in the Amish world as it did in the usual sense? Did he beat her? Cheat on her? Fail to support her in a way befitting a wife? What?

What sins did Luc have?

I thought I knew.

I saw him in my mind's eye. There in the sunshine on market day, all burnished hair, straight white smile, ruddy lips, hooded eyes. Arms and shoulders and thighs bulging into eternity. Everywhere he moved, female eyes followed. They couldn't not follow. It would have been like opposing a powerful force of nature.

And his eyes . . . they had been wise. Knowing. Accepting of his power.

He knew he was attractive to the female sex.

I had seen it in the way he had looked at me.

An invitation? Or a challenge?

And Hester knew him, better than anyone. Did she know his true nature? Could that have been the reason for her confrontation of him that afternoon? I thought back to the scene that we had witnessed, Marcus, Liss, and I. How distraught she was over what he had insisted was "a simple job" that would be "just for the afternoon."

She knew. And she was afraid of losing him.

I was betting on it. Generally speaking, a woman at the very least suspects these things. Even if she doesn't want to admit it.

And Hester knew something about the symbols, too. She'd said as much when I asked her about the many-pointed stars on the Metzger barn.

Could magick have been used in Luc's murder?

Could Hester herself have been involved?

"I am worried about her."

Eli's sudden admission surprised me. I turned my attention to him, still sitting, as I was, within Christine's confines, staring into space.

"She is headstrong, that one. And she does not entirely fit in with our Amish here. She was an outsider when she married Luc, and she never learned to . . ." His voice trailed off, and he frowned. "Our women, they can be hard. Unyielding. Hester was too much her own person. She was different."

There was an edge to his tone that I'd never heard before. Admiration. If I didn't know any better, I might have thought . . . but she was his friend's wife. Eli would never have a thing for his friend's wife.

Would he?

He was a man.

A feeling man.

And he didn't have to act upon his feelings. That was something I knew he would never have done. But people cannot help having the feelings they have. They can only own them and find a way to live with and deal with them.

"Why are you so worried? Hester seems to have a handle on things." Better than I would have done in the same situation, that was for sure.

Eli's big, calloused hands worried the frayed edge of his Carhartt jacket, surprisingly gentle. "The women have turned their backs on her. It is as I thought it might be. They won't help her."

"I don't understand why —"

"They think she has turned away from God because of her ways. They blame her."

"For Luc?"

"And for other things. Cows that have dried up, or milk spoiling in the cans. Sick hogs. Chickens that won't give eggs."

I raised my brows and gaped at him. "You're kidding me! Aren't you? In this day and age?"

He shrugged. "Amish are afraid of Hexencraft, too."

Hexencraft. As in hexes. As in curses.

Hester.

Hester?

"How can they blame her for Luc?" I asked him. "Wasn't Hester home at the time Luc went missing?

"*Ja.* She took the children home. But the women, they think that somehow she invited his death. That she brought it down upon him and upon their family. And they think she is hexing the whole community, bringing shame down upon us all."

"That's ridiculous."

I thought about Hester all the way back to town. I felt connected to her, in a way. An outsider with abilities, living in an unsympathetic world. I wanted to believe that her only crime had been choosing to wed a man unworthy of her affections. A man she could not trust to be faithful to her, if what Eli intimated was true.

Because she had known. How did she live with that? How did she look him in the eye, day after day, knowing that he had been with another woman? Or *women?*

Maybe she hadn't lived with it. Maybe in her way she had done what she could to change her life.

Maybe she had done magic. Or worse.

I didn't like the thought. But what if somehow, in some way, she *was* involved?

CHAPTER 14

I had a surprise waiting for me at the store when I got back. Marion Tabor had arrived at the shop during my absence and had made an instant friend in Liss. The two were chatting away over tall cups of latte, hold the sprinkles, at the counter.

"Marion!" I said as I came around the corner and caught sight of her. I went to her and gave her a hug and a kiss on the cheek. "I don't think I've ever seen you in here before. Did you just now decide to check out our wares, or is this a social call?"

"Neither," Marion said, setting down her cup. "As I was just telling Liss here" — *Liss? My, my, they had become fast friends* — "the activity at the library has been at an all-time high since you and Marcus came by the other night. I'm surprised the patrons have been as blind as they seem to be. The closest anyone has come to saying anything about it is a gentleman who suggested we might think about having a plumber come out. Seems he'd been in the men's bathroom, and Bertie and company decided to have a little fun with him by flushing the toilets — one, two, three, four, right down the line. The question is, was the patron seated at the time? That's what I want to know."

She had a wicked twinkle in her eye at that. I couldn't help laughing. "You, madam, are terrible."

"Hey, the library gig can get a little dry, if a girl doesn't learn how to let down her hair from time to time."

"Laughter is the stuff of life," Liss agreed solemnly.

"Hear, hear. And so is research. Well, it is to a librarian," Marion said in all seriousness. "Speaking of which, that brings me to the real reason I came by. I found this in a dusty old tome in the basement of the Historical Society. From a history of the Rhodes family, formerly a family of note in Stony Mill." Reaching down, she lifted a pink leopard-print canvas tote bag, the depths of which could have hidden a real-life, nonpink leopard, to her ample lap. From inside it she withdrew a lined yellow legal pad, page upon page filled with copious notes in her fine hand.

She settled her reading glasses on the bridge of her nose, cleared her throat, and began to read:

November 12, 1908 — The library continues to be a resounding success and a great source of pleasure for me, as well as for our patrons. I am so very fortunate that Great-Uncle Gerald was able to influence the board on my behalf despite my age and inexperience; otherwise I might never have been allowed this opportunity to prove my value to this community as their <u>very first librarian</u>. Thank you, thank you, Uncle G!

Of course there is the slightest of problems in the boiler room — very slight — but that will all be sorted out eventually, I have the utmost of confidence in that regard. If nothing else, by next June at the latest! A June bride, can you imagine? My dearest Elliott will be so proud. Mummy is taking me to Chicago for the holidays. My trousseau shall be the best this town has ever seen. And to be presented on Elliott's arm as his wife, there will be nothing finer.

Marion looked at us from over her reading glasses. Expectantly.

"Kudos," I said as politely and supportively as possible. "Right up your alley, too. You've always loved being in the know about Stony Mill history."

Marion squinted at me to decide whether I was joking. "Yes, yes, of course. Be that as it may, you're missing my point."

"Oh. Sorry." I walked around the counter and poured myself a cup of orange pekoe, spicing it up with a dash of cinnamon and a dollop of honey. "Er, what was your point? Not that it wasn't interesting or anything," I hastened to assure her.

Marion exchanged a *help me?* glance with Liss, who seemed to have gotten it.

"The point, ducks," Liss explained, "is that the excerpt is from the personal diary of the town's first librarian. A very young woman, with a problem *in the boiler room.*"

Perhaps I was dim, but . . . "Bertie? But he couldn't have been a ghost back then, could he? The library was only built in 1907, if I remember the plaque on the wall correctly, and the fire in the boiler room — didn't that take place in 1909?"

"March of 1909, in fact," Marion clarified, waiting for me to make the connections my brain was so obviously missing out on.

"So," I said, my brain slowly whirring,

"Bertie's ghost wasn't the problem in the boiler room. It was Bertie himself? Live and in person?"

"Bingo!" Marion rifled through her bag, coming up with a folder from which she pulled a photocopy of a grainy, very old-style newspaper article. "Got this from the archives of *The Gazette*."

She passed it over to me. I scanned the article, which seemed to be a description of the fire that overwhelmed the lower level of the library in March of 1909, starting in the boiler room. A great number of volumes had been lost due to water and smoke damage. The article called for donations from the community to help renovate the damaged structure and to replace as many books as they could.

It also listed among the casualties one Bertram R. Norris of 710 East State Street, Stony Mill, aged forty-eight years. *Boiler Room Bertie.*

"The man was certainly tragic," I said. "First he falls for the young librarian, who is promised to another man, and then he dies in a freak fire. What a life."

"Oh, he didn't die in the fire," Marion said. "That was the story passed around in legend, but it wasn't true. He was injured, yes, but he didn't die for another ten years.

319

I have his obit here somewhere," she said, rifling some more. "But take a look at the only fatality listed in the article, farther down."

I read the last few paragraphs more thoroughly. There it was, in the second to last paragraph. Miss Helen Rhodes, aged twenty years, seven months.

"Helen was the librarian? The girl in the diary?" I breathed deeply of the truth and closed my eyes. My chest felt tight, hot. The photocopy began to shake in my hand. What was I doing to myself? I shook it off and opened my eyes. "She never married her Elliott. She died in the fire —"

"That started in the boiler room. And I think she's still there at the library. It was home to her. She never made a life with Elliott, never had children. The library, the books, they were her passion." Marion was getting into the discussion, a light of zeal shining in her eyes. "The fire — do you think that Bertie started it? Is that why he's still there? Out of guilt? Or because Helen is also there? Or is it because his presence is keeping her there, somehow? Keeping her from, what do you call it? Moving on?"

A pensive look came over Liss's features. "Bertie can't be holding Helen there. She died first. Her spirit had already decided not to leave, for whatever reason. It could even have been a case of simple confusion, the swiftness of the fire; perhaps she didn't realize right away that she had passed on. No, I think that Helen's and Bertie's reasons for staying are quite separate and individual."

"I think he loved her." The words popped out of my mouth, unbidden.

"Who, Elliott?" Marion said, frowning. "Well, I'm sure he did; they were engaged, after all —"

"Not Elliott. Bertie. I think it was more than just infatuation. I think he loved her."

"Enough to kill her," Liss asked, watching me closely, "by setting the fire?"

"It was never proven to be deliberately set," Marion said.

The three of us fell into a moment of silence, each absorbed in her own thoughts.

"I don't know," I said at last. "All I get when I think about Bertie is love. He loved her. Pure and simple. I don't get jealousy, I don't get rage. Just love."

"And what do you get when you think about Helen?"

"Fire. Just the fire. Thick, choking, traumatic." I didn't want to close my eyes again, I didn't want to turn inward. But . . . "No, that's all. Nothing else."

"What we need is something that belonged to the librarian. You know, for some good old-fashioned psychometry."

"Psychometry? You mean, you touch it, you feel it or think it?" I asked, frowning.

"The very same."

"I thought that sort of thing was just a joke that magicians do for a captive audience."

Liss gave me a patient, if inscrutable, smile. "Has anything that you've experienced with me been 'just a joke'?"

Ooooh, good point. Touché.

"Marcus is especially good at that sort of thing," Liss was telling Marion conversationally.

I felt my cheeks go hot against my will. I did not need to hear that Marcus was good at touching and feeling anything. Really I didn't.

Oblivious to my embarrassment, Marion said, "I might have just the thing for that, back at the library. You say Marcus has this talent? That nephew of mine is just full of surprises."

I could second that, but instead I changed the subject.

Well, I was about to. The ringing of the store phone eliminated the need.

I was only too happy to say, "I'll get it!"

I picked up the line. "Enchantments Antiques and Fine Gifts. This is Maggie. How can I help you today?"

"Maggie, oh, good, it's you. I was hoping it would be. This is Louisa Murray. Listen, I have a proposition for you. You mentioned that your boss was one of the ladies bidding for the big armoire in the auction up at the market the other day. Is that right?"

"Hi, Louisa. It's good to hear from you. Yes, that's right."

"Perfect. How would she like to own it after all?"

I blinked into space. "I'm sorry?"

"I've been reconsidering the purchase. Buyer's remorse, I guess. It's too big for my little house, really, and I couldn't really afford to pay what I paid — I suppose I just got caught up in the excitement of the auction. And . . . well . . . if you think your boss might like to buy it from me . . ."

"Hold on one sec."

I set the phone down on the counter and put the call on hold. Liss and Marion stopped talking and looked expectantly at me.

"It's Mrs. Murray on the phone," I told Liss.

"Louisa Murray from St. Catherine's?" Marion asked.

"She's the person Mom called for help with our charitable efforts for the Metzger family. We met with her yesterday."

Marion nodded her approval. "Louisa's always been very organized, a key member of the Necessities for the Needful team."

"She has a proposition for you," I said to Liss.

"For me?"

"Mmhmm. Remember the armoire?"

"Eli's armoire?"

"The very same. Louisa is the person who outbid you at the auction. She wants to offer it to you."

Taken aback, my usually unflappable boss could not conceal her surprise. "Really?"

"Something about not having enough room for it, and all."

Liss picked up the phone. Marion excused herself, saying she needed to get back to the library, but I made no bones about listening in.

"This is Felicity Dow. Yes, hello. Congratulations on your winning bid at the auction. Very well done, indeed. I understand from Maggie that you're reconsidering your purchase. Yes. Well, obviously that would suit me. It really is just the thing for the store, and as the piece was built by a friend of mine, it has special significance as well.

Yes. Certainly. I'll have someone come by tomorrow — Oh, no problem whatsoever. This afternoon, then. Yes, thank you. I'm sorry it didn't work for you. Thank you again. Good-bye."

She set the phone down gently on the receiver, lost in thought.

"Well?" I prompted.

She glanced at me over her crescent-moon glasses. "I don't suppose your father is available with his pickup truck this afternoon?"

Smiling, I shook my head. "No, he'll be at work. But I might be able to borrow it. We're picking up the armoire?"

"Aye. We're picking up the armoire. She'd . . . Mrs. Murray would like us to come out as soon as we can."

"What's the rush?" I asked, curious.

"I'm not sure, but there was most definitely a sense of urgency on her part."

I had gotten that same thing from the conversation. Hurry winging its way along the phone lines. Maybe Grace's comments about the spirit of a dead person clinging to an object that was important in life had gotten to Louisa more than she'd let on. That wasn't the kind of thing that Liss would be superstitious about though.

As I'd expected, my dad wasn't home, but my mother told me it would be fine to use his pickup. I was just trying to think who I could get to help with moving heavy furniture when Evie and Tara arrived at the store after school, trailed by a strong, muscle-bound jock, complete with letter jacket.

"Hey, Liss! Hey, Maggie!" Evie called, heading straight for the back office to hang up her things.

Tara followed at a more measured pace, focused on ignoring the boy who was hanging on her every nonuttered word. Upon second glance, I recognized him — Charlie Howell, one of the best and brightest on the high school basketball team. A scant five months ago, Charlie had been completely (and tragically, as it turned out) enamored of Amanda Roberson. Her death had launched him headlong into an emotional loop that I worried he might never find his way out of.

If the soft look lighting his eyes as he gazed at the back of Tara's head was any indication, my worry had been for naught. Time, it seemed, was the great healer of all wounds, especially when one had youth on one's side.

"Hi, Tara. And Charlie — I haven't seen you in quite a while," I said by way of welcome.

He waved at me. "Hey, Ms. O'Neill. How

are ya? You seem to have gotten over that bump on your head."

I put my hand to my scalp, the lump long forgotten. "I did, at that."

Tara slid her glance sideways at her companion, as though trying to make sense of the exchange. I couldn't help noticing that her usually enigmatic smile burned a bit brighter when it turned in Charlie's direction.

It occurred to me that the kids could be the answer to the impromptu change in plans. "Charlie, could we enlist your help while you're here? We have a big armoire we need to pick up and bring to the store. We could use some help, if you're interested. We'd be happy to pay you for the trouble."

Tara quirked her shoulder at him, a pretty movement meant to beguile and intrigue. I wondered where she had learned it. "Do you think you could take the time to help us?" she asked, her voice soft and somehow helpless.

One look at her, and he was a goner. "Sure. Not a problem. Count me in."

"Oh, good," Tara said, winking at me. "That's so sweet of you."

"Okay, great. Thank you. Evie, what about you?" I asked as she parted the velvet curtains. "I need to get my dad's pickup, and then we're going to be picking up a cabinet from a house across town. Wanna come with us?"

"Oh, I'm in, too. The three of us should be able to handle it, shouldn't we?"

I retrieved the handcart we used for boxes from the backroom. Charlie took one look at it and squinched up his face.

"Um, you know, I don't think that's gonna do the trick."

I frowned down at it. "Really?"

"Huh-uh. But hey, I'll bet we have something at the hardware store that could handle it. Let me call my boss and see if we could borrow it for a little while."

He whipped out his cell phone before I had a chance even to say thank you. Tara caught my eye as if to say *Isn't he perfect?* I had to admit, he did seem to have a lot going for him. I was glad for both of them that Amanda's death had not dealt too harsh a blow.

We commandeered the pickup truck from my dad's garage, the cart from the hardware store, and Tony, a friend of Charlie's who seemed to have nothing better to do with his time, and the lot of us drove to Louisa Murray's home on the edge of town. I stepped out of the pickup and stood on the street, looking at the house while I waited for the kids to leap down out of the truck bed. The house and property looked even darker today, even more overgrown beneath the gray sky.

At least there were no smears of manure or egg yolk to deal with today. Louisa must have worked her butt off.

Speak of the devil. Louisa stood just inside the front door, watching us. She looked as though she'd been there a while. I held up a hand in greeting. Seeing me, she backed away from the door. To clear a path for us, I presumed.

Charlie and Tony pulled the handcart out of the bed of the pickup. The two boys were already proving their worth beyond their muscles — they'd thought to bring a number of thick boards to use as a ramp up into the back.

"This the right place?" Charlie asked, looking at the house.

"Uh-huh."

"Someone needs to hack the woods back — it looks like it's going to swallow up the house if they're not careful."

I'd had that same impression.

My four chatty teenagers fell silent as we approached the house.

Louisa opened the door as we drew near. "Thank you for coming so soon," she said to me. "I'm sorry to have to push the transaction on such short notice, but I'm glad it worked out."

"Is everything okay, Mrs. Murray?" I asked her. I sensed a change in the atmosphere in the house from my previous visit, one I couldn't seem to put my finger on. It didn't feel good. I couldn't help wondering what the poor woman had been going through.

"Fine. Everything's fine. In here."

She led us to the craft room off the hallway. The boys stopped and raised their eyebrows.

"Whoa," Tony said.

"Too big for us to handle?" I asked, grimacing as I waited for the answer.

"I'm not sure," said Charlie, circling around the armoire on three sides to get a good look at it. "I hope not."

He braced his hand on the corner and tested the weight by trying to shimmy it back and forth. Tony followed his example, and the two of them set to work.

Evie and Tara stood back and let the boys do their thing while I stood by, worrying and fussing and directing traffic like any mother hen worth her weight in chicken feed. "This way. Mind the door frame. Okay, now, a little to the left. Good, good.

Okay, wait. Maybe a little to the right. Watch out for the" — too late — "plant stand."

Oooh!

I decided that running a bit of interference with Louisa might be a better use of my time.

"By the way, Louisa, I did find the owners of that dog," I told her. "I was so glad not to have to drop it off at a shelter." I didn't mention the Metzger connection, just in case the poor woman was too freaked about the armoire thanks to Grace Mansfield's wagging tongue.

"Did you?" Louisa's gaze cooled measurably. She had a real thing against that dog, that was for sure. It was a shame, really. I had the feeling she could use a little companionship in her life, and a pet seemed the perfect solution. "I do hope they learn to keep the dog under control on their farm now and not allow it to run all over God's creation, threatening innocent people. It was nothing but a pest."

Ah, well. So much for that.

The boys broke a clay pot on their way down the manure-free front steps. Okay, so maybe this interference thing wasn't going to work out as well as I'd hoped. I sent Evie and Tara out to lead the boys through the front yard before they managed to take out what was left of Louisa's prized roses and the picket fence as well.

"I'm sorry it didn't work out for you with the armoire," I told Louisa. "Marion Tabor had mentioned how excited you were to win it, and I know you must have felt very strongly about it to pay so much for it."

Louisa nodded crisply. "Yes, well . . . It's all for the best. As I told Mrs. Dow, it was simply too big. It didn't fit my room at all, and it was too much a reminder of what had happened to that poor man. I just didn't want it around me anymore. Grace Mansfield was right. Who needs a reminder of tragedy such as that? I'm happy to let your boss take it off my hands. I can find something else to suit my needs elsewhere."

Something that didn't have a memory of blood and violence attached. I saw her point.

"Well, it looks like the boys are almost through. I think I'd better go out there and be sure they get it into the back of the truck without mishap."

"Oh, I don't know. They look like very handy boys," Mrs. Murray said, assessing them thoroughly through critical eyes as they strained and shoved, rocked and maneuvered. "You know, I could use a little help around here from time to time."

Poor Mrs. Murray. She was a woman who had lost her husband and who was now striving to make sense of her world without him. It wasn't that she was incapable of understanding about lawn care and home repairs and automobile upkeep. It was just that those things fell outside of her area of comfort. I could totally relate.

A couple of forceful growls, a whoop, and a high five later, the boys had settled the armoire into place. Bungee cords and an old blanket protected the piece from moving too much as we rolled slowly through the streets, avoiding the areas where after-work traffic congregated. Finally we made it downtown and down the hill toward River Street, and I pulled to the curb in front of the store.

"Whew!" Charlie stood up and clapped his hand against the side of the armoire. "I was a little scared going down that last hill, there. This puppy is tippy because it's so tall."

The kids were in the process of hopping down, chattering animatedly among themselves, when a police cruiser pulled up behind us. My heart leapt as Tom got out of the cruiser and started walking toward me.

"Maggie." He nodded.

I smiled at him. "What a surprise — I

didn't expect to see you this afternoon."

"I'm not here for pleasure. I have to ask you for your license and registration, Maggie."

"My — what?"

"License and registration. Please."

CHAPTER 15

He was wearing that no-nonsense, authoritative attitude that drove me crazy — and not in a good way. "Sure. Did I do something wrong . . . Officer?"

The kids were watching with a mixture of amusement and embarrassment and cringing empathy. I sighed. "Why don't you all go inside? Unless Deputy Fielding here is going to need you as witnesses."

Tom was busy writing down my driver's license number and the pickup truck's vehicle registration information, and he barely noticed. "No, that's fine. I'll come and get you if I need you."

"All right, big guy, what's going on?" I asked as soon as they'd disappeared behind the glass door. I wasn't fooled, though — I knew they were there, their noses resting just behind the lacy sheers.

"What's this here in the back?"

I turned my gaze to the left. "Lessee.

Wood, heavy, carved. Looks like furniture to me."

"I see that. Maggie, did you know it's a moving violation to transport people in the back of a pickup truck?"

"Is it?"

"Yes, it is."

"Oh." I bit my lip. "In my defense, I don't usually drive a pickup truck, as you well know, and actually, we were just trying to transport the cabinet safely. Mrs. Murray wanted us to come and get it straightaway, which left us precious little time to plan, and . . . none of this makes a difference, does it."

"Unfortunately, no." He scribbled some more. "You know what they say about ignorance of the law."

Crap.

"I, uh, suppose you're going to give me a ticket."

He leaned a hip against the truck. "I should. If the chief, or one of the other deputies, saw you trail through town, it would have been a done deal. Especially since we're dealing with minors here."

"But you're not going to?"

He shrugged. "No harm, no foul. I'll give you a verbal warning and leave it at that. But if you do it again . . ."

"I won't. Promise. I wouldn't have this time, except we had no other choice." I leaned against the truck, too. "You know, if you weren't in uniform, I could kiss you right now."

A smile twitched at the corner of his mouth, but he stared at the storefront across the street. "Trying to bribe or coerce an officer of the law, Miss O'Neill?"

"No, sir. Not me. Tell you what, how about if I buy you a cup of coffee instead? I have an 'in' with the owner."

I saw his gray eyes flicker toward the store, the flicker that advised caution before all else. He didn't often step over the threshold into Enchantments, but in my opinion it was high time he saw that the store, and Liss, were not threats to his world.

"All right. Sure. A cup of coffee would be great."

Yay! A baby step was, nevertheless, a step in the right direction.

I saw the curtain move as we headed toward the storefront. "Careful, it's bad form to step on the audience," I said as I pushed through the door. "Excuse us, people, coming through."

Evie had the good manners to blush at having been caught. The boys were looking anywhere but out the door. Tara, on the other hand, stared Tom down as though he was the enemy storming the gate.

I smiled at her. "I thought I'd buy Deputy Fielding a cup of coffee before he leaves."

"Why? He doesn't make enough to buy his own coffee busting people for perfectly honest misunderstandings? I mean, geez, Maggie. Why'd you have to bring him in here?" She turned and stormed off toward the office.

I looked to Evie for an explanation, but she just caught her lip between her teeth and shrugged her shoulders.

Charlie cleared his throat. "I, uh, think she's a little worked up about the boys Deputy Fielding took out of school for questioning."

"But I thought — yesterday she seemed to think — you mean she thinks they're innocent?"

"I dunno 'bout that. She does, um, think the cops act before they fully investigate." Charlie gazed toward Tom. "Sorry about that."

Tom, to his credit, said nothing.

Tony looked around the assembled group. "So, uh, I think I need to get going. Places to go. You know."

"You need a ride?" Charlie asked him. "I

think I'll stick around a little while, otherwise."

"Nah, dude. My mom works at the courthouse. I'll just catch a ride with her."

I couldn't say that I blamed them. "Hey, Tony, thanks for your help today. Here, we want you to have this as a token of our appreciation. We couldn't have done it without you." I pressed some money into his hand, holding it there when he tried to refuse it. "Really."

When he had gone, I headed over to the counter to grab a coffee for Tom. "Evie, where did Liss go?"

"Oh, she's upstairs. Looking for a place to put the armoire."

I raised my brows. "She wants it to go upstairs?"

Charlie whistled. "Maybe I should call Tony back here, huh?"

"Well . . ." I let my gaze drift toward Tom.

Tom sighed. "The big thing out front?"

"Uh-huh. Wow, that's so sweet of you to help us!" I said, following Tara's example. I patted Tom's arm as he passed me. Nice, strong . . . perfect. Just what we needed.

Tara emerged from the office just in time to witness my slick female maneuverings. I glanced over at her as Tom passed me, and had to smother a laugh when she gave me a big thumbs-up. Good, that meant she'd risen above her huff.

The trip from the truck into the store was even more eventful than the trip from Louisa Murray's house to the truck. Several *oooofs,* a muffled curse, and a mashed thumb later, Tom and Charlie had managed to push, pull, and force the armoire through to the main aisle, but no farther.

"Dear, dear. This is going to be a little harder than I had anticipated," Liss said, watching the proceedings from behind the safety of the counter.

"Maybe we should rethink the loft idea," I suggested.

Tom and Charlie both nodded emphatically.

Tara and Evie had taken up perches on top of the counter, out of harm's way. Evie sat gracefully with her legs bent to one side, looking delicate and feminine to the max. Tara, with her darker hair and nimble frame, sat alarmingly cross-legged in her short skirt and dark tights, her elbows resting on her knees and her chin resting on her hands. A pixie by nature if I ever saw one.

"Oh, I don't know," Tara said, a wicked gleam in her eye. "That place in the loft was pretty perfect for it."

Tom and Charlie glared at each other. "Yeah," Tom said, "right here is good, I think."

"Couldn't be more perfect," Charlie agreed.

They leaned against the sturdy wooden piece to catch their breath and rest their aching muscles.

"Eli certainly does make sturdy furniture, doesn't he?" Liss marveled, admiring his craftsmanship. She stepped around the counter and ran her hands over it. "It really is beautiful. These carvings that Luc Metzger did, too . . ."

Tara slid off the counter and came nearer. "Hex symbolism again. What is it with all the hex symbols around here lately?"

Liss pulled her glasses down from the top of her head and slid them into place as I moved in closer. "Well, Great Goddess, I do believe she's right."

"Wait. What?" Tom leaped away as though the carving was burning itself into his skin. "What did you say? On this thing, too?"

Charlie looked at us as though he was seeing us in focus for the very first time. "*Hex* symbols? What d'you mean, like curses? And what d'you mean, *too?*"

Tara shrugged. "There's different kinds. Not all are bad. Most are just protective markings. Ask me later, and I'll explain everything."

Six people standing in a circle around a piece of furniture. I'll bet that from the outside we looked pretty strange. The view from where I stood wasn't much better. I studied the carvings more closely, but they just looked like carvings to me. A pinwheel spiral here, a roped chain of ivy there. Plump-bellied birds, four-leaf clovers, and starbursts.

Liss turned her back on the lot of us and retrieved the thick encyclopedia of magical symbols from beneath the counter. "Sigils, symbols, iconic talismans of magical purpose. Of course each magical tradition and region of origin seems to breed new and different meanings. Luc's carvings on the armoire seem to be most similar to the Pow-Wow folk magick. There are several major and recurring themes, but with faint differences." She thumbed quickly through the book until she came upon the section she was looking for, flipped the book open so that the cover lay flat, then spun it around for the perusal of all.

"Hexes," Tom said in a flat voice. "Magical. Symbols."

I nodded. He needed to understand as much as we needed to talk things out. "According to Eli, the Metzgers hailed from the Amish in the Lancaster, Pennsylvania, area. Eli said that the carvings Luc preferred were much more ornate than anything he or any other Amish furniture maker from this area would ever include on furniture. A difference in theologies. I guess I'm as guilty as anyone else, thinking that Amish are Amish are Amish."

"Wow," Charlie muttered, unable to stop looking back and forth between the book on the counter and the carvings in the wood.

Poor kid. I got it. I did. "Charlie, you don't have to stay if this is making you uncomfortable. Really. We know it's a lot to absorb."

We should have been more careful, but Tara had never been reticent about running her mouth with the strength of her convictions, and they were indeed a power to behold.

Charlie cleared his throat and darted a glance at Tara. "Yeah. Yeah, maybe I'd better get going. It's late, and I've got a calc test tomorrow."

" 'Kay."

Tara walked with him toward the door, but their voices drifted back to us. You didn't miss much in the store's controlled space.

"Hey, y'know, we should study together sometime."

" 'Kay," she said, a little brighter.

"Like, uh, maybe this weekend?"

" 'Kay." Even brighter still. In fact, Tara was practically glowing. "Yeah, this weekend. We could do that."

He grinned and took her sleeve delicately between his thumb and forefinger, rocking her arm gently back and forth. " 'Kay. See you at school tomorrow."

" 'Kay."

She practically floated back to us when he was gone. I'd never seen Tara, my favorite Goth girl, float before. It was actually kind of nice — it lit up her entire spirit. Evie and Liss and I smiled broadly, watching her. When she noticed, she retreated back within her usual dark and dangerous persona, and scowled.

"What?" she demanded. "Geez, you're like the Goodwill Ambassadors or something. Haven't you ever seen someone leave before?"

I didn't tell her how nice it was to witness something normal in the midst of all the weirdness. How wonderful it was to see the two of them grab a little bit of romance from the blackness that had threatened to descend upon them last winter. Surely there was hope for us all.

Tom was feeling much less benevolent. "So, now that the kid's gone, anyone here want to tell me what all this hex symbol stuff means? First there's the one at the crime scene, which I have to tell you wigged me right out, and now they're all over this piece of furniture, and —"

"And have you ever been out to the Metzger farm?" I asked him in a calm voice, cutting into the tirade.

Confusion. "Well, no. Not me personally. Chief went out to talk to Mrs. Metzger that night because I was tied up at the scene. It was on my list. Why?"

I struggled to put my thoughts into words. "I think that Mrs. Metzger might be the person responsible for the hex symbol on the tree." I held up a hand as he opened his mouth. "Just an idea," I said before he could challenge further. "I was out at their farm with Eli and the dog — which proved to belong to the Metzger family, by the way, how weird is that? — and I noticed that the Metzgers have quite a number of pretty unusual signs on their barn siding. I've never noticed them around here before, but I suppose I could be wrong. And since they're from the Pennsylvania Amish community . . ."

I let my voice trail off, hoping he would make the same connection I was still formulating in my own head.

His eyes searched my own for hidden meanings, but I didn't often play those games. "So, if Mrs. Metzger is responsible for the hex symbol and maybe, possibly, hex magic, are you saying she knows something about Luc's death as well, just because she knew about his affairs? Because if you're saying that, then I have to tell you — Mrs. Metzger has an alibi, Maggie. Airtight. We've checked it out: upside down, left, right, and sideways. The entire Amish congregation was there that evening, as well as her kids, and later several women from the Amish community whose husbands were out there looking for Luc when he didn't come home."

An airtight alibi. Was there such a thing when magic was involved? *Could* a very strong hex have brought about Luc's murder somehow? Or could it be that there were other forces that could have been employed by one skilled in Pow-Wow magic that perhaps none of us were aware of?

"Wait. Did you just say that Luc had another woman?"

Tom faltered a moment, then his face closed down instantly, as though someone

346

had suddenly slammed the shutters over a bright window. Not good enough, though — because few shutters are successful at completely blocking out all the light from the other side. Glimmers flash between the cracks, peek around edges, squeeze through from the top and bottom, and I could see. And feel. And *know.*

"He did, didn't he?" I said, closely evaluating the play of emotion I saw in him. "I mean, I had wondered that myself, but to know for sure . . ."

Tom shook his head. "We don't know for sure. We're guessing ourselves. All we have to go by are the suspicions Hester Metzger put forth in a letter to her husband. No one else has stepped forward."

"You didn't say anything about a letter before."

The blinds behind his eyes flickered once, and then closed again. He glanced over at Liss and the girls, who were trying to look busy and failing miserably.

"Is there some place we can talk privately?"

Liss cleared her throat. "There's always the loft," she offered helpfully.

I nodded. Silently I led Tom down the short hall and up the stairs. There was a bench there against the gallery railing. I took him by the hand and guided him over.

He sat on the edge of the bench, his spine ramrod straight, as he took in the surroundings. "It doesn't look much different than it did last October."

I looked around, too. The loft was one of my favorite indoor places in the whole world. There was a sense of extreme peace here, a sense of sanctity not often found outside the walls of a very old church. There was energy here, too, of the most benevolent kind. Liss had once told me she'd placed Invisible Threshold wards around the area she used for casting — not even I approached that space without invitation.

"Less broken glass, perhaps," I said with a half smile.

"Less danger?"

I met his searching gaze without hesitation. "Much less. There is nothing to worry about here, Tom. *Trust me.*" *Trust me. Open your mind. Trust in my friends.* Because for me that was the truth at the heart of all this, wasn't it?

"Maggie, I'm trying to. Despite the fact that your boss and her beliefs make me *real* nervous. But you're going to have to understand that I'm a cop. Sometimes there are going to be things I'm not allowed to talk about. Evidence in a murder investigation being one of them."

"Like the letter."

"Yes."

"That Hester wrote to Luc. That you found somewhere, or were given."

Something was making me push those buttons, making me press harder. Maybe I needed him to open up his mind just a little bit. To know that he could. Because I knew that if he couldn't do that much, then I would never be able to completely open my heart and soul to him.

I needed to know, one way or the other.

Exasperated, he leaned back against the railing and just looked at me. He didn't say anything. He didn't have to. His true feelings were coming through so loud and clear, I didn't have to put out any special effort to intercept them. I was picking them up — and more — without any help.

"You were given it," I said, watching his face. "Maybe in his wallet, I'm guessing. Which I wasn't aware you'd found. Unless you were given that, too."

Crossing his arms, Tom shook his head. Stubborn, stubborn, stubborn. "If you're trying to impress me —"

"I'm not."

"— then you're not doing a very good job. What, you took psych in high school, right?

349

It's not all that impressive. The science of body language."

I shrugged. "If that's what you want to call it. Yours is saying a whole lot right now, by the way. You're closing yourself off. No, that's not it. You never opened yourself up to begin with. You don't trust me. You don't trust anyone, do you, Tom?"

"It has nothing to do with that," he started to scoff, but I knew better.

"Doesn't it? There are people connections that go beyond rules and regulations. Beyond science as we know it. Forgive me for saying this, but if we're ever going to mean anything to each other, I really need to know that we have that kind of connection. Or, at the very least, that we have the potential to get there some day."

He was silent a moment, considering my words.

"Tom, listen very carefully, because I have something important to tell you. Whether you believe in them or not, there *are* things in this world that might frighten you — people with abilities, and so much more — but that doesn't mean they're evil, or guided by evil, or even affected by evil. People can be psychic and empathic, and some can even speak with the dead, but still be a part of the goodness that balances out the dark."

"That's what you believe, is it?"

"Yes."

"Why?"

"Because I know these people. Because I know their hearts." It was time to admit the truth. For better or for worse. "And because I'm one of them."

He stared at me, and then, little by little, his mouth dropped open as though he would speak but couldn't form the words.

"I *sense* things. And the sensing, sometimes it gives me information that I otherwise would not have. Feelings. Sometimes the motivation behind a feeling. Like right now, I can feel the fear creeping along your skin, but I know that you're trying very hard to hide it behind bravado because you don't think a man should be afraid of anything. Are you afraid of me, Tom?"

A moment's pause, and then he shook his head. "No."

"Do you believe me when I say that you can trust me? That I would never abuse whatever you might tell me in confidence? Honestly. Most of the time, it's probably going to go in one ear and out the other. You know that, don't you? I don't want to feel like you're intentionally being cautious with every little thing you say to me. I don't want to feel like you're weighing every word, assessing every moment. That's not trust."

Then again, neither was allowing another man to kiss you . . . but I pushed all thoughts of Marcus away.

"No," he said, watching me. "No, it's not."

"Is that what we have?" I asked him quietly.

"I hope not," he answered, just as quietly.

"Do you think you can trust me, just a little bit, despite what I am?"

He took a deep breath, taking my hand as he let it out slowly. Still I could feel the struggle within him. "You were right. We were given the wallet. One of the boys admitted that they had it, but he swore up and down that they'd found it in the woods where they hang out. He as much as admitted to the assault on the other Amish man, but not on Luc Metzger. Wanted to cut a deal with me for handing it over."

I searched his eyes. "Do you believe him? That they'd only found the wallet?"

"I don't know. I don't have enough evidence either way, yet. Suspicion is pretty compelling, though, considering the method of the assault was the same. They had the other man's wallet in their possession, and now they had Luc Metzger's, too. I don't like coincidence." He took a deep breath. "The letter was with the wallet. It was written by Hester to Luc, begging him to leave off the love affair he was engaged in, once and for all. We don't know who he'd been with. No leads there yet. Now," he said, squeezing my fingers tightly, "since we're sharing here, tell me why you suspected he'd had other women."

I looked down at our joined hands. Fingers interlacing, heat, and feeling. "It was a feeling, more than anything. I saw him that morning, at the auction. He was a good-looking guy, you know. Different from all the other Amish men I can remember seeing. He had an aura about him, a confidence in the way he held himself. He oozed it. Then there was the way he looked at women. Like he knew exactly what he had going on. I saw him after, too, when I was buying noodles from Hester."

Briefly I described how he had met my gaze while his wife's back was turned. The directness that seemed intended to let a woman know that he knew just what she thought of him.

Tom absorbed it all, every last word, every last impression and intuition. "The boy I told you about? He took us out to where he said they'd found the wallet, and it did look like there had been foot traffic there. Grass trampled in the area, plants broken, that

353

sort of thing. We know the boys were seen together at a convenience store that evening, and were back for lockdown at the Lodge by their eight-thirty curfew, but there's a span of time there in the early evening that isn't accounted for. The boys are a definite possibility, wanting to cut a deal or no — it could just be they're trying to head off a more serious charge. But I don't know. There's still something about this whole thing that just doesn't feel right. I can't put my finger on it."

Now he was venturing into *my* territory of feeling and emotion, and while I knew it wouldn't last, I was determined to make the most of it.

"Where did the boy say they'd found it?"

"Out in Alden Woods. Inland from where Luc was found. It's a pretty big area — stretches from that county road all the way over to the outside edge of town — and it's a known playground for the teenage boys of Blackhawk. They've been giving us a run for our money lately, that's for sure. We've had loads of complaints coming in, and backlash running counter to the complaints as well."

"Don't they have security measures in place at Blackhawk?" I asked him.

"Yeah, sure. Curfews and lockdowns. But

it seems pretty easy for the boys to get out and about whenever they damn well please."

"So," I said, "exactly what are we dealing with here? Why was Luc killed?"

"Damned if I know. But I'm starting to get that itchy feeling, Maggie. There's something I'm missing, and I hate that. I'm a cross your Ts kind of guy."

I heaved a sigh. "I hate to say this, because I really feel bad for her, but if you look at things from a purely factual perspective, I still think that Hester is a strong possibility, despite the alibi. Revenge is a pretty big motivator. Even among pacifists. A person can easily say 'Turn the other cheek,' but until faced with betrayal of the most hurtful kind, can they know how they might react?"

"A woman scorned?" His mouth tightened into a grim line. "Yeah, but she has all those kids, and a mother's protective instincts are pretty strong, too. Would she really risk their safety as well as her own in order to extract her pound of flesh from a cheating husband when divorce was unlikely? I know it's possible — everything is possible — but is it likely? Pacifist beliefs among the Amish are a pretty hard-line principle. Not something she would turn away from easily. Besides, she's a woman. She could have made him suffer in so many other ways."

Oh, that was sooo chauvinistic.

Pain and suffering had so many different faces. So many different victims. And betrayal had a way of bringing them all to the surface.

"There, um, there are symbols marked in the margins of the letter itself," he confided haltingly. "Like the one on the tree. Maybe you could take a look at them later. Maybe if we understand the symbols, we might understand her state of mind when she wrote the letter. They might be important, and I know no one on the force can help me with them."

It was a step in the right direction. A huge step, for Tom. I knew what it must have cost him. "I'll see what I can do."

CHAPTER 16

The girls didn't say anything until Tom had gone on his way. Then everyone gathered around me as I pretended to concentrate on the day's receipts.

"So?"

I glanced up as Tara leaned her elbows on the counter. "So?"

"What did the Copmeister want?"

Tara wasn't exactly reserved about voicing her opinions on societal influences, so this was nothing new. "What makes you think he wanted something?"

She arched her brow at me. "Are you denying it?"

I glanced at Evie, but she was watching me just as curiously. "Not necessarily. What makes you think he didn't just want the opportunity to kiss me senseless without comment or helpful pointers from the peanut gallery?"

"Him? Please. I don't know what you see

in him, Maggie."

"He has his good points. And besides, I don't know why you think that's any of your business."

She shrugged. "I just want the best for you, that's all."

"Well, that's nice. But I can handle that part of my life on my own. It works out better that way."

"I suppose."

"I mean, you wouldn't want me to make helpful suggestions to you about Charlie Howell, would you?"

She snorted. "Yeah, right. Like I need any help from you. Er, what I mean is" — she backtracked quickly with an apologetic grin — "Charlie and I are taking things slow. I'm a great believer in destiny. If it's meant to be, it's meant to be. I've got the time. Whereas you're getting up there in years, and you're needing things to get a move on. If you get my meaning."

I did. Only too loud and clear. And why did that make me want to make a mad grab for the chocolate display?

I waited until Tara and Evie had gone into the back to take care of a delivery before I spoke to Liss, who had absorbed the entire exchange with quiet amusement. "Would you mind if I borrowed your nephew's book for the evening?" I asked.

"Not at all." She took out a tote bag and put the book inside, tucking tissue paper all around it to disguise it. "There we are. One book of magical symbols, incognito. No one will ever guess." As an afterthought, she grabbed a couple of red candles and a glass tray and wrapped those to tuck into the bag as well. At my raised eyebrows, she said, innocently enough, "Red is for passion and romance, you know. Just in case you wanted to — how did Tara so succinctly put it? — *'Get a move on.'* "

Et tu, Liss? Et tu?

"Thanks. I think."

"Any time, ducks. Don't forget to state your intent in your mind before you light the candles if you want to use them for anything more pertinent than soft lighting. Oh, and if you need any input, just give us a ring. I should be home later this evening."

It wasn't that I didn't want Liss's help, but I had told Tom he could trust me, and I was bound and determined not to say anything about it without his permission.

The book called to me as soon as I got in my car. I took it out of the bag, smoothing my hand over the cover, feeling its heft. The amount of knowledge and scholarship in

359

this thick volume would be enough, I hoped, to steer us in the right direction. A light to guide the way.

I dialed Tom's cell.

"Fielding."

"Hi, it's me," I said when he picked up. "I'm on my way home. I have a book that might help with the symbolism."

"Maggie, you're awesome. Can you leave it with me?"

"Oh. Oh, I don't know that I can do that. It's Liss's book, actually. I told her I was only borrowing it for the night."

"Damn. I'm tied up right now. There's no way I'll be getting out of here for hours."

"Well . . . You know, if you wanted to, you could make a copy of the letter for me. I'd be happy to start sorting through the symbols myself. You can stop by my place when you do get free."

"I don't know," he hedged.

"Did you want to draw out the symbols for me? I could pick them up."

"Well, I guess it wouldn't hurt anything. I'll leave it in an envelope for you at the front desk."

Another huge foray into the realm of trust. "Okay. See you later?"

"Count on it. And Maggie? Thanks."

I hung up, feeling warm and wonderful

and somehow useful. At least, I hoped I would be of use to him.

Tom had everything ready when I arrived at the police station. I picked up the envelope from Jeannette, and was out the door in minutes and on my way again. I couldn't resist peeking inside the envelope in the parking lot, to see what he'd decided to share.

He hadn't bothered drawing out the symbols. He'd given me a photocopy of the letter itself. He did trust me. He did.

I was getting that warm and mushy feeling again. Followed immediately by a moment of guilt when an image of Marcus nudged its way in. What was wrong with me? And where was Grandma Cora's voice of reason when I needed it?

It took every scrap of patience I owned to make myself wait until I reached my apartment on Willow Street before I took the letter out of the envelope.

Silently, feeling a bit voyeuristic but unable to look only at the markings that had baffled Tom, I read the letter that Hester had written to her husband less than a week ago.

My darling Luc,
    I beg of you, don't turn away from me.

Do not think that I don't see the things that you have been doing. I am not blind, unless it is blindness that causes me to love you despite your weakness. You must stop this, for once and for all. You are my husband, in the eyes of God and all the world. You must turn your face away from the temptation that guides you to others for comfort. I am here, and I give myself to you willingly, body, mind, and soul, for you to do with what you will. I give myself to you completely. Once you loved me above all else and you made me yours, and I am yours still. You must see that . . .

Tears streamed down my cheeks with each besotted, gut-wrenching avowal of love and forgiveness. A desperation born of love and mindless devotion settled in my heart, crept along my nerve endings, and lodged in the pit of my stomach. I was shaking by the time I finished the letter, signed so plainly:

Love always,
Your Hester

Simple words, and I felt them all as though I had written them myself. She loved him so much, and still he had turned from her to another woman, despite the fact that she knew of his actions and had pleaded with him to stop, to cast the other woman aside, to love only her.

And now he had gotten himself killed.

The question was, Was it Hester herself who had done the deed?

There were four sigils, each identical, one drawn in each corner of the letter. Surrounding her words. This one was different from the sigil that had been nailed to the tree. That one had possessed a darker feel, one of strength and power.

I didn't need the book for this one.

This symbol was a prescription for love. A ward to preserve it, to strengthen it — I felt sure of it. Within a circle rimmed with a scalloped edge there was an eagle with one wing spread wide and the other wing curved around another bird, reminiscent of a cooing dove or quail. The second bird's full breast was drawn flush with hearts, and what looked like open tulips trailed from its beak. It was very hearts and flowers, very romantic in feel, and the colors that had been filled into the ink drawing — blue, pink, white, and yellow — definitely followed suit.

What was it about love that tied betrayal to it so irrevocably and so often? In my mind's eye, I saw Hester that day at the 4-H fairground at Heritage Park, pink-cheeked and lovely with her wayward lock of auburn hair escaping her tidy white cap. And I saw Luc, too, an angel of a man with a devil riding his back. And I couldn't help but wonder how things had gone so wrong for this young couple.

A beautiful man.

Too beautiful.

Oversexed.

Was he also overhexed?

No more, she had told him.

Just this one last time.

Heartsick, I searched through the book until I found the section Liss had marked earlier: "Folk Magic in America." Needing as much time as possible to gather my thoughts, I began to read the scholarly treatise. How the protective symbols came with settlers from the Old World, mostly Germany and Switzerland, but the magical practices had tended to blend and merge with the mythology of people from other European countries as well. How they were used mainly as protective measures, talismans to ensure fertility, good harvest, even to protect from lightning and bad weather. To draw blessings.

A happy marriage. Faith. Fidelity. Love.

There were others that the book touched

on, but only briefly. Hex signs with darker meanings weren't as prevalent, but the author — Liss's nephew, I kept reminding myself — theorized that it was because that was the nature of the beast. Happier messages needed to be seen repeatedly to be reinforced within one's heart and mind. Just like affirmations could be used to change one's attitude, happy hexes grew stronger the more they were reviewed.

Darker hexes were formulated in silence, and were sheltered by secrecy. Their very strength lay in their concealment. Forbidden by the Amish way of life, they were relegated to the shadow realm of myth and legend. Their existence was suspected but never admitted to. They were the work of the *heverei,* magic with dark purpose — the very thing that most benign hex signs were meant to protect against.

Was the sigil on the tree proof of this? What was its purpose?

That was the problem. As it was taboo for the Pennsylvania Dutch even to speak of their hex symbols with outsiders, there was very little information to go on for these markers of shadowy intent.

I sighed, closing the book at last. Slightly more educated, but only very slightly. The book would be of little to no help in deciphering the meaning of the symbol on the tree. When it came right down to it, the only person who could do that with any certainty was its creator.

CHAPTER 17

I don't know how long I sat there, feeling numb. What had happened? Had Luc gone too far? Had Hester's benevolence and patience somehow been stretched so far that they had suddenly snapped? That *she* had snapped?

Suspicion is such an ugly thing, especially when you desperately don't want it to be true. And the truth of the matter was, when it came right down to it, I didn't want Hester to be guilty. I'd been on the receiving end of betrayal. I knew the desperation, the regret, the self-recrimination. Hester was a victim here, just as much as Luc was. She had to be.

Only the person who created the symbol could know with any certainty . . .

She deserved the chance to speak on her own behalf, didn't she? To explain?

Whoa, what are you thinking, Maggie girl?

Nothing. Except . . .

I couldn't get the sigil on the tree out of my mind. Was it still there? Or had it been removed as evidence?

At least I still had the drawing.

It was still there, just inside the front cover of the book. I took it out and smoothed the wrinkles from the worn scrap of paper. What magic was there in these symbols? What intent? What purpose?

Hester, what were you thinking when you made this?

A thought occurred to me as I studied it. Was it possible? Could looking at it through a more generic universal symbolism help us to decipher it?

It certainly wasn't your usual hex sign, based on a sun wheel design of some sort. It wasn't all hearts and flowers and good feelings, either. That much was definite. The absence of color was one of the most telling features. No matter the magical tradition the world over, black was most often used as a color of shadow, of binding, of protection. This design was fiercer, somehow. Harsher lines. A heavier hand.

My phone rang as I sat there, contemplating. I picked it up and held it to my ear, still focused on the drawing before me.

"Hello?"

"Maggie? That you?"

It was Marion's voice on the other end of the line; I would recognize those forthright tones anywhere. "Hi, Marion. Yes, it's me. What can I do for you?"

"Listen, Maggie. I've been doing some more digging — you know me — and I think I found something. About Bertie."

"Mmhmm?" I was so caught up in my own research, I was only half listening. "You found something about Bertie?"

"And Helen. Maggie, I don't think that Bertie's the one who's causing all the trouble here at the library. I think it's Helen herself."

That information managed to filter its way through. I sat up straighter. "Whoa, wait a minute. Really? But I thought —"

"So did I. But I was directing the focus of my research based on years and years of verbal telling, and of course on the diary, which was Helen's viewpoint only. And you know that in doing research, that logic is totally flawed. *People lie.* They lie, they cheat, they try to purposely misdirect, to pin blame elsewhere. Maggie, what I'm saying is, I am ninety-nine percent certain that Bertie didn't start that fire, even accidentally. I think Helen did it."

I frowned. "But that would mean she caused her own death."

"Accidentally. She didn't mean to, of course. She was getting married! She had the library, a respected fiancé, the future to look forward to. But she also had a thorn in her side whose lovelorn behavior embarrassed her. She set the fire. She meant to pin the blame on Bertie so that she could go to the board of directors to have him terminated for negligence of his duties. Only something went very wrong, and she ended up being caught in the fire and dying at the tender age of twenty. Bertie, I think, always suspected, and when he died years later, I think he made a conscious, or at least subconscious, decision to stay, too."

I sat in silence a moment, absorbing this. "Wow."

"Is that all you have to say?"

"Yeah. Wow with regard to your researching capabilities, wow that so many things have happened in the past that will always remain shrouded in mystery. Just . . . wow. How often do you think stuff like that still happens, that no one ever realizes or discovers?"

"Too much. Too many crimes go unsolved. Too many people get away with things that remain shrouded in secrecy. Just look at all the crime-solving shows on television that deal with cold cases. Thank goodness some of them are getting caught at last, even belatedly, with new technology."

"Why do you suppose she's been popping up so much lately?" I wondered aloud. "Or do you suppose —"

"I think she's been there all along . . . but that may be part of the activity we've always attributed to Bertie was *her*. Or maybe, as Marcus says, things really are stirring up to new levels. Who know for sure?"

I nodded. Who indeed? "So, what will you do about them? Bertie and Helen, I mean."

"I'm going to have a talk with her." I could hear the authority in Marion's voice, and it made me smile. This was her library now, hers and the community's. Not just Helen's. "I'm going to tell her that she's stuck there because of her own actions and her own decision to remain. That if she wants to stay, fine; but she needs to stop trying to scare people, and she needs to coexist peacefully with Bertie."

"Liss could help you send them on their way, if that's what you want."

"I don't want to chase them away. I'm not afraid of them, and there's room in the library for them, too. But I'll keep it in mind, if things get worse. We all just need to get along."

When Marion hung up, I thought about

what she had said, about everyone just needing to get along. That was the trouble when it came right down to it, wasn't it? Personalities getting in the way. Arrogance and conceit and disdain. Greed and ambition and lust. Lust for money. Lust for pleasure. Lust for power.

Control.

Hatred.

Sin.

Not enough good to balance the bad.

I sighed. Where had the balance gone out of whack between Luc and Hester?

I couldn't ask Hester, not without alarming her. But Marion's insistence that she was going to talk to Helen and Bertie triggered something. I suddenly knew who I could ask. I could ask Luc.

I took a deep, deep breath and smoothed my hands over the crinkled edges of the drawing again, closing my eyes. Centering myself. Relaxing. This was the first time I had ever linked with a spirit intentionally.

Think, Maggie. Think.

The first blip of information came faster than I had expected.

Strength.

My eyes flared open as fear of the unknown sluiced through me. There was still time to stop. Was I sure I wanted to do this?

What if I didn't do it right? Was I opening myself up for things I didn't want in my life?

Did I have a choice?

Yes, I did. I did have a choice. And God help me, I was making it.

I closed my eyes. Let my mind open up. Reached out.

Purposely. With intent.

Black. Binding. Protection. Harsher. Heavier.

Rougher.

Where are you, Luc? What can you tell me?

My phone rang again. My eyes flared open.

"Hello." A bit more terse than necessary, perhaps, but I was in the middle of something.

"Maggie? This is Louisa Murray. I hope you don't mind, but your mother gave me your number."

Thank you, Mom. "Not a problem, Louisa. What can I do for you?"

"Well, I was wondering. I was just sitting here, thinking about those boys that you brought with you to help move the armoire. They seemed to be strong, capable, nice boys."

"Yes, they are. Very helpful."

"I was wondering . . . would it be possible for you to pass along their names and numbers? I'd like to get in touch with at least one of them. I have some chores around the house and barn that will be too much for me to take care of on my own. Sometimes a woman needs a man's touch around the home."

"Sure, Mrs. Murray. Listen, why don't I take your number, and I'll pass it along to them."

"You don't trust me?"

The tone bothered me, more than anything. "It's not a question of trust, honest. I don't have their numbers. I'll have to get them from a friend, and it just seems easier to do it this way."

"Oh. Very well, then. As I said, I have a 'Honey Do' list a mile long since Frank died, and it just keeps getting longer. The roof on the barn needs work, the woods need to be cut back, yard work, detailing the car, fixing the cement on the sidewalk and driveway. And then there are things in the house, too, like painting and —"

"Oh, I know, things do stack up, don't they?" I asked, getting antsy to get back to my work.

"They do. Well, thank you for passing the information along. Do what you can do to entice them to contact me. I could really use the manly presence."

"Will do. Good night, Mrs. Murray."

I rang off, feeling relieved, and hoped no one else remembered my phone number tonight.

Now, where was I?

Centering self, reaching out, yada yada. I just hoped I hadn't lost the connection. I mean, I wasn't very good at this. I needed all the concentration I could get.

Black. Binding. Protection. Harsher. Heavier.

Rougher strokes.

Strength.

I opened my eyes and stared down at the drawing of the hex I had copied from the tree until the lines blurred and then disappeared into the page, and I dropped into it, too. So to speak. It's the only way to describe the sensation of what I experienced. The yielding. The surrender. The opening of mind. Of soul.

Luc Metzger, come on down . . .

Strength.

Okay, strength. Got that.

Protection.

Against . . .

What? Or who?

Someone. A threat.

A threat to . . .
Something to hold dear.
Family.
Love.
Both of these things?

I came back into myself, staring down at the symbol and wondering how I could have been so mistaken. The sigil was to protect both love and family.

There were two people from the Pennsylvania *Ordnung* of Amish that I knew of here in Stony Mill. One was Hester Metzger.

The other was Luc Metzger himself.

CHAPTER 18

It was the same kind of mistake that Marion had made in her research that kept us from realizing sooner the truth behind the sigil's creator.

Preconceived notions. Misdirections.

The lines of the markings gave it away more than anything. When compared against the hex on the tree, Hester's drawings on the letter were finer, more precise, made meticulously and with great care. Everything she felt about her husband, she put into those symbols. All the love she felt for him — the passion, the wish for the two of them to be happy together. The eagle, strength. The smaller bird overflowing with hearts and flowers, Hester herself, sheltered beneath his protective wing. Flowing, rippling waves of blue surrounding them. Water? Water was a source of insight, inspiration, communication. Going with the flow.

The sigil on the tree was made with bold

strokes, strong, confrontational. Rough. Harsh. Fierce.

Masculine energy.

Luc's energy.

Hester didn't make that sigil. Luc did.

There was no telling how long it had been there, nor why it was there, on the edge of the woods so near their farm, facing town. Was it to keep some perceived evil away from the farm? Or was it to serve as a reminder to him that something in town was not for him?

Moreover, what kind of coincidence was involved, that he was killed so close by?

It was hidden from sight. If Liss's nephew the scholar was to be believed, sigils were not hidden unless they served a dark purpose.

No, it was not a personal reminder, and it was not to draw a blessing upon his family. It was a ward, placed in secret, that was meant to protect them from harm.

But who was the threat?

The million-dollar question.

I settled against the hard wooden kitchen chair with a sigh and leaned my head against the high back, staring at the ceiling.

It was a woman. It had to be. But who? Did he have an affair with someone in town that went too far? Did he try to break things off, only to have it come to this? To death and ruin?

It was at least half a mile across those woods to the outskirts of town. Half a mile of densely wooded acreage. If the sigil was for protection, why did he choose to hide it there, on the edge of this stretch of woods? Close to the farm, but not on it?

Frowning, I went to the kitchen junk drawer and pulled my Uncle Henry's map from the murky depths. It was something my father insisted I own, something I never thought I'd use in my lifetime. And yet here I was. Given my innate ability to put things away, never to be seen again, I should probably thank my lucky stars that I actually knew where it was.

Uncle Henry maps were like a zoomed version of a regular map. They showed county roads, large tracts of forest, lakes, ponds, and other natural phenomena of interest. Originally created for the use of outdoorsmen, they could be vastly helpful in finding one's way around tricky and sometimes twisty old county roads.

I spread the map out over the kitchen table, sliding my fingertip along the main highway to get my bearings. Once you found your road, it was simple enough to find your way. Most Indiana counties are set up on north-south, east-west grids, with the old "trail" roads being the exceptions to the rules, just to keep things interesting. There it was, County Road 500. And there, right there, was the stretch of woods, just down the way from the Metzger farm.

I followed the woods, colored green (what else?) on the map, toward town. There was one small break from the south, cutting into it, no doubt for one of the newer subdivisions, but other than that, the block of woods was pretty much intact. One half mile solid (nearly) of trees from there all the way over to . . . the Woodhaven subdivision.

Okay, this was getting a little too coincidental for my tastes. The number of recurring themes in my life of late was starting to make me a little nervous.

Something was not adding up. I knew in my mind and in my heart, the same way that I knew that Tom was not going to call me tonight after all his promises, that I was right about that much.

Peaches.

Okay, I had to admit: It was just a little weird that Peaches had ended up at Louisa Murray's house and wouldn't leave.

Yeah, it was weird. As was her reaction to the dog. Why did she dislike her so very much? Peaches was a total sweet pea. Once she settled down and stopped racing around like a chicken with her head cut off, anyone could see that she meant no harm. Why hadn't Louisa just called for the dog to be picked up, if it was causing her such grief? Why had she put up with it for so long?

And then there were the attacks on her property. Okay, so she'd been ratting out the local riffraff, and it was probably just backlash against her dedication to the Good Neighbor Policy, but still . . .

How did this fit in with everything that had been happening?

My Grandma Cora, God rest her soul, was a big jigsaw puzzle lover. She would leave the card table set up for days when she had a puzzle in progress, working on it here and there as she saw fit. Over time, she developed an almost photographic memory for the pieces and their shapes, and how they fit into the overall picture. "You just have to have faith, Margaret," she'd told me over and over again when I huffed out my lower lip at my inability to find the pieces I was looking for. "And you got to have patience. Go off and do something else for a change. Let the pieces come to you."

So I did. I picked up the phone and went into my bedroom and lay down on the bed, staring at the ceiling while I dialed Tom's number.

"Fielding."

"Hey."

"Heeyyyy . . . I'm sorry, Maggie. I don't think I'm going to get out of here in time. It's going to be real late."

My intuition had been right on the money. Imagine that. "That's okay. I kind of figured it was a long shot, anyway."

"You sound down."

I took a deep, cleansing breath and let it out slowly. "Just thinking. You know how you said those Blackhawk boys had been running wild all over that stretch of woods out there? Alden Woods? Isn't it kind of overgrown in there? I was looking at a map, and I don't think it would be all that pleasant to run around in."

"Actually, it isn't so overgrown anymore. There have been a lot of changes in there since that subdivision went in, cutting into it. They've added bike trails, a walking trail. Especially between the new subdivision and the old Woodhaven addition. Of course, over toward the end where Luc Metzger was found things get a little thicker, but even so, it's pretty accessible."

"Oh, really?"

"Yeah. You sure you're all right?"

"Yes, fine. Just thinking, like I said. Goodnight, Tom."

I was still mulling it all over the next morning after a night with little sleep. When I did sleep, it was fitfully, and I dreamed. I don't know if it was the spirit energy of Luc visiting me through dreams, or if I was still connected somehow through my intentional link with him, but I dreamed of being in the woods, looking across the fields toward a collection of buildings a quarter of a mile away while the wind caught in the branches over my head and moaned a somber tune. Looking out with big round eyes. Watching.

I was in the shower before I realized the imagery behind the dream. The owl on the sigil, that was my best guess. Sacred and wise protector, seeing through the darkness. Watching over the Metzger household. Still doing its job, eyes wide open.

When I got to Enchantments, Liss was waiting for me, as usual. We both were early risers, but her rising managed to beat mine nine times out of ten. This morning I didn't even bother with coffee, despite the fact that I could have used the caffeine. I sat down in the old wooden side chair beside the big rolltop desk and faced her.

"I did it last night. Linked with a spirit on purpose for the first time."

Liss looked at me quietly. "I thought you weren't ready."

"Yeah, well, I decided it was time. I was given this tool for a reason. I couldn't justify turning away from it without putting some real effort into trying to understand it. Without trying to understand just what it means in my life."

She smiled proudly. "Brava."

"No congratulations yet. I may change my mind back again the next time something scares me."

"Everyone feels fear at some point in time or another, Maggie. The question is, do you let it control you? Or do you work to understand what you're afraid of?"

Even if it was the monster in the closet?

"Well, anyway. I *think* I managed to link with someone. I'm not sure how to know that for sure."

"There's no real way to know for sure without having someone to corroborate facts. All you can do is trust the knowing. That sense that what you are receiving is true."

"I was hoping there would be more than that. There's no way, then. The person I linked with is passed. Gone."

She pinned me with a hard, assessing gaze. "Luc?"

I nodded, wondering what she was thinking.

"Ah. Did it have something to do with that?" she asked, inclining her nose toward her nephew's book. I had brought it back with me and was now holding it in my lap, my hands folded together over the hard cover.

I nodded. "Something like that. Your nephew is pretty amazing, did you know that? I can't imagine the amount of work that goes into something like this."

"No point in changing the subject," Liss said, her eyes twinkling at me. "I won't ask you if you don't want me to."

"You're pretty amazing, too. No fair doing that when I'm not ready for you, though."

"Doing what?" she asked, the picture of innocence.

I took a deep breath. "I promised Tom I wouldn't say anything without his permission, but it isn't betraying any confidences if I tell you that I think I know who created the sigil on the tree. I had thought at first that it must be Hester . . . but now I know it was Luc himself."

Liss's brows raised as she considered my claim.

"And I think . . . I mean, I know . . . that I need to talk to Hester again. I'm going to call Tom right now and ask him to go with me."

"Do you think he will?"

"If I'm already heading out there before I call him," I said, "he'll have no choice."

"Maggie, be careful."

I nodded as I backed out the door. "For once, I think I know exactly what I'm doing. I'll be back."

CHAPTER 19

"You're what?!"

I had to hold the phone six inches from my ear, but I'd anticipated the explosion and was nothing if not prepared.

"No, absolutely not! You're interfering in something that's none of your concern."

"I don't think she'll talk to you, Tom. She seems to trust me, as much as she trusts anyone else."

"Because you're . . ."

"A sensitive," I supplied.

"Like she is."

"Yes."

"Oh, for God's —" The rest of the curse (or was that a supplication?) was muffled. Probably for the better. "I could understand it better if I thought it was because you found her dog for her. Christ, I knew I shouldn't have let you look at that drawing. I knew it."

"Tom, if I thought it was dangerous to

talk to Hester Metzger about her hex magic habit, do you really think I'd be doing this? I'm not stupid, and neither is she. For heaven's sake, it's broad daylight. She has children. Nothing is going to happen. Besides," I said, saving the most important bit for last, "I don't think she's guilty of anything."

"Oh, of course not. Why would she be?"

I heard the slam of a door through the phone. "What are you doing?"

"What do you think I'm doing? I'm starting the cruiser so I can meet you there."

I cheered inwardly. I so did not want to do this alone. "Thanks, Tom."

"This had better be worth it," he grumbled into the phone.

I flipped my cell phone closed, and tucked it into my jacket pocket. At the next stoplight, I reached into the glove compartment for my palm-sized canister of pepper spray, which joined my cell. Hey, a girl never knows what to expect, and it's better to be prepared than . . . well, it's better to be prepared, that's all.

In the bright light of morning, the Metzger farm looked like a thousand other farms across the area. Nothing strange, nothing unusual. As I slowed my car, I saw Hester leave her house and cross the yard toward the big, faded red barn with its brightly colored hex signs. Taking a deep breath, I tooted my horn as I pulled down the drive. Hester turned at the sound and brought her hand up to shade her eyes, to clear her vision. Hesitantly, she held up her hand in welcome.

I got out of the car. Behind me, from the house, burst her two youngest, Peaches (aka Junior) following hard on their heels.

Hester came closer, and for the first time I noticed that she held an axe in her hands. She placed it, head down, on the ground in front of her feet and rested her hands on the handle. "Miss O'Neill. What a surprise. Is there something I can help you with this morning?"

Peaches ran in circles around the two of us, sniffing happily at my feet, reaching up to lick my fingers as I reached out to greet her, then raced off to the barn.

Hester took her children by the shoulders when they ran up to her. "You two, go after Peaches. She'll need fresh water and food in her dishes, and so will the barn cats. Go on, with you. I'll be there in a minute."

She waited until they did just that before she turned back to me. "Miss O'Neill —"

"Maggie, please."

"Maggie, then. And please call me Hester.

Actually, I'm glad you're here, because it means that I can thank you personally on behalf of my family. Eli told me . . . what you and your friends are doing. I won't insult you by telling you it is not needed. I will only say thank you, and God bless."

I scratched my nose in embarrassment, at a loss as to how to proceed. "Well, you're welcome. We just wanted to help in whatever way we could. Sorry I didn't mention it myself. I wasn't sure how you would respond, hearing it from me." I paused. Looking at the side of the barn, I decided directness was the best approach. "Hester, can I ask you a question?"

"Yes, of course."

"What do your barn symbols mean?"

Hester looked at the signs, a peaceful expression on her face. "They are prayers to God to bring blessings on our home and family. Each little part of the sign has a special meaning, and when they are taken as a whole, they equal a prayer."

I could understand that. Witches recited spells for much the same reasons. And it went right along with all that I had read about hex magic itself.

"Are these examples of your work?" I asked her, looking at the barn.

"*Ja*. I enjoy the creation of them. Luc and

I . . . well, our people come from Pennsylvania. It is not so strange to do this" — she held her hand out, palm up — "out there."

"They're beautiful. You're very good at them."

"Thank you."

"The different elements. What do they mean?"

She looked embarrassed, but she shook her head. "We are not supposed to talk about them outside of our *Ordnung.* Our Order. Many do not like them at all."

"Oh, okay. Fair enough. But are you allowed to talk about whether you have created one or not?"

"*Ja.* That is okay."

"What about the one out in the woods?"

I purposely kept my tone nonthreatening. Curious and light. But her response convinced me I was 100 percent spot on.

She blinked at me. Stunned. Completely and utterly. "There's a sign in the woods? You mean one like mine?"

I nodded. "Well, not exactly like yours. But similar enough. We, uh, had thought that perhaps you had made it."

"We?"

Right on cue, Tom's police cruiser came up the road, spitting gravel, traveling at a far greater speed than I had. But when he had stopped his cruiser and switched off the engine, he assumed his usual, cool-as-a-proverbial-cucumber watchful stance. "Good morning, Mrs. Metzger. Maggie. Beautiful morning, isn't it?"

"Tom, Hester isn't the one who made the sigil in the woods," I said, with no time or patience for police mind games. "I didn't think so — it felt different — but I had to be sure."

Tom's patience was about to snap. I could see it in his eyes. But Hester saved the day.

"Could someone please show me this . . . sign?" she said, stepping forward with fervor in her eye. "I want to see it."

Hester donned a black bonnet and cape, and grabbed a lead for Peaches from a hook just inside the kitchen door. We all piled into Tom's cruiser. A neighbor woman agreed, albeit a little nervously when she saw Hester in Tom's company, to watch the two little ones while Tom drove us over to the crime scene, less than a quarter mile away.

Hester's rosy cheeks paled when the crime scene tape came into view, but she handled herself with dignity. She paused beside it, her head bowed. I tried very hard not to intrude, but her personal boundaries had been weakened by the onslaught of her own emotions, and they bled through easily enough that I was picking things up left and right, whether I wanted to or not. She didn't say anything, but I knew she was thinking about Luc, their marriage, and why he had felt the need to stray when she loved him so much.

After a few moments, she lifted her head, her eyes clear and at peace. She gazed at the wooded expanse stretching before us. "Where is it? I don't see it."

Tom had already pinpointed the trees that obscured it. "Over here."

Big black nose to the ground, Peaches padded alongside Hester's feet as we hopped over the shallow ditch and circled through the trees. Suddenly the dog leaned forward, straining on the end of the leash, leading us straight for the tree.

Tom frowned. "That's amazing. How'd she know?"

I gazed at the sign, still nailed securely to the tree. "My guess is that she's been here before."

Hester stared transfixed at the tree, a thousand thoughts and emotions passing through the depths of her eyes. Her mouth had fallen open, and her breath was shallow. "Luc must have done this. No one else around here makes these symbols."

Skepticism flickered in Tom's eyes. "You're saying you didn't know anything about this?"

"I didn't," she insisted. "But I know what it means."

"And what does it mean?" he pressed.

She just shook her head while the dog tugged at the end of its tether, whining.

"Ma'am, it's in your best interest to be forthcoming with me on this."

"I cannot."

He stared at her. I could almost hear the gears whirring as he worked out his next strategy.

I stepped in and placed my hand on Tom's arm. "She isn't supposed to speak of such things with outsiders, Tom. It's against the rules of their Order. Besides," I said, lowering my voice for his ears alone, "I think I know what it is. What it means."

"You wanna fill me in here?"

Behind us the whining got louder. Peaches was pacing back and forth, becoming agitated. "Peaches, behave yourself," Hester said, giving the leash a gentle tug.

I turned my attention back to Tom, hoping that I was right. That while her Order forbade her from talking about the sigils and their meaning, it didn't prevent her from confirming their meaning if guessed

394

by another.

"There's nothing out there that tells what hex symbols mean, beyond the happy, fluffy images that most know. Love and prosperity. Rain and fertility. But," I explained further, "I think you can look at the images from a more universal viewpoint and get the general gist of things. Look first at the overall theme, and then look at the specifics. The owl. In many cultures, the owl is wisdom, but it also means watchfulness. Protection. All-seeing with its wide, round eyes. Keen sight in the darkness. This owl is black. Black is the color of shadows. Concealment. Stealth. It's also a color of protection, and of binding. Of removing the will of another."

Tom swore softly under his breath. "I was right, then. It's black magic and Satanism."

"No. It's not the same thing. Magic isn't black or white. It all comes down to the intent of the person practicing it."

"Oh, yeah? And what might his intent have been?"

"I think Luc made this to protect something he held dear. His family."

"And how do you come by that?"

"The hearts, not thorns, encircling the owl's head like a crown. Love most sacred."

"And the crossed axes in its claws?"

"Strength and solidarity. Strength united. A united front. The star or pentagram, eternity." I lowered my voice to a mere whisper. I did not want Hester to hear this. She didn't need the reminder. "Remember, Luc was the one who was killed. He's the victim here. And there was someone out there to be afraid of. That much we know is fact."

Tom pressed his lips together, knowing that this much, at least, was irrefutable.

I turned to Hester, who had been listening to my description but not saying anything. "So, did I get it right? Did I understand the sigil correctly?"

Tears glistened in her eyes. She blinked them away, rapidly. "I —"

"We have to know, Hester. Otherwise, someone with a less kind view toward magic might think that Luc was trying to practice dark magic against someone else, that perhaps his chosen method of intimidation backfired against him."

"It would never have been his intent to harm. The hex is what you say — a plea to God above to watch over and protect Luc and our family. The only part of it I do not understand is the roses at the bottom. These aren't of the usual style. These appear to be more literal translations of a rose."

We stood, the three of us, staring at the painted wooden circle, with Peaches winding around our legs, getting more and more antsy the longer we waited.

Roses.

Roses . . . and axes.

"You know, this is weird," Tom said, "and I can't believe I'm saying it, but . . . I think I believe you. Both of you."

I squealed and threw my arms around his neck. He'd done it! He had taken that first big step beyond superstition and intolerance, toward understanding that there were deeper forces at work in the town than what he considered factual reality. Grinning, he let me hug him for a long moment before setting me gently back on my heels and admonishing me. "Don't go getting too excited by that. We still have to figure out who . . . and why . . ."

I nodded. "I keep seeing roses. Flashes of them, in my mind. But the only thing that reference brings to my mind is Louisa Murray. I have ravaged roses on the brain."

"There was that situation with the boys," Tom mused. At Hester's inquiring glance he explained, "There was a complaint about vandalism to a woman's rose bed, less than a mile from here. A little over a week ago. But I don't really see how this can be connected unless Luc vandalized her roses himself."

That didn't make sense to me, either. But . . . "Maybe it isn't meant to be literal," I theorized. "Maybe it is a point of reference Luc is showing me now as confirmation that we're on the right path." I turned to Tom. "The boys who found Luc's wallet and letter . . . did they find them here in these woods?"

He answered me with the briefest of nods.

Peaches whined loudly, and lunged toward the woods. Hester barely kept her hold on the leash. "Peaches, what is wrong with you? Sit, girl." She asked me, "My Luc's wallet? What letter?"

Oh, boy. I looked at Tom. He looked back at me, as if to say, *You let the cat out of the bag. You answer her.* I sighed, knowing I had no other choice. "It was your letter to Luc, Hester. He must have been carrying it in his wallet when he . . . when he died. Some boys found his wallet, and with it, the letter."

"Oh." She bit her lip. "That was a private letter."

I reached out and put my hand on her arm. "I know it was. It must have been hard for you, loving him so much." She was crying softly now, and I needed to fill the silence. "Why did you think he was having an affair?"

She shrugged. "It is no secret that my Luc had an eye on him. He always had. And back in Pennsylvania . . . it was a long time ago, but that was the reason we came to Indiana. I thought we had put all that behind us. But I was receiving notes from the woman in question. Unsigned notes. She was in love with him, she said. Why couldn't I see that he didn't love me anymore? Why couldn't I let him go?" She shook her head, the tears flowing freely now. "Maybe I should have."

How did the sigil fit into all of this?

How did Luc know Louisa?

Tom was apparently wondering the same thing. "Mrs. Metzger, did your husband know Louisa Murray?"

Hester sniffled, working for composure. "I don't know."

"You told me earlier that Luc worked at the RV factory, and that he worked sometimes with Eli Yoder. I understand that he also took odd jobs around town."

"Yes. Whenever we needed extra money for the farm, he would pick up extra work somewhere. He was a wonderful carpenter, my Luc. It was our dream to someday have a fully operating farm. That's why we sacrificed so much."

"Did he ever do work for Louisa Murray?"

She frowned, thinking back. "Well, there was a Murray who needed a roof put on a barn, I think."

"And when was this?"

She shrugged. "I don't know. Last summer, I guess."

"And when did you receive the first information about your husband's affair?"

"September."

"You remember that for certain?"

She met his gaze. "It's not the sort of thing a wife forgets, Deputy Fielding."

He looked at me. "Well? It fits."

But was it real?

I looked at the hex sign, doing its magic over our heads. "This much is certain: Luc felt threatened by something."

"But why would he need protection from Louisa Murray, or any other woman?" Tom persisted. I noticed he had taken out his flip-style notebook. "That's what I don't get. Metzger was a strapping kind of guy."

"I don't think he wanted to hurt her — 'her' meaning whoever was writing those notes to Hester," I commented, jumping in. "Perhaps it was to convince her to back off. To leave him, and his family, alone."

Tom scribbled something in his notebook.

He stood there, staring at it a moment, then gave a self-conscious little laugh. "I can't believe I'm actually considering any of this."

I was surprised that he was, too. Happily surprised. There was hope for Tom yet. "You know, I just spoke with Louisa last night. She asked me . . ." My voice trailed off, and I caught my lip between my teeth as I tried to recall the details of the conversation.

"She asked you what?"

I looked at him. My stomach was suddenly in knots, and I had a bitter taste in my mouth. "She asked me for the names and numbers of the two boys you met the other day. The ones who helped us move the armoire from her house to the store."

His eyes searched mine, his radar on high alert. "Why?"

"She said . . . she said she had some things around her house that she needed help with. Nothing unusual there, considering her husband died about a year ago. But — oh, why didn't I think this was weird earlier? The way she said it. Something about how sometimes you just need a man's touch around the home. Oh. Oh! And she mentioned needing work done on her barn roof, but . . . but when I was rescuing Peaches that night, she mentioned having a new roof put on the barn a year or so ago."

Could it be? Could Louisa Murray have been having an affair with Luc? Sweet and mild Louisa Murray, St. Catherine's Leading Lady of Charity, who looked like a younger version of my mother, for heaven's sake? Could she have been taken in by an oversexed Amish lothario? My mind struggled to wrap around the concept. But, assuming that it was possible, was it also possible that something had gone wrong? That she had been more serious than he was about the affair?

A woman usually was.

Before I could pursue this thought any further, Peaches went on high alert, staring fierce-eyed into the woods. In an instant, her entire personality seemed to morph before our eyes, from mild-mannered goofball to attack dog. She made a mighty lunge, yanking the leash straight off Hester's wrist, and took off into the underbrush, barking ferociously.

"Peaches! No! Peaches, come back! Come!" Hester clapped her hands. "Peaches, come!"

But it was no use. Hester turned this way and that, as though trying to decide which way to go. I stopped her with a hand on her arm. "She's too fast. You'll never be able to catch up with her." Already her barks were growing fainter as she followed whatever trail had caught her attention.

"I have to try. The children will be heartbroken if she's gone again. She could get run over out there."

Or worse. I caught her eye. "The last time, she was hanging around Louisa Murray's barn. That's where I picked her up that night. She's lucky I came along when I did. Mrs. Murray was going after her with a broom."

Hester's eyes widened. "Luc used to take Peaches with him as often as he could. She went missing that night."

As one we turned to Tom.

I was so proud of him — he hesitated only a moment before making his decision.

"You two go back to the farm and wait for me there. I'll get the dog."

And more, I hoped.

CHAPTER 20

Tom pulled away with a spit of gravel from beneath his tires, leaving us to stare after him. A part of me was glad that I was not, for once, going to be in the thick of things, embroiled in a situation not of my making. Another part of me was champing at the bit, wanting to see how it all played out.

Curiosity killed the cat, Margaret dear.

While Hester paced, I phoned Liss to let her know where I was and that I would be held up just a little while longer. And then I called my mother.

"Mom," I said, breathless, "I need to ask you something."

"Margaret? What is it? What's going on?"

"Mom, just listen to me and don't ask any questions. Has Mrs. Murray had any kind of relationship since her husband died?"

"Louisa Murray? No. Well, not publicly. Not that I know of."

"What do you mean, not 'publicly'?" I

narrowed my eyes, wishing I could see into my mother's. "What do you know, Mom?"

"Well, nothing, really. There was a rumor, a few years back, but that's all it was. A rumor. Back when her husband was still living. Of course he'd been ill for quite a while with his liver attacks, and she tended to him the whole time without a single complaint. Nothing ever came of the rumor — you know how they are — and eventually it just faded away."

You hear a lot of stories in small towns. Some true, some not so much. Some based in fact, some based on lies and jealousy. It was the ones that you heard over and over again that you tended to worry about. Or the ones that gathered more tinder to feed the fading coals. New stories to add to the old fires.

"I don't remember anything like that."

"Well, you wouldn't. Too busy with your own life. It must have been, I don't know, eight years ago now. They say she became fixated on a man in her neighborhood. A younger man, with a young family. Sent him love letters and everything. But that's all water under the bridge. I've never heard another thing attached to Louisa's name that anyone could consider bad."

"What happened to the family?"

"Moved away, I guess. That summer."

That bad feeling that had been twisting through me? It was tightening to a breaking point. Something was about to give. I knew it.

"Thanks, Mom. Gotta go. 'Bye."

Hester was staring into the woods, a distant look in her eyes. "Peaches . . ."

"Will be fine," I assured her. "Tom will be there in no time flat."

She turned to me, her expression fierce. "We could cut through. He has to go all the way around."

"Tom asked us to stay here." Not that that had stopped me before, but I was supposed to be turning over a new leaf. Minding my own beeswax. Heeding the wisdom of others, and any number of other clichés.

A series of barks sounded, closer than expected.

"I think I can call her," Hester said, hunching down to peer through the underbrush into the deeper gloom of the woods. "She's not far, I don't think."

I wondered whether I should tell Hester about what my mother had said. Tom should know for sure, I decided. I thumbed through the menu on my cell and texted a message to him, short and sweet. *LM obsessed w/man B4. Luv Ltrs & all. Famly moved 2 get away. 8 yrs ago.* The message completed, I pressed Send and looked up.

Hester was gone.

"Hester?"

But it was too late. Hester, it appeared, was as headstrong and determined to make her own way as I was. "Peaches, come here, girl!" I heard her call from somewhere close by. "Peeeeeeaches!"

I had two choices. I could stay where I was, allowing Hester to blunder her way toward Louisa Murray's house alone, or I could try to catch up with her and do what I could to convince her to leave the chase to Tom.

Was Louisa Murray a threat? I didn't know for sure. But I wasn't sure that any of us, least of all Hester, should take that chance.

I couldn't let her go it alone. I had to follow. Threat or no, there was a reassuring kind of safety in numbers.

Following Hester's lead, I turned and started pushing and ducking my way through the underbrush and low-hanging branches. It was amazing how quickly these old logging woods became dense, how much sunlight was filtered out by layers of . . . I glanced up. No, not filtered by leaves; it was too early in the year for anything more than a pale green wash of color from newly spreading leaf buds. High above, the daylight was leaving us as the hazy clouds darkened and swirled their way into a thick and ominous state of being. Storm clouds.

April showers bring May flowers.

Ahead of me I saw a flash of blue skirt and sensed movement. I headed in that direction.

Tom was right. There were paths cut through these woods. I stumbled across one as I hurried to follow Hester as best I could. Things went much faster once I wasn't forced to fight against clinging vines and snagging brambles.

Was that smoke I smelled?

I redoubled my efforts. I was clutching my side by the time I finally caught up with Hester I don't know how many minutes later. Actually, I really didn't want to know how many minutes — this was the longest and farthest I had run since Mrs. Hooper's gym class (aka The Torture Chamber) in the ninth grade. It was better to not know these things.

Hester wasn't making it easy for me. Living a clean and active lifestyle must make a huge difference — she was barely breaking a sweat when I grabbed her arm. She swung around to face me, a strange fierceness in her eyes. "Fire. Do you not smell the smoke?"

She was right. The acrid scent and eye-burning haze clung like swaths of wispy batting to the tree limbs above our heads.

"We should go back," I wheezed, trying to ignore the stitch in my side.

"We are nearly there. Come on, Maggie. I can hear her."

I hoped she meant Peaches.

For some reason, I found myself following her. She no longer dashed, but prowled along the path toward a grove of tall pines looming ahead of us. A flicker of light caught my eye at ground level. Definitely a fire, but not a big one. Who in the heck would be roasting marshmallows with a storm coming?

I knew the answer in my mind, but I was just trying to keep my spirits up, dontcha know. Trust me. It works if you work it.

Considering her earlier headlong dash, Hester was being downright guarded now. We were walking cautiously, placing our feet carefully before shifting our weight into the next step, trying to keep noise at a minimum as we eased toward the pines; keeping ourselves out of a clear line of vision from the fire, just in case. I didn't know if whoever set the fire was paying heed to the woods around them or not, but I didn't want to draw attention to our presence if I could help it. We hid behind tree trunks that were not nearly wide enough and listened for signs of life.

Nothing except a rumble of thunder.

Where in the name of heaven was Peaches?

I took a deep breath and peered around the edge of the tree, letting my breath come out in a whoosh of relief when I found no one there — just the snap, crackle, and pop of the fire itself. It was in a small clearing between the pines, a makeshift fire pit at its center, lined with fieldstones. The trees made the safety measure of the stones a moot point — in a dry season, an upwafting spark could send the trees up like torches.

With that thought came the first soft patter of raindrops all around, and another low rumble.

Hester went straight toward the fire pit. I waited a moment, still not certain that we weren't being watched. I didn't like this place; it felt dark, even darker than our hasty path through the woods, and it wasn't just an effect of the storm rising above us. This was astral dark, energy dark, bad feelings and bad intent dark, and I didn't like it. It reminded me all too much of the dream I had had the night before, and I shivered, remembering.

Big round eyes. The sigil.

"Look." Hester stood at the edge of the pit. I edged closer. The wood used to fuel the fire must have been wet, because the flames weren't spreading well along its length. Surrounding the branches were three small boxes. Pink. Frilly. Photo boxes.

Hester reached her bare hand out to nudge the smoldering boxes away from the flames. I caught her arm. "Wait." I picked up a decent sized stick and knocked the boxes aside. "Those photo boxes belong to Louisa Murray, I'm sure of it," I murmured. "I saw some exactly like them at her house just the other day. She's a photo-and-scrapbooking fiend."

I wondered if Hester would even understand the explanation, living, as she did, apart from hobby fads and trends.

I squatted down and carefully poked at the boxes with the stick. Whispers of smoke slithered from the heavy-duty cardboard frames, but whatever flames had licked at them had gone out. I wasn't taking any chances on burning myself — the stick would have to do all the work for now.

It was enough. The first lid popped off when I knocked the box sideways. A plume of smoke and cinders emerged, along with a spill of photographs. The edges were slightly crisped, but the damage had gone no further. I flicked them away from the flames before they could get too close.

Hester reached out and took one. "It's a picture of our farm."

It was, and there were more like it. Many more. Different distances, different perspectives, different zoom settings. And then there were pictures of Hester. The children. But most important . . .

Luc.

Luc driving the buggy, wonderfully aloof in his black, round-brimmed hat. Luc walking the fields. Luc riding an old-style bicycle. Luc, in coveralls, crossing a street, a hardhat in one hand and a metal lunchbox in the other. Luc kneeling, a hammer in hand, atop the roof of a barn.

Luc, Luc, and more Luc.

Big round eyes looking out from the depths of the forest at the farm buildings some distance away.

The dream again. And then it hit me. I hadn't been dream-linking to the imagery on the sigil, guided by Luc's spirit.

It was Louisa.

Louisa, watching the Metzger farm from the woods, the big, round eyes of her binoculars and telephoto lenses bringing everything into crisp focus.

"We have to get these to Tom," I said.

"Maggie?"

"Yeah?" I asked, sifting through to get a good sampling. She tapped me on the shoulder, repeatedly. "What is it?" I glanced up finally as I tucked the photos into my jacket.

And looked straight into Louisa Murray's surprised stare.

"What's this?" she asked, circling warily around us. She held a hoe in one hand, a can of kerosene in the other, and had a bag slung over her shoulder. She shrugged out from under the bag and let it fall to the earth at her feet. "What are you doing here?"

I scrambled to my feet, using the stick as leverage, my brain whirring frantically in a search for an acceptable response. Anything that wouldn't raise her suspicions over-much. Of course that was probably a lost cause, since she had seen me tuck the photos inside my jacket. My eye was drawn to the hoe in her hand, and I groaned. Why hadn't I looked up sooner?

Hester was much less intimidated. She stepped forward, her eyes blazing with a cold light beneath the simple black bonnet. "You killed my Luc."

Oh, shit! My eyes widened to maximum potential.

Louisa laughed in disbelief, but I could see the secrets in her eyes. I could hear their whispers. I knew their truth. "What are you saying?"

I cleared my throat. "Hester —" I said, touching her cape.

But Hester was in no mood to mince words. "My Luc. You killed him."

"You don't know what you're talking about."

Hester reached down to the crisped photos and grabbed a handful, then threw them in Louisa's face. "I know. I know what you are."

Louisa's face froze into a tight mask, reptilian in its absence of feeling. "And what am I?"

"A brazen woman. One who seeks and takes away. You killed my Luc."

Louisa sneered at the photos that had bounced off her proper little jacket. "Those are just pictures. A few harmless pictures," she said with a dismissive wave of her hand. "Maggie, tell her."

Another handful of pictures. "I don't need Maggie to tell me. I can see for myself." Hester advanced on Louisa, flicking the pictures at her, one by one.

Louisa tried a different tack. Her expression softened slightly, her voice became a coax. "This is all a mistake. We are collecting things for you . . . money . . . for you and your family . . . to make up for what was done to you."

"You. Can. *Never.* Make. Up. For. What. You. Did. To. Me."

Hester stood there a moment, eyes blazing, and then she dropped to her knees in the wet dirt, surprising both Louisa and me. She rocked back and forth on her hands and knees, breathing deeply, becoming someone, *something* else. As we watched, spellbound, she began to etch lines into the earth, deeper and deeper.

Symbols. Magical symbols.

Hex marks the spot.

"What are you doing?" Louisa flexed her fingers around the handle of the hoe. "Stop that. *Stop. That.*"

Hester didn't appear to hear, or if she did, she didn't heed the warning in Louisa's voice. Maybe she should have, because in the next instant Louisa snapped.

What happened next came in a kind of slow motion that would have dazzled and bewitched and bemused even the most experienced magical practitioner. The kerosene can dropped to the ground with a metallic thunk. Louisa's fingers gripped the handle of the hoe, once, twice. Her lips pulled back over her teeth in a primal snarl. Her face contorted. Flattened. I saw a shift, as though another face was superimposed over the top of hers or under hers, the features merging so that you couldn't tell where one started and the other stopped. The hoe came down across her body, dropping into her waiting palm. For a moment the hoe hovered there in her hands, and I knew in an instant what she was about to do. I stumbled over my own feet, one hand in my pocket scrabbling for the canister of pepper spray I just remembered I'd brought with me. Too late . . . too late. I hit the ground hard, tucked my shoulder under at the last second, and rolled over just in time to see Louisa swing the hoe back in a stance that would have made a home run hitter proud, her gaze pinpoint focused on Hester, oblivious on the ground before her.

"Noooooooooooo!"

The shriek tore from my lips; I felt it. I know I did. But it was quite another shriek that I heard screaming through the storm-whipped forest. A huge brown shape arced down from the pines, six feet wide if it was an inch.

The owl is a symbol of protection . . .

Before Louisa could initiate the forward motion of the deadly swing she intended for Hester, the shape zoomed down, dive-bombing at her full speed, startling her so badly that she stumbled backward. Her scrambling feet tripped against the canister of kerosene as she sought purchase, knocking it over. The golden liquid burbled out against the dampened earth and trickled into the deeply cut symbol that Hester was still etching. We all watched, transfixed, as it filled the symbol and then continued on down a little hillock none of us had seen, in a straight line toward . . .

I grabbed Hester by the shoulder, pulling her backward, away from her sigil, just in time. The line of kerosene ignited instantly, flames licking along the path it had taken, gathering speed and force as it rushed toward its target.

Louisa reacted a split second too slowly. The kerosene that had spilled beneath her feet had soaked into her shoes and the hems of her slacks. The flames of the fire she had set to remove all evidence of her guilty conscience proved her undoing. She screamed, stamping her feet, but the flames only licked higher. Before I could think or react, she turned and ran, legs ablaze, back toward her property at the edge of the woods.

Hester and I stared after her, and suddenly the slow-mo effect dissipated. Time and space returned to normal, as abruptly as they had turned moments ago, and with the return came tremors of adrenaline, shaking my body to its core. I realized my mouth was hanging open; I closed it, hard enough to make my teeth hurt.

I turned to Hester, and noticed with more than a little relief that the *otherness* was leaving her eyes as well. "What happened?" I asked her.

She shook her head, a tiny frown crimping her brows. "I — I don't know."

"We should go after her," I said, still trying to get my feet and body to follow the intent being set by my mind.

Hester shook her head again. Turning away, she began to walk, slowly and wordlessly, along the path toward her home.

Later — much later — after I used my cell to call 911, after Tom's colleagues on the force came and found Louisa Murray sitting in agony under a stream of water pouring from her outside faucet, after the ambulance carted her away for the medical care she was going to need so badly, and after I reconnected with Tom (who had found Peaches wandering along the road to the north, happily hunting for bunnies, while Hester and I stumbled into the path of danger; and who would, I hoped, in time forgive me for my unintentional disobedience) . . . after all of that, I sat alone in my dark apartment, replaying the events in the woods in my head. Muddling. Wondering.

Worrying.

Louisa had found God again in the midst of the flames. Sitting beneath the cold, streaming water, her teeth gritted against the pain, she told anyone who would listen how she had been shown the evil of her ways in a split second of shocking reality. She repeated over and over the tale of how she had asked Luc to come to her house to fix some loose shingles on the roof that he and his crew had replaced the summer before. A ruse, of course. She told the story of his rejection of her, and she explained how she took his life in a fit of blind desperation and rage. Like a broken tape recorder, she told it over, and over, and over again.

Louisa had seen the light, and it scared the hell out of her.

But it wasn't Louisa's admission that was troubling me. It was the words of wisdom that Marion had imparted that were swimming freestyle through my brain:

People lie. They lie, they cheat, they try to purposely misdirect, to pin blame elsewhere.

It was Hester's final, brutal hex that guided my inner eye and molded the thoughts into a useful pattern and helped me to see, for once and for all. It was the hex that reminded me once again so clearly that magic itself is neither black nor white. That it can be used to protect or heal, as was Luc's intent with his sigil in the woods, or it can be used to inflict harm or pain, *as was Hester's.*

It all came down to the intent housed in the heart and soul of the practitioner . . . and sweet, innocent Hester was not as pure of heart as everyone, including me, wanted to believe.

Hester, who had suffered the addition of insult to the injury of Luc's supposed affair each time an anonymous letter came to her, had recognized instantly that her only chance for justice was about to pass her by as we awaited word from Tom, and it was in that split second that she decided to act.

Only I had witnessed the speed with which Hester had traveled the paths in the woods, a speed I was hard pressed to imitate as I followed. Only I had seen her face in the shadow of the pines as she traced a mysterious pattern upon the hard forest floor. Only I had seen the giant owl that she had conjured from the very air itself that had helped to bring about Louisa's fall from grace.

Only I had seen the strangeness in her eyes . . . and only I suspected that her final, forceful hex had been intended to kill.

Hester had done nothing illegal that afternoon. But was she innocent of wrong-doing?

Of one thing I was certain — I would never look at innocence in quite the same way ever again.

When the story behind Luc Metzger's murder was released to the public, it spread across town like wildfire, blazing trails along telephone wires and burning up the cellular airwaves. Some claimed to be shocked by the very nature of Louisa Murray's admissions. It was too much for them to absorb — the knowledge that a respectable woman, a churchgoing woman, could have earthly needs that could consume her mind in such a way as to drive her to the greatest sin of all. The women of the Ladies Auxiliary of St. Catherine's, of course, claimed to have suspected her true nature all along. After all, not a one had truly forgotten her previous fall from grace while her poor, sick husband had been rotting away in his bed. Lust was one thing. But even my mother could not forgive a woman who could present a saintly face to the world while pursuing a man who belonged to another woman.

Community saints are held to higher standards than the rest of us. They should never admit to having . . . needs.

But Louisa's needs had been suppressed far too long. Was Luc's death something that had been predestined? An event set into motion by the wheels of fate long ago? Some would blame the restrictive environment Louisa had been trying to escape when she left home at the age of seventeen to marry her much older husband. Could she ever have been happy with someone twice her age? And his illness must have been quite a blow, striking in the prime of her life.

Because if she had had needs before, they most certainly didn't die when he did.

It must have seemed so innocent when the infatuation first hooked her. Luc's was the kind of male beauty that's rare, and rare equals precious to many people. Rare meant desirable. Prized. Something worth having.

From the safety of the house, from the safety of the woods, Louisa had watched Luc while he worked, becoming more and more captivated. She followed him, trailed him, hunted him. And she persuaded herself that he had appeared in her life for a reason. He was there to make her forget all the disappointments and regrets of her past. He was brought there by God to make things better.

Luc was meant to be hers.

Eventually she had become so convinced of these things that nothing mattered, except being with him. She became a victim of the lies she told herself.

Yes, I could feel sorry for Louisa. I could pity her. I could understand her.

But forgiveness? That was another thing entirely.

How could anyone forgive a woman who had relentlessly pursued a married man who innocently happened across her path? A man with a wife and small children, who did everything he could to gently turn away her embarrassing advances? A man with a history of temptation, though Louisa probably didn't know that. She knew only that she needed, and she wanted, and didn't she deserve some happiness in her life? And so she'd taken pictures of him as he'd worked on her barn, and she'd enticed, and she'd pursued. For months. And when it became clear that she could never have the beautiful, young, vital man that she wanted to fill the physical void she felt in her life, she lured him to her home under the pretense of another job that needed tending to. She tried one last time to seduce him, and failed. All the way back through the darkening woods she pleaded with him to see beyond their age difference, to see her for the pleasure she could give him. And when he refused her, his face hard with disgust, she snapped. She seized the hammer from the toolbox he held, and she swung it. She took his life in the torment and aching agony of her own desperation.

So, no, forgiveness was too much to ask. I would leave that to Luc Metzger's fellow Amish, who in the coming months would lobby the court for mercy to be shown to Louisa.

They were much better at forgiveness than I was. I was going to have to work on that.

Hester, of course, was not in attendance. Perhaps she needed to work on that, too.

EPILOGUE

It was two weeks since Louisa Murray had been taken into custody for the murder of Luc Metzger, and the mood in town had lightened considerably. People waved at passersby from their newly tidied lawns and smiled at each other at the grocery store. Even the sky looked bluer, and the sun was somehow brighter. Sunnier. And of course the weather had warmed even more as spring tightened its hold on the earth.

Such short memories we all had.

The weekend after Louisa's arrest I'd gone to Easter Mass with my mother, knowing it would make her happy. But as I sat in the pew in my Sunday best, going through the motions while the priest talked about faith and rebirth and redemption, I could hear only the echoes of what had been stirred up in Stony Mill, and I was left to wonder why. Why here? Why now? What had we all done to deserve to be put through this? Three murders. Three murders in six months. Were they over? Was the thing that had brought this misery to us satisfied? Was it done?

The sky was blue. The sun was bright. The world was still turning. We had to act as though nothing was wrong, pick up the pieces, and go on with our lives. Because that's what we do, we who are left behind.

We survive.

None of that mattered today, on this Beltane Eve, as dozens of Liss's friends from near and far gathered to celebrate the Maying, the quickening and blossoming of the Earth.

"How do I look?" I asked Liss as I held my hands up to the wreath of flowers pinned atop my head. Ribbons dripped down my back to the waist of my plain white cotton dress. I felt like a girl again, fresh and untried, and not the young, quasi-sophisticated, semi-worldly woman I was supposed to be. A girl with daisies in her hair.

Liss smiled at me, as beautiful as ever in a simple sheath of pure silver, a color that echoed the elegant streaks in her auburn hair. "Gorgeous, of course, ducks. Are you sure you don't mind coming tonight?"

Tonight was the celebration of May Day

that Liss was holding in the beautiful sacred glen on her property, where she held her very personal outdoor rituals. May Day — Beltane, some call it still, a remnant of the Old Ways, the fifth Sabbat on the wheel of the year. Beltane, fire festival of fertility, of personal growth, of love and passion. This would be my first true experience of a real witchy ritual, something that went beyond Liss's and Marcus's N.I.G.H.T.S. meeting circles. I didn't know quite what to expect, but I knew I wasn't afraid. Not of Liss.

Marcus, on the other hand . . .

Forcing Marcus from my thoughts for the time being, I shook my head, smiling at Liss. "I'm so glad you invited me."

"Good." Liss paused, considering me. A twinkle appeared in her eyes. "You know, Maggie, there's something I've been meaning to ask you for a while now."

"Is there?" I stuck another pin into the wreath of flowers, determined that it would stay in place through the night. It was too pretty not to.

"Mmm. There really isn't a good way to say this, so I suppose the best way is simply to come right out and ask you. Maggie, how are things between you and Tom? Settled? Or no?"

I blinked into the eyes that were peering

so inquisitively into mine in the mirror. "Uh . . . well . . . I don't know quite how to answer that."

"In situations like this, brutal honesty is the only sensible approach."

She was asking me to be sensible when I could hardly make out my own feelings. I thought about Tom, about how much closer he had come to trusting me — and how much farther we still had to go. "The truth is . . . they're not settled. Not really. Oh, I think he might like them to be, and sometimes, so would I . . . and yet there's always something there, holding us back," I confided, feeling a rush of relief in the doing. "*Both* of us. Even when I think we've worked beyond things." Case in point, the Easter dinner with my family that Tom had skipped out on, much to my mother's disappointment. Something else had come up to claim Tom's attention, which left me wondering just how ready he was for any serious relationship. Maybe being single was too new for him. Maybe he was clueless to a woman's needs. Maybe he was already married to his job as a cop and didn't have the guts to tell me.

Sigh.

I straightened my spine, determined not to let ghosts, even those haunting relationships, ruin my evening. "Anyway, there you have it," I said. "The truth, the whole truth, and nothing but the truth."

"So help you Goddess?" she said, twinkling again.

"So mote it be," I answered, more at ease now with the solemn plea than ever before. I paused a moment, then cocked my head in her direction. "As long as we're in the mood for an honest exchange . . ."

"Aye?"

"How are things between you and Marcus? Settled? Or no?"

She gazed at me for several moments, surprise in her wise blue eyes. Just when I was sure I had overstepped my bounds, she threw her head back and let loose a great long peal of laughter. "Oh, my dear," she said at last, wiping the tears from her eyes, "I'm very sorry, but . . . what on earth ever made you think *that?*"

My mouth fell open. "You mean . . . ?"

"Never. Not once. Oh, Marcus is a wonderful friend whom I would trust with my life, but good Goddess, he's young enough to be my son." She chuckled again, long enough that my cheeks started to burn.

We sat in silence for a few minutes, each absorbed in her own thoughts. I had no idea what Liss was thinking, but I was surfing back through wave after wave of memory, going back over all the times I had ever seen Liss and Marcus together, trying to determine how I had become so certain that they were seeing each other.

Liss cleared her throat. "So. Would the question you asked have a motive behind it? Oh, I might as well come straight out and say this, too. Maggie, are you by any chance attracted to Marcus?"

"No!" I bit my lip. "No, no. Well, I mean, he's a wonderful friend, and I would trust him with my life, but . . ."

But what? He was too scary? Too forbidden?

Too much everything.

I swallowed hard. "Nope, not me."

Liss smiled at me and went back to tidying her hair. "Oh. That's too bad."

I couldn't let that just pass, could I? "Why? Why is that too bad?" I asked, trying not to sound too curious.

She just shrugged and went about her business. I figured that if she could, I should be able to do the same.

Of course I hadn't seen Marcus yet, so I had no idea that the sight of him garbed in nothing more than narrow leather breeches was going to affect me so strongly.

My heartbeat caught in my throat as he

stalked up to the altar as Liss's high priest. He had an almost animalistic grace and power. His dark hair was loose around his shoulders, shining in the golden light of the May fire. His naked chest, dusted lightly with dark hair, was drawn with spirals that led into twisting vines that traversed the length of his abdomen and (*steady now*) even lower. His cheek had the bewitching mark of a dragon, breathing the fire of life. His eyes glittered like blue topaz in the firelight as he met my gaze over the altar. I couldn't breathe, but felt no need to. It was enough to be swept along on the eddies and gusts of the breath of life that was being celebrated with the night's ritual.

The earth tonight was blooming anew. Stony Mill was blooming anew as well. In time, perhaps, so would I.

When the ritual was done, someone broke out a set of Celtic pipes; someone else, a deep-timbred drum. Lilting music soon filled the air, and with it came dancing. And laughter. Lots of laughter.

I wasn't surprised when Marcus appeared beside me, as silent as a panther approaching his prey. "Hey," I said softly.

"Hey back."

"You've been away."

"Duty calls sometimes."

431

I nodded.

"Dance?"

I glanced up in surprise and found his hand extended in offer.

His teeth flashed wolfishly in the muted light. "I'm not going to bite you, you know."

Embarrassed that he had caught the gist of my thoughts, I made a face but accepted his hand. It felt warm and hard beneath mine.

It was just a dance . . .

"Unless you want me to."

Uhhhh . . .

I cleared my throat. "I'm not really sure how to dance to music like this."

He spun me around into his arms and locked me into place. His eyes bored into mine. "Just move your feet to the music . . . and enjoy."

I could do that.

So on this warm spring night, while most of Stony Mill was asleep in their beds or finishing a beer to the chatter of late-night comedians, a few of us celebrated in the Old Ways, the way people had done for eons. Embracing the new and chasing away the old shadows with music and fire and laughter.

It was a survivor's way.

It was the only way.

432

ABOUT THE AUTHOR

A born aficionado of all things paranormal, **Madelyn Alt** is the bestselling author of the Bewitching Mysteries. Madelyn is fortunate enough to be able to spend her days writing tales of the mysterious, and evenings, too, when the spirit moves her. She loves chocolate, Siamese cats, a shivering-good ghost story, the magic in the world around us, and sometimes, more chocolate.

Madelyn writes from her home, an 1870s Victorian in Northeast Indiana, where she lives with her husband and four sons. She can be found most days either hard at work on the next Bewitching Mystery or puttering around in her garden. For more information, please visit her on the web at www.MadelynAlt.com.

The employees of Thorndike Press hope you have enjoyed this Large Print book. All our Thorndike and Wheeler Large Print titles are designed for easy reading, and all our books are made to last. Other Thorndike Press Large Print books are available at your library, through selected bookstores, or directly from us.

For information about titles, please call:
(800) 223-1244

or visit our Web site at:
http://gale.cengage.com/thorndike

To share your comments, please write:
Publisher
Thorndike Press
295 Kennedy Memorial Drive
Waterville, ME 04901